THE CHARGE

SHARON BAYLISS

A Division of **Whampa, LLC**
P.O. Box 2540
Dulles, VA 20101
Tel/Fax: 800-998-2509
http://curiosityquills.com

Cover design by Michelle Johnson

ISBN 978-1-62007-202-8 (ebook)
ISBN 978-1-62007-203-5 (paperback)
ISBN 978-1-62007-204-2 (hardcover)

For my husband and sons,

my reason for everything.

TABLE OF CONTENTS

CHAPTER ONE

hen Warren arrived outside his mother's apartment, he saw Luke Skywalker's face plastered against the window. For some reason, his mother had taped his old *Star Wars* comforter over the patio glass. He didn't pause too long to wonder why. His mother suffered from what his brother called *severe eccentricity*, a condition that sometimes included blacking out windows with old sheets for no obvious reason.

Warren always came home when his mother asked, in part because she tended to do things like make bacon in the toaster and start fires. However, if she called him today for anything less than a toaster fire, he would head right back to campus to enjoy the first day after finals the way he had intended to—drunk and poolside.

He wiped his feet like his mother taught him, even though the revolting brown carpeting didn't show much. He kind of missed the crappiness of the apartment he grew up in, although he didn't know why, because crappy also described his new apartment in Eugene. Still, to him, home smelled like pine trees intermingled with pool chlorine and exhaust from the laundry room.

His mother stood in the kitchen beside their yellow nineteen-eighties stove and a refrigerator that always looked too small next to Warren and his other too-tall family members. She held a box of uncooked spaghetti and didn't respond to his presence right away. The box of spaghetti looked worn and crushed, as if his mother had stood there and squeezed the box for a while. The wrinkle between her eyes had grown deeper, and a few more strands of gray had found their way into her waist-length black hair.

Warren took the box of spaghetti out of her hands.

"I will make you dinner," she said.

"I'm not hungry."

Two Red Bulls churned in Warren's hungover and now worried stomach.

"What's wrong?" he asked.

Please don't say cancer. At six-foot-five, Warren had grown too tall for most childish things, but losing his mama still felt like the worst thing that could possibly happen.

"It's Isaac," she said.

Warren's hands began to sweat.

"What's wrong with him?"

Okay, maybe losing his little brother felt like the worst thing that could possibly happen.

His mother took Warren by the hand and led him into their apartment's only bedroom. She had slept on the couch for fourteen years, and Warren and Isaac had shared this room. A bleach-stained towel hung over a broken window. Through the gap, Warren saw the courtyard full of pine trees where they had played as kids—the courtyard where Isaac collected specimens to look at under his microscope while Warren hit mud balls with his baseball bat.

Glass surrounded a brownish-red smudge on the carpet. Blood.

"What is this?" Warren asked.

"Someone took him."

Warren's breath caught in his throat.

"He came home to visit. Said he felt sick. I tried to get off work, but I couldn't find anyone to cover my shift." Her voice took on a higher, more urgent pitch. "When I came home, he was gone."

"You mean someone actually broke in and took him?"

"Yes."

"He's sixteen years old and freaking six-foot-four. You don't just abduct a guy like that for no reason. What the hell for?"

She shook her head, her eyes on the spot of blood.

"Did you call the police?" His voice got higher and louder too.

"Yes, I called 9-1-1, like you told me to for an emergency. Isaac put the numbers on the phone so I wouldn't forget. They came and asked me questions and took pictures."

"What did the police say?" Warren asked.

"Just to call if anything new happens."

"It doesn't make sense. He's nice to everyone. Keeps his head down. This is bullshit." He realized he had yelled. "I'm sorry. I didn't mean to curse."

"It's okay."

Warren knelt to get a better look at the blood smudge, careful to avoid the glass.

His mother sat on the floor next to him and took his hand.

He didn't notice his hand shook until she held it firmly.

She pulled him into a hug and squeezed tightly.

"I love you," she said.

"I know. I love you, too, Mom."

"I think you should go."

"What? No. I'm not going anywhere." She got confused at the grocery store on her best days. She needed him now. And he needed her.

"They'll come for you, too," she said in a near-whisper.

He pulled away from her. "What aren't you telling me?"

"Nothing. I'm just worried. I don't want to lose you, too."

She didn't lie well, and only one topic caused her to act this evasive.

"Does this have anything to do with my father?"

She paused for what seemed like a full minute, and then finally gave the same answer she always gave when they asked about their father.

"No. Your father is dead. He died in Waterloo when the bomb hit Texas."

CHAPTER TWO

arren's mother told him to get out of Portland, drive across the Canadian border, and check into a hotel using a fake name. He had no intention of doing any of that. He didn't know if she lied on purpose, or had just gotten confused, but he suspected his mom hadn't told him the whole story. Regardless, blood smeared his bedroom floor. And no one messed with Warren's brother. He had protected Isaac from bullies ever since the little dork decided to wear a cape and top hat to school in third grade, and that wouldn't stop now that Isaac towered over just about any bully. Warren planned to find his brother, and then kick the ass of whoever caused that smudge.

Isaac's phone rang and rang without answer, and Warren gradually lost hope that Isaac sat on his couch watching science documentaries or whatever boring thing he would do on a Saturday night. But just in case, Warren decided to start by visiting Isaac's apartment in the Commonwealth of California.

He patted the hood of his fifteen-year-old Camry and gave it a little pep talk. *You've got an eleven-hour drive ahead of you. But I know you can do it, I have faith in you.*

On the drive, Warren topped off the Red Bulls in his stomach with a Venti Iced Americano. When he finished the coffee, his heart raced and he wondered how much caffeine it took to kill a man. About thirty miles from the border, Warren saw an official Oregon road sign that said, *Warning: Entering Texas Empire in Twenty Miles*. And then another one, a little later: *Warning: This Road Leads To The Texas Empire. Turn Around Now To Remain in The U.S.* The signs plus the caffeine kept his heart rate up. He didn't know if these warnings remained in effect or were just left there from before the bomb. Now that the Texas Empire had fallen, the Texas territory of California had become a territory of the United States. *So it should be safe. Right?*

With all the worrying about his brother, he hadn't stopped to think about entering the old Texas Empire for the first time since his family had escaped as refugees fourteen years ago. He'd made a few bad choices in high school, but he had never joined the forbidden road trips to California to see if the Texas Empire drinking age of sixteen remained in effect. His mother didn't set too many rules, so he didn't mind following the one rule she enforced—"Don't go to Texas. It's a bad, bad place."

Now only a few miles from the border, he wished he had asked her why, exactly. He knew the United States and the Texas Empire hated each other like a snake and a mongoose, although the country that played the snake in the story changed, depending on who told it. But Warren's American high school history class painted Texans as cartoon villains. They called the Texas Empire a lawless place where the convenience stores sold heroin, prostitutes roamed the streets, and people played roulette at McDonald's. Worst of all, of course, Texas was a monarchy, where leadership passed down from father to son. Their ancestors had founded America in the first place because they didn't like Kings telling them what to do, so they didn't like it in Texas either. Warren's history teacher hadn't convinced him to hate Texas. He felt the two hundred years of conflict simmering between the lines, and he didn't get worked up about politics. Live and let live.

The California border had a massive cement fence that could keep out a T. rex or a herd of zombies, and the United States government probably thought the Texas Empire had both. The deserted guard station could have housed a Wal-Mart. In the vacant window of the guard station hung a sign that said, *Border Open: Enter At Your Own Risk.*

For some reason, Warren held his breath while he crossed the border, and then expelled it loudly after he entered. The signs got to him. He had to chill out. Isaac lived here and went to school here. The land on this side of the border looked the same as the land he just passed through. He didn't sprout wings or see little green men on the side of the road as soon as he crossed.

The highway looked smoothed out from recent repair, with new United States green highway signs alongside the old Texas Empire blue ones. He couldn't see much in the darkness, so he couldn't spot any potential zombies or T. rexes prowling outside.

Eventually he had to pee, so he stopped and set foot on Texas Empire soil for the first time in fourteen years. The gas station sold guns and liquor, plus a lot of Texas Empire-themed knickknacks placed to either entice tourists or frighten them into turning around. One T-shirt had the entire North American continent colored in with the Texas flag and said, *We're coming for you.* Another one said simply, *Screw you, America.* Other than feeling bullied by T-shirts, peeing at a Texas Empire gas station didn't seem different from peeing in an American one. They had M&Ms and Doritos and Coca-Cola and Purell dispensers, and no heroin.

Warren reached Palo Alto in the early morning and wondered if he should second-guess doubting his history teacher. He saw abandoned cars with broken windows and people openly selling drugs. Really openly. At a stoplight, one man pressed a laminated menu of narcotics to Warren's car window. It looked professionally made, like the menus Warren handed out at the microbrewery-slash-restaurant he worked at.

But aside from the drugs-to-go, Palo Alto didn't seem too bad. Colorful buildings popped up among the lush green landscape. They even had Starbucks. He drove by the Palace of the Lord of California. Once the monarchy fell, the Governor of the Commonwealth of California lived here instead of a Lord, but he still got to live in the palace. The building looked like an over-blown Spanish mission, with red tile roofs, stucco walls, and lots of archways and palm trees. Not a bad way to live.

Isaac lived in a yellow, cube-like apartment complex, near Pike University where he went to school. Isaac had an IQ of 162, so he began college at the same time Warren did. He had a funky brain, like his mind took steroids. Warren would watch him scrawling notes or solving puzzles, and his eyes would jet back and forth so fast they looked like they vibrated. Isaac's smarts and premature grown-up-ness made him seem like the older brother . . . or even Warren's grandfather, on occasion. He said stuff to Warren like, "You would be a genius, too, if you applied yourself even an iota."

Even in the weak early morning sun, people lay by the pool, and Warren felt their eyes on him as he walked by. But people looked at him everywhere he went. Warren knew he stood out. He had hair so black it had a blue sheen, and pale blue eyes. That, plus his height, made him somewhat of a spectacle. Unlike Isaac, who tended to slouch and wear a lot of gray, Warren had no problem standing as tall as he could. He smiled at some pretty girls in bikinis. They smiled, but then grabbed their towels and shoes and headed straight for a first-floor apartment. He couldn't imagine why they would run from him like they had seen the bogeyman, but women frequently did things that baffled him.

Warren climbed the stairs to the second floor and found Isaac's apartment. He turned the knob, then tried to open the door, but found it locked, of course. What had he expected? Did he think he would show up, knock on the door, and Isaac would explain how the whole thing had been a misunderstanding? He rammed the side of his body into the door a few times, more out of frustration than anything. The door looked sturdy and probably had at least one solid lock. Warren might resemble Superman a little, but he couldn't break down doors.

"Are you Warren?" A small redheaded girl stood in the doorway of the neighboring apartment. Her petite stature and pink pajama pants made her look about fourteen years old, but most likely she attended Pike University, too.

"Do you know me?" Warren asked.

"I know Isaac has a brother named Warren. And you have to be his brother. You look just like him."

"Yeah, that's me."

"I'm Jessica. I go to school with Isaac."

"Are you friends with him?" Warren had found Isaac's first friend, and a female to boot—a historic moment.

"I suppose. We've worked on group projects together."

"Do you have a key to his apartment?"

"No. Why? Where is he?"

Warren didn't want to say the words out loud. He stared at her awkwardly for a moment before responding. "He's missing. We think he may have been kidnapped."

Her mouth parted in shock. "Kidnapped? Are you serious? I saw him yesterday."

"I'm trying to find out any information about what might have happened. Could I talk to you for a minute?"

She glanced inside her apartment, and then back at him warily. He didn't blame her. He had not slept, had drunk enough caffeine to get an elephant wired, and just tried to knock down a door. Maybe those girls downstairs *had* seen the bogeyman.

"You don't have to invite me in if you don't want to," Warren said.

"It's okay. My roommates are home."

The inside of the apartment matched the girl. Stuffed animals littered the couch and it smelled like a day spa.

"Do you want anything to drink?" she asked politely.

Tired and strung out on caffeine, Warren couldn't even tell if he was thirsty.

"No, thanks." He sank into the plush, white couch. "You're from the U.S., too, aren't you?" Warren asked.

"How did you know?"

Warren shrugged. "You've just have a lot of nice stuff."

"I'm from Duluth, Minnesota. I came here for their robotics program. They don't have anything comparable in the U.S. And I don't know what makes you think they don't have nice stuff in the Empire. They have all the same stores. They have more stores, in fact. Fewer tax laws, although a lot of that is changing, of course."

"You're studying robotics?" Warren didn't know science geeks came in such a fluffy, pink variety.

She nodded.

"Isaac came here for the genetics program," Warren said. "They don't have as many regulations on human genetic manipulation, or whatever."

"Yeah." She chuckled to herself, like she thought of a private joke. "I want to help," Jessica said. "I know you are close with your brother. He doesn't talk much, but he mentioned you to me a few times."

"Do you know of anyone who wanted to hurt him?"

"I barely know anyone who *knows* him, let alone wants to hurt him."

Warren rubbed his forehead absent-mindedly. The tiredness hit him like a wave and he wanted to lie down and sleep right there on her couch.

"But something strange did happen," she continued. "Last night, I talked to Isaac. He actually called me, which he never does. I went over to his apartment, and he was really sick. He could barely make it to the door to let me in. He thought that maybe I should take him to the hospital."

"Why didn't you?" Warren couldn't conceal a touch of anger in his voice.

"I'm sorry. Maybe I should have. But he changed his mind. Decided he was just having a panic attack."

"What was wrong with him?'

"I don't know. He just kept saying he felt funny. He said something about adrenaline and his skin burning, but mostly he just kept saying he felt funny. He had turned off all the lights and electronics in his apartment. It was dark and he . . . scared me a little, so I left."

"Do you think it was a panic attack?" Panic attacks didn't seem completely out of character. At sixteen, Isaac lived alone and went to college in a strange place. He could have cracked up a little.

Jessica shrugged. "I don't know. What does a person feel like when they have a panic attack?"

"I'm no expert. But, maybe short of breath, fast heartbeat . . . panicky."

"No, I mean, how do they feel to someone else? What does their skin feel like?"

"What do you mean?"

"I grabbed his hand to help him up. His hand felt really hot."

"You mean he had a fever?"

"No. It was hot, but it was more than that. His hand vibrated. And touching him made my heart beat fast, too, and the hairs on my arm stood on end."

CHAPTER THREE

After Warren talked to Jessica, he talked to the woman in the apartment office. He convinced her to let him into Isaac's apartment pretty easily, but not because of his winning smile or talent for persuasion. Isaac had listed Warren as his *in case of emergency* contact person. Warren couldn't charm someone out of keys anyway, in his present state. He felt agitated. Irritable. His brain ran hot. He needed some real food and some sleep.

Warren unlocked the door to Isaac's apartment, and then turned on the light. The apartment smelled like Isaac, one of those mild scents a person and their house share that no one noticed unless they paid attention. For Isaac, it smelled vaguely of lab chemicals and something spicy, like cloves. The smell seemed to bring Isaac into the room itself, and Warren pictured him in his kitchen making the same dry toast and black coffee he ate every morning. Warren missed his brother so much his chest hurt.

But he didn't enter Isaac's apartment to feel sad. He needed clues. Aside from the distinct Isaac-ness of the apartment, he didn't have many personal items. Warren doubted he'd find fingerprints in the immaculate apartment, even if he had the tools or know-how for something like that. Management could have used this apartment as the generic model to show to prospective renters, except for a photo of Warren, Isaac, and their mother at Isaac's high school graduation. Isaac didn't talk much about his personal life, and Warren now suspected he didn't have one. The kidnapping wasn't about something personal.

Isaac did have something of value worth taking—his brain. Warren had no proof, but he guessed Isaac had done something like invent a time machine or something even more amazing, like cure male pattern baldness, and someone wanted to steal the idea for profit. Knowing Isaac, he came up with something so complicated that they couldn't just steal his notes. They would need Isaac to build the invention for them.

Even in the small apartment, Isaac had set up some kind of lab; Warren just knew that. Sure enough, he saw a blue light and heard a humming sound from down the hall. Isaac slept in the smaller, second bedroom and lab equipment and computers filled the master bedroom. Heavy plastic covered the carpet, and Isaac appeared to have installed his own sprinkler system. Warren hoped for some obvious sign that someone had searched the lab, but couldn't find one. Nothing appeared out of place. On the silver table in the middle of the room sat nothing but microscopes and other equipment Warren couldn't name. Unless a giant blinking arrow led him to a clue, Warren wouldn't find anything. The lab made Warren's head hurt even more. He wondered if some chemical leaked, because the room seemed to glow oddly.

He heard a knock at the door. Warren's heart kicked into high gear, like someone animated it with jumper cables. For some reason, the back of his left knee started to tingle. Warren wondered if he should have bought a gun at the convenience store. Everyone else in the Texas Empire probably had one, including whoever knocked on the door. He picked up a microscope with a heavy base and wielded it as he approached the door. The microscope probably cost more than Warren's rent, but that didn't seem too important just now.

Through the peephole, he saw the petite figure of Jessica and put down the microscope. He opened the door.

"I saw you go in," she said.

For some reason, she looked even smaller than before.

"Yeah?" Warren asked.

"I know this is the last thing I should be asking you, but Isaac was helping me with some of my research. I left my notes in his lab. I wouldn't ask, but I'm submitting my doctoral dissertation next week. I'll go crazy if I don't double-check everything."

"Doctoral dissertation? How old are you?"

"Twenty-four. I know I look young. I graduated high school early, and I got my undergrad and Master's degree in four years combined."

"So you're a genius." He may have underestimated her. But he didn't feel too badly about it. She looked like a life-sized American Girl doll. "If that's true, what is 345 times 769?"

She laughed nervously. "I'm not a mathematical savant."

"345 times 769, and I'll believe you're a genius and let you in." Warren didn't know why he tried to stop her from coming in, but for some reason he couldn't pinpoint, he wanted to be far away from her. His head felt hazy with agitation, and he could feel a vein behind his eye pulse irregularly.

"You're twice my size and you don't want to be alone around *me*?"

"Size can be misleading."

"That is true." She took a deep breath and closed her eyes. "265,305."

"You know what, I don't know if that's right. But you can come in."

"Thank you."

He followed her back to the lab. At least he knew Isaac had let her in before, because she walked straight toward it with no hesitation.

She sighed when she entered the room. "I left them on the table, but he must have filed them somewhere. He hates clutter."

"I know. He spends most of his time at home following me and my mom around with a dust pan."

She opened the file cabinet and handed Warren a stack of papers.

"He's got this thing so full, I can't even read the labels," she said. She continued to thumb through the files.

Warren looked at the papers in his hands. He saw tables of numbers and some images with black lines that looked like DNA tests. The black lines on the paper seemed to wiggle. He felt like crap. Maybe the caffeine overdose had set in.

He tried to hand the papers back to Jessica, but she pushed them back toward him . . . God knew why. The irritation he had felt all afternoon peaked. For some reason, he imagined throwing Jessica against the wall just to see her break. The thought scared him. He didn't think things like that. His fingers tingled. He put the papers on the counter and shook his hands to rid himself of the sensation.

"Why are you shaking your hands like that?" Jessica asked. She had turned and gave him a look that made him think she could read minds.

"Oh. I don't know."

"Isaac did that. When he got sick." Jessica stepped back from him and looked at the door.

He hoped she would run. For the first time in his life, he felt . . . dangerous. He could crush Jessica's tiny hands like eggshells.

"You should go," he said.

Jessica didn't argue. She handed him the stack of papers once again and then left so fast she practically dematerialized.

Warren's eyes felt like they might melt out of his skull, so he didn't trust he had read the file correctly at first, but after a few blinks, he realized one of the DNA results had his name on it. Another test had Isaac's name, and another one for their mother. Isaac had put marks by some of the numbers in the table and also on the image with the lines. Isaac had written *the blue chromosome* in handwriting a little messier than usual, on his and Warren's test results. Warren couldn't imagine why Isaac had tested their DNA. For some reason he couldn't explain, it made him angry and he ripped the test results into a pile of confetti.

Warren went to sleep in Isaac's bed and slept fitfully. His dreams and even his waking thoughts didn't seem like they came from his own subconscious. He dreamed of a desert with sharp red cliffs. He jumped on a rock because he saw a scorpion. Black smoke filled the sky. When he woke up, his eyes still felt dry from the smoke and dust. He had almost no memories of anything before he lived in Oregon. Maybe a memory from when he had lived in the Texas Empire had slipped through.

When Warren closed his eyes again, he returned to his desert dream. Night had fallen, and the wind across the rocks sounded like howling. A toddler version of Isaac slept on the ground nearby. Warren had surrounded him in a ring of rocks in a child's attempt to keep scorpions off his little brother. Warren lay down next to Isaac and put his hand on his back so he could feel him breathing.

A monster leaned on a rock, watching them. Warren heard other monsters talking in grunts nearby. The monsters looked like people, but Warren knew better. The giants had violet eyes. Most of them couldn't speak. Warren had seen them kill—mostly animals, but some people, too. They could grab a deer and kill it with their hands.

The sunrise turned the smoke in the sky a bright red. A female monster kneeled next to Warren. He closed his eyes and pretended to sleep. She stroked his hair and hummed. She had only a vague sense of what a song sounded like. Her undulating moan had no rhythm or sequence.

Then, the song gained shape and sounded clearer. Now the woman hummed the tune to *Swing Low, Sweet Chariot*. The breathy and off-key tune comforted him deep down. His mother used to sing him that song.

With a jolt, Warren realized the dream had ended. A woman had her hand on his forehead. He swung at her, but she caught his wrist in mid-air and brought his arm to a painful halt.

"Calm down honey, it's me."

"Mom?"

"Yes."

"I almost hit you," Warren said as he rubbed his wrist.

"No, not really."

"That was a freakishly good deflection."

"You have to be a strong woman to work in assisted living," she said. "Mr. Walker weighs nearly three hundred pounds and I help move him in and out of his chair."

"What are you doing here?"

"I followed you. You didn't go to Canada."

Warren ran his hands through his hair. Sweat soaked Warren's head and the pillow. The feeling of agitation had not improved.

"No. I didn't go to Canada."

"You have to do a better job at running."

"You tell me to leave Isaac and save myself but you won't even tell me what I'm running from." He went from asleep to angry very quickly. His hands shook. "Stop lying to me!"

She moved closer to Warren and gently cradled his face in both hands. "Don't ever forget that you are a good man. A great man." Her words sounded rehearsed. "I've come to say goodbye."

"What?"

"I have been so honored to care for you. I love you so much. And no matter what anyone says, I know it is real love."

"Why would anyone say it's not real? You're my mother. Who doubts a mother loves her son?" Warren laughed, but didn't know why. "Mom, come on. What is this? I know you love me, Mom, you didn't have to come all the way down here to tell me that. You're being paranoid. You always think the worst. There is no reason for anyone to hurt Isaac. There is an explanation for this, I promise."

"If you see me again, do you promise to still call me Mom?"

All of his ambient anger seemed to come to a point of light. His frustration with his mother, his anger about Isaac's disappearance, and all the extra rage that had coursed through him all day came together. Without thinking, he raised his hand to strike his mother, something he would never, ever do. But before his fist hit flesh, she grabbed his arm and brought it to an abrupt halt once again.

"I'm so sorry," he said. "I don't know why I did that."

"Will you promise to always call me Mom?" she asked again.

"Of course."

She leaned in and kissed him on the cheek. "I love you."

By the time Warren untangled himself from the covers, she had left the room. He rushed out to follow her but the door had already closed.

CHAPTER FOUR

Will Cole sat on the couch and put his head between his knees. He listened carefully for the sounds of the elevator so he would have time to compose himself before the door opened. He figured all guys feared introducing their girlfriend to their mother. But not all guys had the President of the United States for a mother, and a girlfriend on the terrorism watch list.

He heard the sounds of the elevator moving closer and before the ding sounded, Will stood and posed with a smile. His girlfriend, Lena Lowell, along with several armed members of the Secret Service, exited the elevator. Apparently not fazed by the small army around her, Lena approached Will and kissed him like they had met at a café for brunch.

"You look really pretty," Will said.

"Is this outfit okay?" She brushed invisible dust off the shoulder of a royal blue dress that hugged her curves pleasantly. The blue made the ample helping of red in her blonde hair look brighter.

"It's perfect. I hope it wasn't too expensive. I didn't know you were going to buy something new. You should have told me, I would have bought it for you."

"Well, I wasn't going to wear a Texas Freedom T-shirt."

Will eyed the guards cautiously, but they didn't react. Secret Service knew all about her affiliation with the radical Texas Freedom Campaign, but he wished she would let the elephant in the room sit quietly.

"Besides, you know how I feel about you buying me things." She leaned close to him. "You're nervous. You have those little red patches at the base of your neck that you get when you're nervous."

Will rubbed his neck. He hated having a tell. The guards must have gotten some instruction in their earpieces that Will couldn't hear, because they re-entered the elevator with a sudden lack of concern for the possible terrorist in the President's private quarters.

Will wouldn't miss the White House. Living in the most securely protected home in the United States made it hard to have any fun. The same army of guards that kept invaders out had also kept Will in a painful state of good behavior. And if he did manage to sneak past them, an even more frightening army of paparazzi waited outside. He had just turned eighteen, and would move out in the fall to begin college. It couldn't come soon enough.

He might live in the White House again one day, but when he did, the Secret Service guards would work for *him*.

"I'm not worried," Will said. "You and my mother actually have a lot in common. I'm sure you'll get along great."

"That would be a little creepy if I thought it were true," Lena said.

Will's phone vibrated against his leg and he jumped.

The word *Mom* flashed on his phone.

"She's not coming," Will said. He let out an audible sigh of relief.

"How do you know? You didn't even answer it yet," Lena asked.

The low, gruff voice on the other line surprised Will. "Mr. Cole?"

"Uh, yes?"

"Everett Ward, Secret Service. Your mother regrets that she cannot attend lunch with your lady friend. She is preparing to make a statement."

"About what? Did something happen?"

"She asked me to tell you not to worry. Everything will be okay."

"What's going on?"

"Just turn on the television."

"Which channel?"

"All of them. Good afternoon to you, sir."

The Secret Service agent ended the call abruptly.

"What's wrong?" Lena asked.

Will guessed that his skin had grown even patchier. He tried not to worry. The President didn't have the luxury of turning off the news. She had to worry about all the crap that went on in the world, which meant addressing a crisis every few days.

Will went into his bedroom and Lena followed him. He turned on the television. Sure enough, every channel showed the same footage.

A newswoman stood somewhere dark. He could only see her pale, excited face against the black background. On the bottom of the screen, it said, *Live from Waterloo* in big green letters.

Will felt like his heart stopped beating entirely.

Lena gasped and kneeled down close to the screen, like she wanted to dive in. On the other hand, Will wanted to back out of the room. Or better, back in time to five minutes ago when his biggest problem was introducing Lena to his mother.

"What is this?" Will asked.

"Oh my God, I know her," Lena said. "That's Rochelle. She was one of the ones that planned to . . . ."

"What?"

"Look at the marble floors," the woman on the television said, and the camera scanned the floors. "It is amazing what beautiful things they built underground. I wish that I could give you a sense of how big this room is, but without proper lighting, it's hard."

"Where are they, that still has marble floors?" Will asked no one in particular. "It's not the palace, is it? The palace wouldn't be there anymore."

Lena looked too entranced to reply. The camera continued to span the area, picking up only portions of the large room. A chandelier, some carpeting, and walls that had a faint sparkle like granite. A tiny light illuminated so little; any sort of monster could sneak up and grab that reporter.

"I don't understand." Will felt like his heart beat in his tongue.

"The Texas Freedom Campaign. They broke into the closed territory to film a documentary. They wanted to prove that people still lived in Texas who need help," Lena said. "I don't see people, but that doesn't look like abandoned rubble. We were right. It's not uninhabited."

"You did this?" Will asked. His didn't like how wounded his voice sounded.

Lena turned around to face him, but turned her head to look back at the screen every few seconds. "No, *I* didn't do this. The unpaid interns don't exactly make the big decisions for the Texas Freedom Campaign."

"Why didn't you warn me?"

"It was just a rumor I heard. I didn't want to worry you." She squeezed his hand. "You have nothing to be afraid of it. Their government is gone . . . *they're* gone."

"Did you hear that?" the reporter asked. She abruptly halted her description of her surroundings and stared at something off camera.

"What?" Will responded like she spoke directly to him. He tried to breathe as quietly as possible so he wouldn't miss a single sound.

"*What was that?*" asked a man's voice, presumably the man who held the camera.

The woman turned to face the camera, her face washed out by the small light, looking half-afraid and half-exhilarated. Will imagined the entire country holding its breath with him, also glued to the TV.

Rochelle and the cameraman stayed silent for a long time, and then the camera started to scan the room again. More carpet, marble, tiled ceilings. Then, Will heard a sound, too, a metallic sound. He didn't want to say it, afraid to even think it, but it sounded like someone cocking a gun. He slid down on his knees to watch the screen more closely, and Lena kneeled beside him. Will wanted to grab the light and start looking around that room himself.

"Raul," said the woman in a terrified whisper. "I think there is someone over there."

Raul continued to scan the room, more and more frantically.

"Where?" Raul said in a raspy whisper.

In a split second, several things happened at once. The camera stopped on the face of a pale man with black eyes, pointing a gun. The man shouted something Will didn't understand, and then the feed went out, leaving an empty blue screen with the words *Connection Lost* in red.

Will watched the empty blue screen with even more attention than the actual feed. He leaned so far forward, his forehead nearly touched the television. He breathed through his teeth and didn't blink. A reporter behind a desk replaced the empty blue screen. She began with a somber tone. "As I'm sure you saw a moment ago, we lost connection with—"

"Oh, come on!" Lena said. "Go back to the live feed."

"It doesn't mean anything. It could be anything," Will said vaguely. He felt someone grab his hand and he pulled it away, startled.

"Relax. It's just me," Lena said.

"I'm sorry."

Lena opened her mouth to say something, but just settled on a sympathetic look.

Will hated sympathy.

"It's nothing to panic about," Will said, unsure of who he intended to console. "People probably moved into the impact zone after the smoke cleared. Everyone within a hundred miles of the Capitol when the bomb struck died on impact."

As soon as he said it, he remembered Lena's parents lived within a hundred miles of the Capitol when the bomb struck. But she didn't react to the statement. He assumed any hope she held that her parents somehow survived had died many years before.

Lena flipped through the channels.

"What are you doing?" he asked.

"I wanted to see if any other networks have anything new."

"Please, just leave it."

"Okay." She handed him the remote and paced. She didn't blink as much as usual and her excitement looked like it could bubble out of her ears at any moment. At the TFC headquarters she would probably do a cartwheel, but she reined in her enthusiasm for him.

Will had made a controversial choice when he asked Lena out. Due to her affiliations and beliefs, some even suspected Lena of espionage. Will wondered himself sometimes, but not too much. Yes, she had approached *him*, but she had just wanted support for a TFC-sponsored bill and wanted to know if he'd talk to some of his contacts in the Capitol. She hadn't flirted. Just business. He had to ask her out three times before she said yes. Perhaps, after eighteen years of not ruffling any feathers, he wanted to do rebellion big, and chose the most scandalous girlfriend possible. Either way, *he* had convinced *her* to give him a chance. If she planned to weasel her way close to his family for any dark purpose, she had done a great job of hiding it.

"Why are you looking at me like that?" Lena asked.

"I . . . I don't know."

"I know this is awkward. I can leave if you want me to. But I don't think I should. I'm here for you."

"I don't want you to leave," Will said. "My mom said this would happen eventually. I don't know if she knows something I don't. But she knew."

"Or like Senator Brighton says, 'cockroaches and Texans are hard to kill.' I guess this proves him right," she said with smug satisfaction.

The feed returned. Lena stopped pacing and sat down. The same *Live* stamp appeared on the bottom on the screen. The camera illuminated nothing more than glossy white paint, like the wall of an office. Will guessed the camera sat on a table or other stable surface, instead of held by the shaky cameraman. The minutes passed, and Will's anxiety mounted. The shot of the single bare wall seemed like deliberate torture.

"What is your name?" asked a deep, male voice.

The sudden voice shot through Will's body like an electric current. Will and Lena leaned closer to the TV in synchrony. The view on the screen stayed the same, but now Will heard the almost imperceptible sound of breathing.

"Rochelle Blake," said the voice of the female reporter. The screen still showed nothing but wall. Rochelle and the man stayed off-camera.

"Why are you here, Rochelle?" The man's words wove through the darkness like liquid. His voiced stayed calm, not angry or purposefully intimidating. In fact, his voice sounded warm and inviting.

"We are investigative reporters from the United States. We just came to . . . look."

"What were you looking for?" he asked.

"Anything of interest."

The image moved, as if someone lifted the camera off the table. A small hint of static marred the screen, and Will feared the feed would drop again, but the static cleared. The woman came into view, and Will guessed that the male questioner now filmed her. She looked unharmed and sat unrestrained in a plain wooden chair, with the same white wall behind her, her beige, sleeveless blouse and pants almost blending in. She looked up at the camera with wide eyes, full of reverent fear. Will had the sense the man tortured them on purpose, staying off the screen himself, putting her in the most uninteresting chair he could find, keeping the room dark, all to make the entire world squirm.

"Did you find anything of interest?" He had a melodic accent, easy to recognize as upper-class Texan.

"Yes," she said.

He chuckled lightly. The camera left Rochelle's face and momentarily scanned the wall again before becoming still, aimed back at Rochelle. The man walked in range of the camera and stood next to Rochelle. He had the deep black—almost bluish—hair, nearly translucent blue eyes, and towering frame distinctive of the Texas Empire's royal family, the Wildes.

Next to the average-looking Rochelle, the man appeared especially larger-than-life. His massive body moved like air and his unblemished skin seemed to glow faintly. Aside from that, he looked surprisingly normal. He wore a black suit with a gray shirt and no tie, and appeared clean and well groomed. Other than his unusual size, he could have walked into a coffee shop on Capitol Hill and looked like he belonged.

Rochelle continued to gaze up at him in admiration, and he smiled down at her. He looked amused, as if he relished the shockwave of terror that must be rippling through the United States.

The appearance of this man confirmed Will's greatest fear. Will's father had dropped a bomb on Texas that killed millions of people and still missed his target. At least one member of the brutal royal family that had ruled and terrorized the Texas Empire for almost two hundred years had survived.

Still grinning down at Rochelle, the man put his hand on her shoulder. Upon his touch, she shuddered and gasped, a strange reaction, almost indecent, and Will couldn't tell whether or not his touch had caused her pain or pleasure. He lifted his hand, and a noticeable red flush remained on her skin.

"It's been nice talking with you, Rochelle," he said simply. He walked back to the camera, and the blue screen with the *Connection Lost* message reappeared once again.

CHAPTER FIVE

Warren stared at the blue screen with the *Connection Lost* message. Without really thinking about it, he got up and walked to Isaac's refrigerator to look for a beer. Even wine would work. Isaac didn't have any beer, but Warren did find a dusty bottle of whiskey tucked into a cabinet. Even better. He took two shots and went to the bathroom mirror . . . or floated to the bathroom mirror. Even without the alcohol hitting him yet, he felt like he glided an inch above the floor.

He gripped the sides of the sink to keep himself from passing out or floating up. He knew what he looked like. But he must have never looked in a mirror properly until that moment. If he had looked in a mirror before, he certainly would have noticed. Of course, he could explain it away. The Wildes didn't have a monopoly on black hair, blue eyes, and impressive height. Surely, plenty of other people in the world had those features. But logical reasoning didn't help. After seeing that man, Warren knew instinctively he had found another of his own kind, as obvious as the fact that he had two hands and ten fingers. Failing to notice something obvious for eighteen years unsettled him. It made Warren wonder what other obvious things he had missed. Like, the world really was flat or that down was really up and he had walked on his hands his whole life.

He went back to the television and flipped through a few channels of anchors and pundits speculating on what the return of the Wildes meant. Warren tired of their opinions quickly. He had no interest in the feelings and reactions of random people whose lives would not change in the slightest when his life had just turned on its head.

He called his mother. It went to voicemail immediately. He couldn't think of anything to say, so he hung up. She owed him some explanations. But, at least he could admit his mother had not overreacted when she told him to run. The list of people who might want to kill him and his brother just exploded. The Wildes had pissed people off for a long time—the Lords of the territories, Texas revolutionaries, the Mexican government, Native American tribes, and of course, the good old U.S. of A. He threw his clothes back into his duffel bag, along with the photo from graduation, with the intention of driving straight back to the United States as fast as he could.

CHAPTER SIX

ill watched a documentary about the ocean. A week ago, the face of that Wilde man first graced the television screen, and the news channels showed almost nothing else since. Will usually liked to watch CNN, MSNBC, and a little bit of BBC World, to familiarize himself with any topic that might come up in conversation. But the past week, he had given up watching the news entirely because they covered nothing but those six minutes of live feed non-stop, twenty-four hours a day.

Shortly after Will turned five, an international tribunal tried his father for war crimes. After years of Cold War between the United States and the Texas Empire, United States intelligence discovered definitive proof of weapons of mass destruction within the Texas Empire and collected information that the then-King of Texas planned to reignite conflict between the two nations in order to claim additional United States soil in the name of the Texas Empire. These threats, compounded by bitter hatred for the Texas monarchy roused by the Blue Scare of the nineteen-nineties, led to a dangerous backroom standoff between the two nations.

Many believed that the King of Texas never really intended to use the weapons, and the two entities could have eventually resolved the conflict through diplomatic discussion, but on the twelfth day of the standoff, the United States launched a bomb at the capital of the Texas Empire. No one knew exactly what happened in the top-secret meetings that led to the bombing, but the President at the time and his cabinet placed blame on Will's father, General William Cole. They accused him of using "manipulation and deception to circumvent Presidential orders and launch the bomb without proper authority." Some conspiracy theorists claimed that General Cole could not have worked alone and that the President made him a scapegoat to cover up a massive, deadly mistake made by the entire administration. True or not, Will's father did not contest the charges against him.

Will knew all this now, but at the time, his mother had simply told Will that his father had made a very bad mistake, the kind of mistake too bad to just say, "I'm sorry." Even still, his father never had said *sorry*. Will had read the transcripts of the trial, so he knew that for a fact.

His father had said, "Although I regret the loss of life, I do not regret my actions. I have no doubt that King Antony Wilde would have followed through on his threats and attacked the United States capital. The hesitancy of the President was about to kill us all. If I hadn't acted, none of us would be here today. I have a son. I had no choice."

I have a son. I had no choice. Will memorized every word. Nothing else remained of his father other than the recorded words from the trial. An international tribunal found his father guilty of the "wanton destruction of human life not justified by military necessity," then sentenced him to death. Will didn't get to say goodbye to his father before the execution. His mother had said, "Daddy says he loves you very much, and to be a good boy. You'll see him again in Heaven."

Heaven. Yeah, right. But what should she say? Be a bad boy and maybe you'll get to see Daddy again in Hell?

Tired of learning about the mating habits of whales, Will turned back to *The Weather Channel*. The date on the left side of the screen made Will's stomach flip.

"Oh, no," he said to his empty living room. He called Lena, and she didn't pick up, probably already mad at him. He called the TFC office with a fake name, and the woman he talked to said Lena took the day off for her birthday and planned to spend it with family.

Will thanked her and hung up. The line about family gave him pause. He figured the woman had to mean Lena's former foster family.

After Will rang the doorbell at the foster home, he realized he shouldn't have gone there. He stood on the porch in his designer clothes among the scattered faded toys and children's swimsuits drying on the railing, feeling like the world's biggest jerk. A boy opened the curtain and looked at him with a classic gaping mouth and shut the curtain again, quickly. Then, two little girls also peeked out at him through the curtain. He smiled and tried to look nonthreatening. Lena had told him her foster mother had come from the Texas territory and like to take in Texan foster children. She had lost her own children in the bomb, and took in children who had lost their parents the same way. Will's father may have killed the parents of every single person inside, at least the older ones. And he stood on the porch with yellow roses.

Lena opened the door. She held an infant on her hip who wore a birthday hat. To Will's intense relief, Lena smiled.

"What are you doing here?" she asked, still smiling.

He handed her the flowers. "Happy birthday."

A black woman in her fifties came to the door, took the infant from Lena, and positioned her body so she shielded the baby from Will. Her face scrunched in such a way that Will thought she might spit on him.

Will did what he always did when he met someone new. He gave the woman a winning smile and held out his hand. "You must be Ms. Jones. I'm glad we finally get to meet. I'm Will Cole."

After a moment she squeezed just the tips of his fingers and nodded curtly. She pointed to the intersection down the block. "You need to put a stop sign there," she said to Will. "We've got children playing here. I filled out a form at the City Hall, but they haven't done a thing."

"Maggie, he's not in charge of stop signs," Lena said.

"I'd be happy to look into it," Will said.

"It's a lovely day," Maggie said pointedly. "Why don't the two of you go for a stroll?" She pushed Lena out the door, then shut it.

Lena hugged Will tighter than he expected. He didn't realize until then he'd barely touched her since the Texas footage. While she pressed herself up against him, he made a mental vow to not go without touching her for that long again.

"You've been such a zombie. I thought you had drifted away from me for good," she said.

"I'm sorry. I didn't mean to be a . . . zombie. I shouldn't have come here, either. It was inappropriate."

"Yeah, probably," Lena said. "I'm going to go put these in water, then let's get off the porch before you get shot."

"Where do you want to go?"

"Maybe just a walk. Want some ice cream?"

"Sure."

Ancient oak trees lined the sidewalks, shading them from the intense summer sun. The sound of children splashing around in backyard pools and the scent of various mid-day barbeques made him feel almost like a normal person—a normal person with a Secret Service SUV following ten feet behind him.

"Are there a lot of new kids at your foster home?" Will asked.

"Yes. It already seems really different," she said sadly.

"Do you miss it? I thought you hated it there."

"I did. Or I thought I did. It's just so quiet in my apartment. I'm not used to it. Do you know that I've never had a room to myself? At least, not since I lived with my parents. Now I have a whole apartment to myself. It's lonely."

"Well, when I start at Yale, you won't need to spend so many nights alone."

She bumped her hip into him playfully. "You're not afraid of the paparazzi catching you on your walk of shame?"

"I'll wear a disguise."

She laughed.

"And somehow you still plan to warm my bed from Connecticut?"

"We don't have to think about that now. We have all summer."

Lena rolled her eyes.

Will didn't see the problem with going to different colleges. He could afford the airfare for the short plane ride.

"I heard you got to make your first public statement for the Texas Freedom Campaign. I'm sorry, I didn't see it," Will said. "Did it go well?"

"You don't want to talk about that," Lena said.

Will smiled. "I suppose I don't."

Lena summarized the plot of a book she had read and went on to talk about a swimsuit she thought about buying, but ultimately didn't. She discussed her ice cream flavor preferences and asked him about his. She always knew the right thing to say. She even knew the right time to talk about nothing. Her emotional IQ always impressed him. She would make a great First Lady.

They waited behind a few children at the ice cream stand. Will appreciated that the brightly colored flavor choices distracted the children from noticing that the people behind them frequently appeared in tabloid magazines. As they neared the front of the line, Will saw the Secret Service agents head toward them. Secret Service usually kept their distance when Will tried to do normal things like go on dates. He wondered if they just wanted a Rocket Pop. He grabbed Lena's hand and pulled her out of the line to go meet them.

"I'm so sorry to disturb you, Mr. Cole," said one of the guards, "but a car is coming for you. It will be here very shortly."

"I didn't call for a car."

"The President sent for you."

"What for?"

"I'm sorry, sir, I'm afraid I don't know."

Will looked at Lena. "I'm so sorry."

"It's fine," she said. "You can take me to dinner tonight."

"Come with me."

"Now?"

A black sedan with tinted windows pulled up beside them, with two police escorts.

Will grabbed Lena's hand and pulled her into the car with him. He didn't even look at the guards to see their reaction. They probably didn't approve, but he doubted they had the proper authority to drag her out of the car. Will guessed right. The driver glanced back and hesitated for only a moment before he started the car.

"I'm in a tank top and flip-flops," Lena said.

"That's not against the law."

"I can't meet your mom like this."

"I'm not dressed up, either," he said.

"Your outfit probably cost more than my rent."

Will put his hand on her leg. "I'm spending your eighteenth birthday with you," he said firmly.

He called his mother three times in rapid succession, which all went straight to voicemail. He called the head of security, who spared him about two sentences to tell him that someone would brief him upon arrival. As they got closer to the city center, he noticed more police around than usual, posted along the streets, waiting for something. Without knowing what they waited for, Will began to share their apparent sense of anticipation.

They turned toward the towering white dome of the Capitol building. Police covered the Mall. They entered the secure underground garage, and the driver stopped by an illuminated elevator shaft.

Will jumped out and ran around the car so he could open the door for Lena. They got in the elevator.

When they reached the ground level, the sight of his childhood friend, Victory Brighton, hit him like a spotlight—as it always did. She did her best to avoid extra attention. She tied her white-hot blonde hair back in a twist, and the ruffled blouse she wore under her business suit went all the way up to her neck. However, when it came to downplaying her beauty, Victory failed every single day. But she didn't fail at much else.

She rationed out smiles like she had a limited supply, but she flashed a brief one at Will that caused all the blood to leave his brain.

"Hi," Victory said to Will. She nodded to Lena politely, her smile gone as quickly as it came.

Lena smiled and nodded back. They had met on a few occasions but Will tried to avoid it. Although he had no plans to cheat on Lena—and Victory would decline any advances he made, anyway—at some point, he feared Lena would notice he could barely see straight around Victory. Fortunately, Victory didn't make small talk. She nodded again and then continued walking down the hall.

The head of security swept toward Will, with a flock of guards behind him.

"The President has ordered you to the safe room," he said.

The words seemed to come from behind Will and punch him in the in the back of the neck.

"Why?" His heart rate spiked.

"I will explain on the way. We don't have much time."

"If there is a terror threat, why aren't you evacuating the grounds? This place is full of Capitol staff." He gestured toward Victory.

"It's not a terror threat. Just a precaution. Follow me."

He pulled Lena along with him and one of the guards actually grabbed her arm to hold her back. By the look on Lena's face, for one terrifying moment Will thought Lena might actually hit the guard, but when he released her arm, she slapped him with nothing more than a murderous look.

"It's a classified location," said the head of security. "Just you."

Will had no intention of leaving Lena, Victory, or really any of the people in the Capitol vulnerable while he went to an underground hidey hole.

"No," Will said.

"It's not my rule, it's the law," he said. "No one aside from the President and her family can know the location of the safe room. And I wouldn't worry about your girl. If anyone in this building is safe, it's her."

Will had the feeling he insinuated something cruel, but didn't know what. The head of security shoved him into the elevator and closed the door before he could even tell Lena goodbye.

CHAPTER SEVEN

ena agreed with the people who hated Texans on one count—Texans were like cockroaches, but only because they didn't go down easy. Texans survived everything. And they never forgot . . . anything. Remember the Alamo. Remember Goliad. Remember the Mexican-Texan War. Remember the Gold War. And so on and so forth. Texans stayed alive no matter what, through many years of devastating economic depression, countless natural disasters, and nine wars, including the Texas Civil War, the First and Second American-Texan Wars, and then, finally, a catastrophic bombing of their capital fourteen years ago. If that meant they were like cockroaches, Lena could live with that. Cockroaches existed long before the humans and would probably exist long after. As the saying went, "At the end of time, all that's left will be cockroaches and Texans."

The Texas Empire had only one rightful destiny, freedom from the tyranny of Wilde royal family as an independent democratic nation, and Lena planned to live to see it happen. In fact, she would make damn well sure of it. She didn't care that as an eighteen-year-old girl just out of the foster care system, she looked like she belonged behind a pair of pom-poms instead of behind a podium. In fact, all this worked to her advantage. People saw her as a sad, sweet, little orphan. She used this quality to sneak up on big bad people her whole life, and recently it had paid off big time.

The Texas Freedom Campaign chose her as one of their spokespeople, a group of camera-friendly young people with tear-jerking stories of survival who toured the United States getting support for their home nation. Which meant she now got to work for the TFC and earn an impressive college scholarship. In the fall, she would study Political Science, with a minor in History, at the University of Virginia.

Lena rubbed her bare arms. Her tank top and flip-flops made her self-conscious. She considered herself a political figure, not a lost college co-ed. With all her big talk though, right now, she had to admit that more than air conditioning had caused goose bumps to erupt all over her arms. Lena didn't know why the arrogant-looking guy in the black suit had called her safe; that couldn't be further from the truth.

The United States government and most of its people considered her a dangerous radical, but that didn't bother her much anymore. The Blue Scare hatemongering of the twentieth century had led many people, especially the stupid ones, to believe horrible things about Texas; many thought that cattle would do a better job running a free nation than Texans. That hate ran off her skin like water. But last week, a whole new enemy came into her life—the only people less in favor of a free, democratic Texas than the United States—the Wildes. The TFC wanted to help a forgotten territory build a democratic government, but now the movement seemed like a revolution against the Texas monarchy, and historically, those ended . . . poorly. Lena liked nothing more than taking down the big, bad guy . . . the bigger and badder, the better . . . but taking down the King? She loved a challenge, but she also wanted to live to see nineteen.

Lena headed down the hallway and caught sight of a familiar name printed on a gold-plated placard outside a large, mahogany office door. *Senator Samuel Brighton, Staff Office.* Lena didn't know Will's friend Victory well, but she didn't know anyone else in the building that hadn't retreated to a secret underground chamber. Lena walked in the open door. The room had a burned smell, like an overheated copy machine mixed with a coffeepot left too long on the burner.

"May I help you?" asked the frizzy-haired receptionist.

"Is Victory here?"

The receptionist looked her up and down. Maybe she considered calling a Legislative Aide by her given name presumptuous. Lena's appearance probably caused some suspicion—after all, a spokesperson from the TFC had walked into the office of the TFC's most vehement opponent—in flip-flops, no less.

"Lena?" Victory leaned against the doorframe of her office. Lena found Victory hard to like. Her eyes had the perpetual look of knowing everything and finding it all boring. At twenty, she already had a political science degree from Harvard and would start law school in the fall. During the session, she worked as a Legislative Aide for her senator father. Lena hated to admit it, but even though nepotism had surely played its part in Victory's success, she had also probably worked hard to get what she had, and deserved it.

Something had always bothered Lena about Victory. Lena shook the chills off her back. The feeling reminded her of waking up from a nightmare she couldn't remember . . . afraid, but not sure why.

"Are you here to see me?" Victory asked.

"I hope I'm not interrupting."

"No. Come in."

Lena took a seat in an overlarge, musty-smelling chair in Victory's office. "They took Will to the safe room. I hoped I could hide out in here for a while."

"The safe room?"

"Yeah. You know what's going on?" Lena asked.

"Hmm." Victory purred the sound and stared into the empty space to the left of Lena's face. "I think so." She leaned toward Lena as if about to tell her a secret. Victory's eyes sparkled with intensity and her cheeks reddened. "It's quite odd. I know I should be afraid. Or angry. But I feel . . . good."

The intercom on her desk buzzed with the sound of crackling electricity. They both stared at it.

The receptionist came in. "Something is wrong with the phones," she said.

The fluorescent lights dimmed, then brightened erratically.

"The legend is true," Victory said. "Come on."

Victory grabbed Lena's arm and pulled her out of the office. Even in her heels, Victory had no problem reaching a full run, while Lena slipped and skidded along the granite floors in her wake. The lights in this hall flickered, too.

Lena slammed into Victory's back when she stopped running suddenly. Guards stood sentinel at the end of the hallway. They waved them back.

"The Great Rotunda is closed; you'll have to turn around," said one of the men.

Victory didn't stop to argue; she grabbed Lena's arm yet again to whip her around, then dashed back down the hall and into a tiny cement stairwell. Lena gasped for breath as she struggled to keep up.

They reached the top of the stairs. Victory stopped in front of a small door. She pulled a ring of keys out of her jacket pocket and tried them in turn.

"I think I have the key to this lock, I just don't—" The next key she tried worked, and she turned the knob. "Be as quiet and inconspicuous as you can. I don't think they thought to block off this area, but if they see us up here, they might tell us to get down."

Victory opened the door, and Lena saw a wall of gold. They walked out onto a narrow balcony around the gold-plated rotunda. Victory ducked down and sat with her knees folded under her. Lena sat down beside her. Fortunately, heights didn't bother her too much. If they did, she might have passed out from panic. The balcony ledge measured about three feet wide and the miniature railing didn't even block their view, sitting down. The army of guards still stood around in the central hallway, so whatever Victory wanted to see must not have passed through yet.

"So what are we waiting for?" Lena whispered.

Victory put her finger to her lip to shush her, and then used the same finger to point down the hallway. The lights flickered again. The guards looked down the hallway at something Lena couldn't see.

The guards in the rotunda stopped staring down the hallway and backed up to line the walls, regaining their composure. The click of a woman's heels echoed before a man and woman entered.

Lena recognized the Wilde man from the video feed. He walked alongside a woman who looked related to him, tall and graceful, with shiny black hair worn freely down her back. The man wore a classic black business suit with a blue tie, and the woman wore a body-hugging black dress that sat on the line between office and nightclub wear. The woman's heels clicked with an odd echo that made it sound as if she walked on the ceiling.

The woman paused to glance up at the glistening gold rotunda, and she appeared to spot Lena and Victory. She stopped dead. Lena had the impression the woman looked more at Victory than at her. The woman nudged her companion, and he looked, also. Apparently not concerned about whatever had bothered her, he gently guided her forward by placing his hand at the small of her back. They continued down the hall, and the sound of her heels faded.

Lena's legs had gone numb, folded under her and Victory had to help her stand. Lena noticed flushed patches on Victory's chest and neck.

Lena followed Victory back to her office and sat back down in the musty chair.

"Wow," Lena said.

Victory leaned forward in her chair and absently tapped the desk panel with her foot.

"You must be cold in that top," Victory said unexpectedly, examining Lena's little red tank.

Lena felt her cheeks get hot. "We were going for a walk when they came for Will."

"I've never felt anything like that before," Victory said.

"What?"

"The charge in the air when they arrived. It must be even stronger than it was for their ancestors. I never read anything about feeling it from that far away. I thought they had to touch you. I could feel it as soon as they landed here, and I didn't even know they were coming." Victory took a deep, steadying breath. "My heart is still racing."

She ran her hands through her hair, and her neat twist started to frizz.

Lena stared at her, completely nonplussed. Sure, she had felt fear and anxiety waiting for them to come, but because Will had rushed off to the safe room and all the police and commotion, not from some mysterious *charge*.

"You felt it, didn't you?" Victory asked.

"No. What are you talking about?"

"Wildes give off energy . . . an electrical charge. That's why the lights and phones malfunctioned. You're sure you didn't feel it?"

"No, I didn't feel anything."

"You have never heard of their power. Public schools," she said, shaking her head. "Why *do* you think that people have been trying to exterminate the Wilde bloodline for almost two hundred years?"

Lena had the urge to walk out of the office. She hated it when people called her dumb. Besides, she knew the answer.

"The Texas Empire and the United States have hated each other ever since the first Texas President, Matthias Wilde, opposed statehood after the Texas revolution and made himself King, instead. It didn't help that both countries believed in manifest destiny and wanted the West. They fought over land and gold deposits in the nineteenth century, and then fought over ideals in the twentieth century—monarchy versus democracy. They have almost two centuries' of conflict worth hating each other for. As for the legend that they have superpowers, of course I have heard of that. When I was a child, they would tell us that the King created hurricanes, tornadoes, and droughts to keep Texans too busy rebuilding and trying to survive to have time for revolution. But it's just an urban legend."

"I made you angry." Victory pulled a book from her shelf, *The Wilde Dynasty: A Complete History,* and handed it Lena. Lena thumbed through the musty-smelling book. Each section featured a different prominent Wilde, with lots of pictures and a biography ripe with scandals such as extramarital affairs, murder, and accusations of homosexuality with a tone that implied the writer considered it as much of an abomination as the first two. Victory watched her with eyes that seemed to see through Lena's skin and gave no explanation as to why she had handed her the book.

"What are you showing me?" Lena asked.

"Look at them."

"I'm not sure I'm supposed to be looking at," Lena said.

"What do the Wildes have in common?"

Lena glanced back at the book. She thought, *they are all so sexy I wish I could jump into this book,* but knew not to say that aloud. They all had the same black hair and blue eyes with a handsome, classic bone structure. No big noses or weak chins, just always pleasing, strong features. And *tall.* All the men looked at least six-foot-five.

In family photo after family photo, the men looked the same, different enough Lena could tell them apart, but only just. The Wilde daughters had more variety. Once in a while, she found a blonde, or a petite one, but they mostly looked the same, too, tall and lean with long sheets of black hair and striking blue eyes. The wives from other families came in a variety of shapes and colors, but their bloodline appeared to dissolve in the mix because the children always looked exactly like their fathers.

"They look the same?" Lena asked.

Victory continued to stare at Lena.

"They're gone," Victory said wistfully and slumped into her chair.

"What?" Lena asked.

"The visitors. I can't feel them anymore."

Lena heard Will's voice in the other room. Victory jumped up and hurried toward him. Annoyed that Victory dashed over to greet her boyfriend before she could, Lena followed her out to see Will looking as excited and jittery as Victory. A flush covered his pale skin, too, and sweat darkened his blond hair.

"Did you feel that?" Will asked. His gaze locked into Victory's.

Fury bubbled in Lena at the sight of their shared excitement. She didn't consider herself to have any special powers, but she did have an uncanny knack for perception. Why didn't she feel what they felt?

Lena wrapped her arm around Will to remind him she existed. He squeezed her back, harder than she would have expected. He felt . . . different. He had more body heat than an hour ago. Although, she wouldn't describe it as *heat*. She might call it . . . a charge, as if electricity ran through him. The mystical energy Victory mentioned seemed to have stuck to him.

"Apparently, my mom invited them. Her opponents will not like that." Will laughed in a too-excited way, like he'd had too much to drink.

"Why?" Lena asked.

"Because it's controversial to invite them here," Will said. "And possibly dangerous."

"No, I understand *that*. I meant why did she invite them?"

"Diplomacy."

"So the U.S. will give them back the Texas Empire, just like that?"

"I wasn't in the meeting," Will said. "I don't know what they discussed."

"Victory." The man's voice from the doorway caused the fiery energy in the room to fizzle at once. Lena knew Senator Brighton's face well. Two years ago, his presidential campaign ads had drilled into her consciousness so deeply that, upon seeing him, she could still hear him say, "I live for God, family, and country. I am every man."

His campaign ads showed an attractively weathered working man with a sparkle in his gray eyes and a full head of thick blond hair—with just the right touch of gray—sitting on a front porch or leaning up against a fence telling the country he will make it all okay. He seemed like the father she had always dreamed about, strong enough to fight off the monsters and gentle enough to stroke her hair and comfort her after the battle.

This man seemed so different, it rattled her brainwashed subconscious. His eyes bulged slightly out of his purplish face and his pit stains stretched all the way down to his waist.

When he noticed Lena and Will, he smiled broadly, wiped his hand on his slacks, and reached it out toward Will. Will shook it.

"It's a scorcher today," the Senator said. "I bet I could throw some steaks on the sidewalk and they would sizzle."

Will laughed in a way Lena hadn't heard before. Convincing, but having heard the real thing, Lena thought the laugh sounded fake.

"Yes, sir," he said.

Will gestured toward Lena. "This is Lena Lowell."

"Why, of course." The Senator took her hand and actually kissed it, like in old movies.

Lena needed a lot of willpower not to wipe her hand on her shorts.

"My dear, you look as pretty as a glass of ice-cold lemonade."

"Thanks," Lena said with the slight hint of a question mark at the end. For a first meeting with a man whose public position involved open hatred of the Texas Empire, and often of Lena herself, she found it underwhelming. But she supposed he wouldn't go at her with a pitchfork in the middle of the Capitol.

"I'd love to visit with you both, but I'm afraid I must have a word with Miss Victory here," the Senator said.

Will and Lena murmured brief goodbyes to Victory, who had managed to shed all of her previous enthusiasm and would have blended in well with the mannequins in a display window.

"Do you want to finish that walk?" Will took Lena's hand.

Lena shrugged.

"Come on." He led her out of the office, but they didn't get very far. He grabbed her around the waist and pulled her against him. Before she could object, he kissed her. He had one hand firmly wrapped around her back and the other hand holding her head to press her into his kiss.

It didn't occur to her to resist. His spontaneous eruption of passion caused a thrill of excitement to rush into her abdomen. She returned his embrace and his kiss. But as he started to move his hand up the front of her shirt, discretion got the better of her. She pulled his hand away.

"Will," she whispered. "What are you doing?"

"Kissing you."

"In the middle of the Capitol? In the hallway?"

He just smiled and pressed himself against her. "Should we find a closet, then?

Maybe she would find his passion sexy in another time and place. As a matter of fact, the thought of her I-don't-want-to-do-anything-that-might-come-out-in-a-campaign-later boyfriend wanting to have sex in a Capitol closet tempted her quite a bit. But she had the feeling that something other than her had gotten him all worked up.

"This isn't the best time for me. I'm too stressed from everything. I just want to go home."

"There's nothing to stress about, it's all okay."

"Yeah, but still." Lena pulled away from him and readjusted her top.

"Are you mad?" he asked, his own tone angry.

"No." She lied, but she didn't know exactly what had made her so mad, so she couldn't hold her own in an argument. "I'll call you later."

"Hang on." He grabbed her arm. "Seriously, what did I do?"

"Nothing, really. I'm just tired."

Will glared at her for a moment. She had never seen a look like that on him before. But he just shook his head and sighed. "Can I at least call you a car, or did you want to walk fifteen miles?"

CHAPTER EIGHT

arren glared at his reflection in the side mirror of his Camry. He loved the old car and how it refused to die and the way it still smelled like pizza from his old delivery job, but he didn't think he wanted to spend the rest of his life inside. But at that point, he had no better plan. The media had plastered Saul Wilde's face everywhere and Warren looked just like the bastard. He didn't feel safe ducking into a convenience store to buy a chili dog and take a leak, let alone go back to his job. He wanted to go home and pretend nothing had happened, for as long as possible. But he knew better. And he still needed to find Isaac. Unfortunately, he didn't have a damn clue how to do that. Although the list of possible suspects had expanded, he still had no idea who took him and why, or where they had taken him. And his mom still hadn't returned his calls.

He scanned his memory for any hints his mother might have dropped that she dated a prince or something. Which seemed so unlike her. He couldn't judge his own mother well, but he figured men might find her attractive. Still, he couldn't imagine she would catch the eye of royalty. She hardly brushed her hair or put on makeup, and Warren suspected that she might be mildly mentally challenged. She just didn't understand enough words. Statements like,

"I need to rent a tux and limo for prom," left her baffled. He had needed to define the words *tux*, *limo*, and *prom*, like she never heard them before in her life.

He rubbed the crick in his neck, from sleeping with his head against the glass on the driver's side window. He could smell his own dried sweat, mingling with the old pizza. People seriously underestimated the value of beds and showers. He had made it to Colorado, the boring no-mountains side, a good distance from the border of the former Texas Empire Deseret Territory, after skirting the Texas border indecisively for a week.

He turned on the engine and pulled out from behind the bowling alley where he had parked to sleep. He didn't know when it opened, but wanted to get out of the way, just in case. Something seemed a little off about the car. Heat radiated from the console. He pulled off the road at the next exit to check the engine. When he took the keys out of the ignition, the heat seemed to dissipate quickly, but a tingling sensation spread through his fingers.

He opened the hood and stared at the engine. He didn't know much about cars, but he didn't see flames, so that seemed promising. The tingling sensation crawled up his arm, from his fingers to his ears. He shook the feeling away. He had probably screwed with his body by eating nothing but fast food and convenience store fodder for over a week now.

He got back in the car and pulled into yet another convenience store. The sun had barely risen, so the sunglasses made it hard to see, but he put them on anyway, along with his trusty University of Oregon cap. He would have to take a shower really soon or his smell would attract more attention than his looks. The freshly brewed coffee inside the store smelled amazing. Good coffee improved any situation. He grabbed a V8 to treat his body with a shot of veggies, and opted for a granola bar instead of lining his arteries with more sausage biscuits. Something in the store caused the tingling to return. A little patch on the back of his neck tingled now, and another patch on the side of his face.

He brought his breakfast to the counter, and the young woman waiting behind the register didn't smile. Either his lack of bathing or his I'm-about-to-rob-you appearance had diminished his charming effect on women. A photo on *Star* magazine caught his attention and he grabbed it instinctively. *Will Cole Heartbroken—New evidence that Lena has left him in his time of need.* The picture of Lena caught his notice. When he looked at her, the odd feeling of tingly heat seemed to rush from his head all the way down his abdomen. Sure, a cute girl might cause that kind of reaction. He liked her look. Girl-next-door-ish. Pretty smile. And tall and curvy enough that he wouldn't worry about breaking her. But plenty of girls in the world fit those characteristics.

"Would you like that, too?" asked the cashier.

"Sure." He tossed it on the counter. He probably should have said no, because he didn't have much cash left.

He made it only a few miles down the road when he had to pull over. The feeling of heat became painful. His hands burned and he stared at them, half expecting them to burst into flames. The tingling increased to a fever pitch in his back, like his skin teemed with insects. Even the morning sunlight seemed unbearable, and he pressed his hands over his eyes. His heart beat so hard, he could hear it. This could be a heart attack. Or a panic attack.

Someone touched Warren's forehead. He thought he felt not only the hand itself, but also the life force within the hand. The force alleviated the fire in his own body, like the hand sucked out the terrible tingling sensation. He opened his eyes. The light blinded him. He didn't even remember passing out.

"Warren, are you awake?"

The voice surprised him, and he forced himself to focus on the person speaking.

His mother looked down on him. She appeared to have pulled him into the front passenger seat of her own rusty station wagon. She had the seat pushed all the way back, and she leaned over him from the driver's side. Her long black hair fell onto his chest. He saw his car on the side of the road in front of them.

"Mom?"

"Are you okay? I found you passed out. It's like your energy turned up too high."

Warren didn't really understand that description but it sounded surprisingly accurate. She kissed him on the cheek and gave him the best hug she could from their respective positions. As he acclimated himself to his surroundings, he realized the tingling sensation had faded. But his body still felt tired and achy, like he had the flu. The more aware he became, the less sense it all made.

"You told me you were abandoning me," Warren said.

"I would never abandon you. I can always feel your energy. When we're close, in the same city, I can feel your general direction. If we're very close, in the same building, I can tell what room you're in. When you and Isaac went away to college I didn't like that I couldn't feel you all the time. But I could still feel you distantly. Like little candles flickering. I didn't know where you were, exactly, but I liked just knowing you were out there somewhere."

What the hell? He had heard bat-mothers could find their babies in a cave of millions just by the sound of their squeaks. But a human woman with no sonar could not do that.

"I can't feel Isaac anymore," she continued. "But that probably just means he's too far. I really hope that's what it means."

Her face scrunched up like her thoughts caused physical pain. "I feared they could track my energy signature, too, and I didn't want my closeness to make it easier to find you. That's why I had to say goodbye. I have followed your energy from a distance. But this morning, it changed. You started growing brighter. Until you didn't flicker like a candle anymore. You swelled to a fireball. I pinpointed your location from many miles away. It was easy."

"Mom, are you okay?" This crossed the line between eccentric and needing psychotropic medications.

She suddenly sat upright and very still, like a deer that spotted a hunter.

A black SUV pulled over behind them.

"Stay here," she said.

Even in Warren's condition, it seemed wrong for his forty-five-year-old mother to greet the strangers. He should protect her. He grabbed her arm. "No, I'll talk to them. I mean, they're probably just good Samaritans seeing if we need help."

"Stay here," she said again. The command felt hypnotic. She had trained him to mind her quite well over the last eighteen years.

Three men and one woman exited the SUV. They wore what looked like all-black army fatigues. They had guns in holsters around their waists. One of the men wielded a black square that looked like a phone, but he held it up like a weapon.

Warren followed his mother out of the car. He had to hold himself up against the side of the car to keep from toppling over, but he couldn't let his mother face these people alone.

"You need any help, ma'am?" said one of the men. He had a Southern accent that tugged on Warren's deepest memories.

Then, many things happened very quickly. All four of the soldiers looked at Warren. Although he had hoped to intimidate them, their reaction surprised him. They stared for only second or two, but in that moment, they looked at him with awe, like children looking at a well-stocked Christmas tree. The female soldier drew her gun and aimed it at Warren. But she didn't have a chance to pull the trigger.

Warren's mother—the one who had rocked him and sung him lullabies and had packed his lunch box every morning before school—pounced several feet in the air like a jungle cat and attacked the woman. She first grabbed the woman's gun arm and twisted it until Warren heard it break. Then, she threw her against the side of the car by her ponytail, breaking the window. The woman crumpled on the ground, blood oozing from the back of her head.

"Caebellum," said the man who spoke first. "Kill it."

The man without the black box pointed his gun at Warren's mother. His hands shook and he didn't shoot fast enough. Warren's mother lunged toward him and grabbed him around the neck. She took his shoulder in one hand and his head in the other and pulled his head back . . . way too far. The man fell, his head lolling to the side.

She looked up at the remaining two men and waited. She breathed in and out through her teeth and didn't look human.

The men dropped their guns in surrender. She stepped back from them, perhaps to imply they could go. She didn't stop them from taking the bodies of their fallen brethren into the SUV. The SUV turned and went back the way it came.

Except for some blood on the gravel, it might have never happened. Warren's mind had so much trouble digesting what he had witnessed, he had to fight off oblivion. He wanted to ask his mother if she wanted to get lunch and repress the whole memory of what just happened. She stared down at the ground by Warren's feet, her mouth set in a pained frown. Warren noticed blood on her sandals and he couldn't take it anymore. He leaned over and retched.

She came over and rubbed his back. "I'm sorry," she said. "But I couldn't let them take you."

He stepped away from her. "What the fuck are you? What have you done with my mother?"

She grimaced like he had hit her. "You really don't remember, then?"

Tears brimmed in her eyes. Warren didn't remember the last time he had seen her cry. She reached her finger toward her eye and Warren flinched, expecting anything. She pulled out one brown contact, and then another. She looked back at him with bright violet irises, which popped in contrast against the white part, reddening from her tears. That shade of violet couldn't exist on a human without the use of cosmetic lenses.

"What about now?" she asked.

Warren said nothing. He felt like he might retch again if he opened his mouth. He feared his mother. The only parent he had, his ultimate protector.

"Do you remember your real mother at all? Your real father?"

The words didn't hit him very hard. His real mother? No. He only remembered the woman standing before him. And he didn't remember any father.

She moved closer to him, tears falling freely from her alien eyes.

"Some of the others didn't want to follow through with my brother's wishes. They wanted to drop you and Isaac in the river. Said you were destined for darkness. Destined to be killers. But I already loved you. And I already knew that you were not bad. I wanted to be your real mother. I wanted to raise you to become good men. Honorable. Compassionate." She straightened herself up and held her head high. "And I did it. All by myself."

Warren turned his back to her, went to his car, turned the ignition and drove away.

CHAPTER NINE

arren's mother . . . or the woman he had always called his mother . . . followed him to the motel he decided to stop at. When he parked by the office, his mother parked nearby but didn't get out of her car. It didn't look like she would stop him from checking in. Warren didn't care anymore about anyone recognizing him as a Wilde. He wanted a shower, a bed, and television, and didn't give a crap about anything else.

He put on his sunglasses and entered the office. The young woman behind the desk smiled at him. He fake-smiled back at her, and whatever she might have thought of him, good manners or good customer service prevailed and she checked him in with cash and the expired ID of a twenty-two-year-old man named Travis Ellis, not a perfect match for Warren, but a white man with dark hair, anyway.

He fastened both locks on his room door and put up the *Do not disturb* sign for good measure. He doubted the sign would keep the soldiers away, and he now knew his mother could rip the door off the hinges. He looked out the window. His mother's car remained in the lot, but he didn't see her. He closed the curtains and took a long, very hot shower.

After his shower he felt mildly better, but only because he'd rather be scared and clean than scared and dirty. He flipped through the channels looking for something that wouldn't make him think too hard and settled on an old Simpsons rerun.

Warren heard a light knock on the door, but ignored it.

Then, after a minute, the knock came again and his mother said, "Warren?"

He crawled out from the covers and looked out the peephole.

The wrinkle between her eyes had grown more pronounced than ever. She held a Wendy's bag. "Are you okay?"

Warren didn't say anything.

"I know you don't want to talk to me. But I have to tell you. They found you like I did. Isaac, too. I think so, anyway. Are you listening?"

Warren still didn't say anything, but she continued.

"Wildes give off energy. It makes you easier to find, but it's still hard. Even if their equipment works as well as my senses, they have to be close. And if the new King is looking for others, he'll have no idea where to look. He's done something to make your energy hotter so they can find you easier. That's why you felt sick. The sicker you feel, the closer they are, I bet."

"What do you mean, we give off energy?"

At the sound of his voice, he saw her put her hands and cheek against the door.

"I'm sorry, I don't know how to explain. It's in your genes."

"Why is the King looking for us?"

"I don't know. Maybe he doesn't want someone else to take the throne."

It seemed like a stupid reason. Warren wanted to become King of the Texas Empire about as much as he wanted a double root canal and chest wax. He wanted to go back to Eugene. Go back to his job at the brewery. He would finally call that girl, Kristie, he had met at a party two weeks ago and if she forgave him for taking so long to call, he would ask her out. He wanted to do all that, the simple things. Go to college. Date pretty girls he met at parties. Play fantasy football. Ride his bike through the massive pine trees in the parks in Eugene. He missed his awesome life.

"I don't want to stay away from you, Warren. But Caebellum can be tracked, too. Since they know I'm with you, they might use my signature to try and narrow down your location."

"What the fuck is Caebellum?" Warren asked. He had never talked to his mother like that, but she didn't seem to notice or care.

"The King kept us hushed up. The royal family didn't like the U.S. to know the stuff they came up with. They're so smart, they can come up with things the U.S. can't. But they didn't come up with us, not exactly. During the U.S. Cold War, they made soldiers who were stronger than regular people, with science. And Lord Pike stole the science and created us. We were supposed to kill the Wildes, but they won. Killed most of us. I haven't hurt a person since I left the Empire. But you're my son. I would kill anyone who tried to hurt you and I'm not sorry."

Warren said nothing.

"It's how I can track you. We were designed like that so we could . . . hunt you. Hunt Wildes."

She stared at the door with her brow furrowed. Maybe she waited for him to say something.

"I thought you might be hungry," she said. "I'll leave it outside your door."

Warren watched her put down the bag and walk away.

Warren picked at his Wendy's meal and watched the rest of the Simpsons episode. He didn't feel like eating. He needed to get his head on straight. His life turning upside down couldn't distract him any longer. He now knew exactly what had happened to Isaac.

He pictured the scene. Isaac, sixteen years old and all alone in a strange town with no friends, suddenly inflicted with a painful burning tingling he couldn't explain with his medical reference books.

So he did the only thing he could think of. He went home to his mother. He complained about the light, so she blacked out the windows the best she could. She should have known. She should have figured it out faster and not left him alone. She had failed them in so many ways.

She went to work because she feared losing her job. Didn't think about losing her son. She left him alone. When they came to the door, Isaac knew to fear them. He hid in his old room. They came in through the window. Then, the blood.

Warren had thought about that smudge of blood a lot. He had thought about its pattern and diameter. Always checking it in his memory to make sure the blood loss couldn't have killed him. No. They probably had hit him and Isaac bled onto the carpet when he fell.

His little brother.

And then? What? She said they wanted to eliminate competition for the throne. *Eliminate.* The word stuck in him like a rock lodged between his ribs. But they could have killed him then. They could have made it look like a random murder or even an accident that no one could trace to the King. But they hadn't. No, they hadn't wanted to kill him. They took him for some other purpose, which meant they must have kept him alive.

Alone. Waiting. Warren just had to find him.

Warren's skin felt hot and cold at the same time, and that didn't have anything to do with any mysterious energy. He wanted to act. If he knew Isaac's location, he would drive right there and start flinging his fists around.

If the King had ordered Isaac's kidnapping, then Warren assumed that Isaac's kidnappers would take him to the King. Before the bomb, anyway, the King had lived in a palace in Waterloo. Should he just drive to Waterloo, look for a palace, and barge in asking for Isaac? In a movie or epic novel, the hero would quest to the King's Palace and somehow defeat all the King's soldiers by himself and rescue Isaac from a dungeon, perhaps guarded by a dragon. For some reason, he thought he thought he needed a slightly better plan or at least a magic sword.

He flipped through the channels and stopped abruptly when he saw Lena Lowell's face on the screen, the girl from the magazine. The girlfriend of the son of the President.

A reporter interviewed her on a news show. Lena wore her golden blonde hair down in loose waves. Girls could probably buy glow in a bottle these days but her skin seemed to radiate its own sunshine.

Caught up in watching her lips move, he didn't really hear her words right away. When he started listening, what he heard surprised him. From the tabloids, he knew she dated Will Cole, and therefore he thought they would share girl talk about going on dates with Secret Service in tow. But at the bottom of the screen he read, *Lena Lowell: Representative of the Texas Freedom Campaign (TFC)*.

"Opponents of the TFC long believed that the land inside the impact zone was uninhabitable and unpopulated, and that the surviving Texans did not have the infrastructure to sustain a Commonwealth, let alone a free nation," said the female interviewer. "What do you say to them now?"

"Now that our reporters have proved that the Texas territory is not a barren wasteland, the U.S. government is out of excuses for not providing immediate assistance to the people still living there, including assistance with building a new government. If they don't act, now that there is proof, they must concede that they don't wish to assist Texas due to sheer bigotry," Lena said.

"Although you are from the Texas territory, you left there at age four. Many of your cohorts at TFC are other young Texans who were smuggled out by missionaries after the blast. With all due respect, you can't possibly know enough about the Texas people to make any judgment."

"I haven't lived in Texas for most of my life, but I have studied it plenty. Enough to know far more about Texans that most politicians today. Many Americans believe that Texans are anarchists who believe the West should stay wild. Americans think Texans are stupid people who prefer to suffer under a state of lawlessness and the whims of monarchs than admit that American values are superior. They were wrong on many counts. We know so much more about the real Texas Empire now. All its territories, except for the Texas territory, have become Commonwealths or states. The territories of New Mexico, California, Deseret, Nevada, and Navajo have proved to excel as Commonwealths. And we have found that they can to govern themselves effectively and justly. And of course, the Louisiana and Arkansas Territories, who joined the Texas Empire during the American Civil War, have re-entered the Union as states without any problems. Unlike what many Americans believe, the Texas Empire had a governmental infrastructure and provided many of the same services as our government, so the transition was not difficult. In addition, a switch to democracy isn't too much of a stretch, because in many ways, the people already ran the Texas Empire due to the monarchy's belief in laissez-faire government."

"Yes, but the monarchs owned so much of the capital that you can hardly say the people had any true power," said the interviewer. "The monarchy had control over the economy through ownership of corporate monopolies that stifled true free enterprise. As their opponents used to say, who needs high taxes when you can set prices at whatever you like?"

"Well, with Texas as a free nation, that wouldn't be an issue. And the technological advancements kept proprietary by the monarchy could benefit everyone. Waterloo was the epicenter of technology for the entire Texas Empire. Perhaps more of their resources have survived the bombing than we believe. The technology and proprietary knowledge kept in Waterloo is worth saving."

"And what do you say to those within the pro-Texas camp who call you an inappropriate spokesperson for TFC because of your associations with the Cole family? Some even call you a traitor."

If the woman had asked Warren that question, he probably would have said something along the lines of, "Screw you, lady," but Lena remained poised. Her composure reminded Warren of the President.

She smiled. "I certainly understand that many Texans will never forgive William Cole, *Senior,* for his actions. I count myself among them. But Will and I met while he worked with the TFC to support a bill, a bill that passed, to send needed aid to the Commonwealths. He is not his father."

"But the President herself does not support the TFC."

"Not yet. She has said that she would be open to the Texas territory becoming a Commonwealth if they can show proof of an ability to sustain it, but she does not believe that it's fertile ground for an independent democracy."

"I suppose it can't hurt to have a direct line to the President to share your views."

"It is a great opportunity."

"And what do you say to Saul Wilde, who calls himself King?"

Lena hesitated and had a very brief look of fear on her face—her only moment of lost composure. "The TFC has no message for him. We do not presume to be his enemy. He has never spoken publically and we have no knowledge of his intentions, or whether or not he actually calls himself King."

"You're speaking in Oklahoma City next weekend, correct?"

"Yes, that's right. It's the next stop in the TFC tour."

"Thank you for being here."

After only a few minutes of watching her, Warren felt more hopeful without really knowing why. He had the gut feeling she could help him, like a giant blinking arrow hovered over her head. He could stop in Oklahoma City on his way to Waterloo, anyway.

CHAPTER TEN

Will pitched an invisible object at the television screen and a tank exploded in a fiery orange spray of pixels. The speakers rattled the floor with the sound, and the explosion seemed to reverberate in Will's brain. His temples pulsed with pain. His mouth filled with saliva and he thought he might vomit.

He turned off his video game. He had tried to play through his discomfort, but he didn't want to vomit all over the carpet. He had felt crappy all afternoon, but tried to ignore it. The sickness he felt differed from a cold or stomach bug, and that strangeness bothered him more than the feeling itself.

"Uh . . . ." Will blinked a few times. Turning off the television didn't ease the sensation of brightness. The brightness seemed to come from behind his own eyes. He became oddly aware of his heart beating. He couldn't literally hear it, but its presence seemed more . . . obvious . . . than usual.

Then, the energy inside him and everything around him seemed to surge to an unbearable brightness. He could no longer tell where his own energy ended and the rest of the world's began. He feared his soul would rush away from him in the surge. He thought he might have slid onto the floor, but he could have slid on the surface of the sun, for all he could tell.

Will hadn't answered Lena's calls. After four unanswered calls and a handful of ignored texts over the course of a day and a half, she got pissed off and worried enough to track him down herself, a tricky task for a *terrorist* whose boyfriend lived in the White House.

After a security check where a female guard cupped Lena's breasts to look for hidden weapons in her bra, they finally allowed Lena to enter the private quarters. She found Will holed up in his bedroom, with all the lights off and the curtains drawn. Upon seeing him, she felt her face get hot without knowing why. She felt like she'd walked in on something too private to see.

He lay in bed, curled on his side. Shadows colored the skin under his eyes, like he had kept them open all night. He slowly adjusted his position to look at her.

"What's wrong?" she asked.

He grunted and shrugged one shoulder. "I think I have the flu."

"Did you see a doctor?"

"No."

"I'll take you."

"No!" he shouted.

She didn't appreciate him shouting at her, but he looked so sick, she would give him a pass. She ran her hands through his sweaty hair. She didn't know if she imagined it, but she thought she felt that charge again, like the one she felt on him the Capitol, like he vibrated almost imperceptibly.

"You do feel a little . . . hot or something."

The intercom buzzed to life by Will's bed.

"Victory Brighton is here to see you," said the voice through the intercom.

"Ugh," Will said. "Okay, I guess. Lena, would you let her in when she comes up?"

Lena met Victory in the main living area. If Lena followed her instincts, she would have run, because the little voice in her head screamed, *danger.*

Victory stared at Lena. She wore her long blonde hair down and loose strands flew everywhere. She had indentations on her hands where it looked like she had dug her own nails into her skin.

"What are you doing here?" Victory asked.

"I'm Will's girlfriend," Lena said firmly.

"Where's Will?"

"His bedroom. He's not feeling well."

Victory rubbed her temples as if this information stressed her immensely.

"Sick how?"

"The flu."

"It's not the flu." Victory moved close to Lena. So close, Lena thought she felt a charge radiating from Victory's body, too, although she couldn't imagine why.

"You know it's not the flu," she whispered in Lena's ear.

Goosebumps popped up all over Lena's body.

In an odd reversal of mood, Victory took Lena's hand delicately and pulled her into an embrace. Victory entwined her fingers in Lena's hair.

"What's happening to me?" Victory whispered.

Lena couldn't breathe, let alone say anything to answer her. She definitely felt the charge emanating from Victory now, reverberating through her. Lena's heart beat uncomfortably fast, as if hit with an electric current. Victory leaned her face very close to Lena's neck, as if smelling her, and Lena felt her lips lightly brush against Lena's skin.

In another sudden reversal, Victory pushed back from her and tossed her hand away violently.

"Why are you with Will?" she asked.

"What do you mean?" Lena managed to choke out.

"You don't love him."

"I . . . ."

"Why are you really with him?"

The left side of Lena's face exploded in pain and she tasted blood in her mouth. She saw her blood trickle onto the carpet and realized Victory had hit her. Victory yanked Lena's head back up by her hair and struck a second blow to her face.

Lena needed a moment to recover from the shock of it all before she could fight back, but she managed to land a punch on Victory's jaw. Lena's hand throbbed in pain and she couldn't imagine she had hurt Victory more than she had hurt her own hand.

"What the hell?" Will asked, leaning against the wall in the hallway.

"I'm sorry," Victory said vaguely and turned around and left, clutching her face.

CHAPTER ELEVEN

Warren didn't claim to pay attention all the time in history class, but he knew about the Eternal War of Oklahoma. Way back when, when the U.S. first made Oklahoma a U.S. Territory, they had a disagreement with Texas about which branch of the Red River constituted the border between the U.S. and the Texas Empire. They *never* resolved their disagreement, and for more than one hundred years, the Texas Empire and the United States drew their maps differently. Over the years, they fought several bloody battles over the land, giving the area the nickname The Bloody Red. In fact, King Reven used this disagreement over land as an excuse to make the first move in the Second American-Texan War. He invaded The Bloody Red, and then just kept on moving.

They didn't actively fight over this land for the whole time, but even in times when the two nations shared a period of peace, each one still kept a minor occupation of soldiers on guard. Warren pictured one Texas Empire soldier sitting in a chair on one side and one U.S. soldier sitting in a chair on the other side, both punching the clock day in and day out, but there to prove that yes, neither country will ever give up on this ugly, random piece of land. It also meant neither country had official claim of the area, making it an inland international waters, where people traveled from miles around to dump bodies and such. People often referred to land around the border between Oklahoma and Texas as The Worst Place on Earth.

Oklahoma City still looked bomb-worn from the Second American-Texan War. The city didn't seem to have anything left over from before the war except for a few empty lots still filled with old foundations and miscellaneous rubble.

Warren walked into the Oklahoma City Hilton. The owners rebuilt the hotel in 2007 to look like the historic hotel that had occupied that spot before the war, an old-style hotel that felt so fresh and new and had a fake quality, like a movie set or a Disneyland attraction.

Warren put on his sunglasses, even though the sun had set. Texas Freedom supporters had overrun the hotel to attend the rally, and he needed to keep his famously familiar appearance hidden. He couldn't help but smile at the scene in the lobby. He felt hope bubbling from every corner. Texas had definitely survived in this lobby. Loud talking. Loud laughter. Some guy in a cowboy hat played a guitar. The doormen constantly stopped people from walking outside with full beer glasses, still ignoring U.S. laws about public drinking after years of living there. The TFC supporters had tied red ribbons to everything. Ponytails. Luggage. Belt loops. Someone had even tied red ribbons around the banister of the stairwell. The red ribbon was the symbol of the TFC, and had once been a symbol for Texas revolutionaries. Red symbolized passion—freedom at any cost.

He went to the bar and ordered a beer and the bartender didn't card him. His freakish height had some advantages. He had passed for twenty-one, at least some of the time, since his sixteenth birthday. He saw a couple of girls not much older than he was glancing at him from where they stood by the wall. He could tell by their smiling and whispering that they glanced at him for the reasons Warren liked, and not because they had recognized him as kin to their ruthless overlords.

He smiled at them and walked over. They wore red ribbons in their hair and Texas flag T-shirts. He didn't have too many special skills, but he could flirt well enough to get the information he wanted. He didn't like to use people like that, but he had a noble cause. Men had done worse for less.

"Hi," he said. The simplest pick-up lines often worked the best. "I'm Travis."

"Hi," they both echoed back.

"I'm Josie," said the smaller girl. "And this is Madison."

"You're here for the rally?" he asked.

Josie nodded and sipped her beer. "We intern for the TFC. What about you?"

"I live around here. Just wanted to check it out."

"Are you from Oklahoma or from Texas?" asked Madison.

"Texas," he said cautiously.

They nodded approvingly.

Warren didn't know where Josie came from, but her genes had mixed nicely into a combination of cappuccino skin and auburn hair. Madison had long brown hair, big brown eyes with thick lashes, and breasts that might cause her to topple over any minute. But it was all a waste. Warren didn't want to so much as lay a finger on either one of them. Thank God a few feet separated him from their invasive energy.

Between his mother's bizarre explanation and what he had experienced, he concluded that the King had some sort of device that made people of Wilde descent feel like crap. As his mom had said, Wildes had some kind of extra energy in them that other people didn't, and the King had a device that amplified this energy so he could track down the Wildes. In his head, Warren called this device *the amplifier.*

Lately, it seemed like the King had his energy amplifier thing on all the time, but not on as high, or perhaps it had moved farther away. Warren wondered if the soldiers had moved on to track down someone else. Either way, he could walk around without passing out, but touching people sucked.

Yet another girl, with dark blonde hair and too much eye makeup, joined the girls.

"Kristen, this is Travis," Josie said, "He's one of us."

Kristen reached her hand out to Warren, and he hesitated. He knew it would feel awful to touch her, but what would it feel like to her? Warren shook her hand as quickly as he could manage. When he touched her, he felt vulnerable. Too alive. He could feel life, or his soul, or whatever made him different from a corpse, pulsating inside him. The awareness of his life force made his soul feel more tenuous, like a stiff wind could blow it away.

All living things gave off energy, and closeness forced a connection between his energy and the energy inside the other living thing. Electrical things gave off energy, too, which seemed uncomfortably intense, but felt markedly different than life energy. The electricity that ran a computer differed from the electricity than ran a person. He couldn't explain the science of it . . . if he could call it science, even though Isaac probably wouldn't . . . but he could tell the difference as easily as he could tell the difference between red and blue. Electrical devices always felt the same, but the energy of people pulsed with unpredictable patterns and rich emotions. Touching something alive with the amplifier on made him feel more vulnerable than he ever had in his life, including the first time he'd let a woman see him naked.

Kristen pulled her hand away quickly.

He guessed she must have felt something, but she didn't comment. Probably she couldn't explain what she felt or thought it would make her sound crazy.

She eyed him with a touch of fear.

"What's with the sunglasses?" Kristen asked.

He would need to get some brown contacts, like his so-called mother had done.

"I know it's a little strange," he said. "I have a photosensitivity."

"What color are your eyes?" Josie leaned close to him, and he felt her energy wafting toward him like an odor. He shuddered. "Wait. Let me guess. Brown?"

"I knew you'd get it on the first guess," Warren said. "Brown with little flecks of gold and green. They are quite spectacular. Too bad you can only see them with the lights off."

"I've never heard of anyone with photosensitivity," Kristen said. "Does that mean you can't go out in the sun?"

"Like a vampire," Madison said.

Warren would have to learn how to lie better. Instead of a Wilde, he would go undercover as a vampire? *Much better.*

"It's just my eyes with the condition," Warren said.

"It's lucky your eyes are brown," Kristen said. "If they were blue, you would look exactly like a Wilde."

"Oh my God, you're right," Josie said. "You look like Saul Wilde."

Warren laughed. "I don't think so. Besides, I don't know many Wildes who support the TFC." He pointed to his *Free Texas* T-shirt. "Let me get you ladies some drinks."

Lots of drinks.

Will peered out at Victory through a crack in his bedroom door. She had waited until Lena left for Oklahoma City to show her face again. A good idea, since Lena said she hadn't fought back enough and itched for a re-match. He had ignored Victory's calls. But, he would have to talk to her again sometime.

"Thank you," she said when he opened the door all the way. She wore a stained T-shirt and some kind of stretchy exercise pants, and her hair didn't look washed. For most women, this indicated a bad day, but for Victory, the disarray meant something much more serious. She had it together—always—and never seemed to understand why the other humans needed things like days off and sweat pants. He considered her beautiful all put together, but that paled in comparison to how beautiful she looked falling apart. He wanted to hold her and stroke her hair while she told him about her problems. But that couldn't happen.

"Come in," he said coldly.

"I came to apologize for my inappropriate behavior. Is Lena all right?"

"Well, she's pissed. She thought she might have to cancel Oklahoma City because of the bruise on her face. She covered it up with makeup, but fair warning, she told me if anyone notices it, she's going to tell the truth so the paparazzi don't think I beat her."

"That is understandable, I suppose."

"What the hell is wrong with you? She said she didn't say anything to provoke you. Are you . . . jealous of her or something?"

"I'm glad you're with her," Victory said. "You deserve to be with someone who wants to be with you."

Ouch.

"Then why?"

"Something is wrong with me. I can't think straight. I feel emotions with more intensity than I normally do."

"So, more than not at all?"

She ignored his jab. "But you *do* know what I mean. Don't you? The same thing is happening to you."

"I have the flu. Why is that so hard for everyone to understand?"

"Your capacity for denial is staggering," she said.

"I'm fine."

"Come here. Come closer to me."

"Why?" He stayed a few feet from her, as a rule. That was the only way to go cold turkey. No Victory. Just his Lena-patch. And for some reason he didn't quite understand, touching Victory now seemed more dangerous than usual. She had a quality about her he couldn't explain. He instinctively felt like touching her might burn his skin, but that made no sense.

She held out her hand. "Come."

He inched closer to her and put his hand in hers. His heart beat like they were doing much more than holding hands. The brightness that emanated from her didn't feel intrusive. She felt like him, his other—the only two members of the same species.

She pulled him in closer and kissed him. Their first kiss, and Will didn't have time to prepare for it. He tried to focus on her kiss, wanting to remember everything about her taste and the shape her lips. Far too soon, the kiss ended.

She stayed in his arms and looked into his eyes. Her eyes . . . so much like his.

"I felt something," she said. "I thought maybe . . . I wanted you. I was wrong."

CHAPTER TWELVE

ublic speaking always boosted Lena's mood. She loved the high stakes. The touch of fear. The thrill of a room full of people hanging on her every word. After she finished her turn on stage, the adrenaline numbed the pain in her jaw. She walked back from the park with Vance, the private security guard Will had hired for her while she travelled with the campaign. Halfway back, the sodden gray sky burst open.

Soaked from the rain, she shivered when they entered the air-conditioned lobby. Lena knew her makeup slid down her face, and breathed a sigh of relief when no paparazzi braved the rain to get a look at her. They seemed to like following her even more than Will, probably because she didn't have a Secret Service detail.

"What happened to your face?" Vance asked.

The makeup covering her bruise must have washed off.

"I got in a fight with some girl."

"Cool," he said, a little too excitedly.

"Yeah, well, we didn't roll around on the floor ripping each other's clothes off or anything. It lasted about five seconds. It was really pathetic."

"I think I'll picture it my way, thanks."

"I don't like that my security guard thrills about me getting beat up. It's your job to prevent that sort of thing."

He held up his hands. "I'm not responsible for things that happen off the clock."

Vance walked her up to her hotel room and reminded her that she could find him in the room across the hall.

After a hot bath and some yoga, Lena stripped down to her underwear and a TFC T-shirt, then crawled under the covers. She kept the lamp on by her bed and tried to sleep. Sleep didn't come easily. She suffered with nightmares her entire life. Always about home. Her subconscious mind had the uncanny ability to transport her right back to Texas, right after the bomb. It remembered every detail, even when her waking mind did not. The smell of smoke. The black sky. Dead bodies rotting in the streets. Fresh grief from losing her parents. As real and crisp as if it had happened yesterday.

The rain battered her windows and the wind knocked the patio chair on her balcony into the window every few minutes. She would relax, and then notice a shadow or lump of clothes that scared her and sent her heart racing back to a state of complete vigilance. Her terror increased to the point that it defied logic. She hated that she couldn't get used to sleeping in a room alone. She focused on her breathing to calm herself, and counted: four seconds inhale, four seconds exhale, and so on.

The sound of the rain intensified. The jolt of fear that ran through her body seemed to stop her heart for a moment. She saw someone on the balcony.

She froze. Every detail became vivid. She felt like she watched him from outside her body. He opened the patio door and came inside. The rain had drenched his clothes, and he shivered in the cold of her air-conditioned room.

He closed the door slowly and whispered, "Please don't panic."

It reminded Lena of the dream where she wanted to run, but couldn't. She couldn't talk or scream. She just lay there, frozen.

"I'm sorry I have to scare you like this," he said again, in a whisper. "I didn't know what else to do."

He slowly walked closer, as if to avoid frightening a small animal.

In the light of her lamp, she saw him completely now. His eyes stood out in contrast with his pitch-black hair, a cool, almost translucent blue. He looked like a Wilde, no question. The men in the photos had looked more formal and kempt, but his casual college-guy appearance didn't mask his true identity. He wore cargo shorts and a *Free Texas* T-shirt. He held a pair of soaked suede flip-flops in his hand. He raised his other hand in front of him, as if in surrender. He didn't fool her. Her work with the TFC had pissed off the Wildes, and he had come to exact his revenge.

Her blood rushed back to her brain and she found her voice.

"Vance!" She screeched. "Vance!" She shot out of bed and ran toward the door.

The man stepped into her path and pressed himself up against the door like a barricade.

"He went to the vending machine downstairs," the man said. "I have about only three minutes to get you to listen to me before he comes back."

He spoke with a theatrical calm, like he wanted to hypnotize her.

She searched for something she could use as a weapon. For the first time, she thought gun rights advocates had a really good point. She picked up a lamp and threw it at him as hard as she could. He turned, and it hit him in the back, but he didn't seem hurt. Of course not; he looked like a freaking building.

"Please listen. My name is Warren King. I'm not here to hurt you. And if you're not convinced of that in the next few minutes, your guard will return, and you can call out to him."

"You're one of them," Lena said.

He winced. "Yes. But it's not like that. Please hear me out." He spoke quickly. "I'm like you, not like them. I was born in Texas, but I'm from the U.S. I'm in my freshman year at the University of Oregon. I work as a waiter at a microbrewery, and I deliver pizzas.

Or, I did do all those things before this shit. I barely remember Texas at all."

He paused to breathe.

She picked up the remote control and wielded it like a laser gun. Her logic told her to scream her throat raw, but in her gut, she believed him. If she hadn't so recently made the wrong choice by ignoring her instincts with Victory, she might have cried out. Besides, now that she had a good look at him, something about him comforted her; he seemed almost . . . familiar.

"Thank you for not screaming," he said. "I just want to talk to you for a few minutes . . . . Do you want to put on pants?"

Lena looked down at her bare legs. She hurriedly pulled on the closest piece of clothing she could find, a black skirt, which clashed with her T-shirt.

"What do you want?" she asked.

"I need your help. They kidnapped my brother. Wait . . . let me back up. Saul Wilde . . . you know, the man from the footage . . . is looking for me, and anyone like me. People with their blood."

"What do you think I can do about it?"

"I don't know much about this kind of thing. But I know that the United States has a duty to protect its citizens from foreign enemies. Just because I'm distantly related to people they don't like, they can't just let an enemy nation capture an American citizen. We must have some rights to protect us."

"I still don't see how I can help."

"You're the best I could think of," he said, exasperated. "I don't just don't want to walk into a police station or go the Capitol and ask for help. They wouldn't trust my face. They'd put me in handcuffs before I got through the door. I've seen you on TV. I know you date the President's son. You could take a message to him or the President herself. Let her know what they're doing."

"What could she do? Declare war, just to get your brother back?"

His eyes flashed with danger. "Well, what should I do? Just never see my brother again? Let them take me?"

"What makes you think I would want to help the Wildes? You know I work for the TFC, right?"

"That's another reason I thought you could help. If the President won't, maybe the TFC? At least they could help me get into Texas so I can find my brother. You got in to take that footage. I think they took my brother to the King. I need help getting to Waterloo without being caught by the U.S. or the Texas Empire."

Lena shook her head. "You plan to just go to Waterloo and take your brother back? That's so stupid, you *have* to be lying."

"Listen." He stepped toward her and took her hand.

She jerked away immediately, but the touch lasted long enough for her to notice something strange about it. It felt like the nerves in her hands suddenly went wild, and a hot sensation surged through her fingers.

"I'm sorry," he said. "I didn't mean to touch you. I shouldn't have done that. I know it seems like a long shot, but that's just how desperate I am. I practically killed myself climbing from balcony to balcony. I'm begging you."

His ice-blue eyes locked into hers, and she had trouble looking away. His formidable height and wild black hair made him frightening, but his eyes made him look like a scared little boy. Something in them reminded her of Will. She had the urge to take care of him, to wrap his wet, shivering body in a blanket and run her fingers through his tangled hair.

"I don't know," she said. "I suppose I can think about it."

He exhaled audibly and smiled. His smile made him even more endearing. He looked innocent and simple, at odds with the rest of his appearance.

Lena felt foggy. She couldn't tell if he really did have some power to control her mind, or if he just charmed her more easily than she would have thought. He made a small movement that gave her the impression he wanted to touch her again, but pulled back.

The sound of a soda can opening came from just behind the door.

Warren brought his voice down to a whisper, so quiet Lena almost had to read his lips. "So you'll do this for me?"

She nodded.

"Thank you," he said. "I don't want to tell you how to find me. I'll find you."

He went back out onto the balcony and disappeared into the storm.

CHAPTER THIRTEEN

Warren watched Lena walk by with her security guard, resolutely keeping her eyes away from him. He sipped his Jack and Coke at the bar, trying not to look as rejected as he felt. He had followed her to Nashville and left a note under her door asking her to meet him. He wanted to know if she'd talked to the President yet, or someone at the TFC, if she had found out anything that might help him. He supposed it had been a long shot. A mile long. And now he had wasted a whole week on his idea to ask Lena for help.

At least the bartender hadn't ID'ed him, and the guy poured whiskey with a heavy hand. A couple of twenty-something girls wearing copious makeup glanced at him from across the bar. He missed his old self, the self that wouldn't care if one particular girl ignored him when he had a whole world full of perfectly good women to discover. But he couldn't muster enthusiasm for any of them. His fingers burned from the bartender's energy whenever he walked by, and he knew the closeness of those girls would hurt even worse. He didn't take home strange girls, anyway. He wanted to, sometimes, but didn't. But even the thought of sleeping with beautiful strangers didn't entice him now that he knew their life forces would touch. No condom protected against that.

Only one person he had met recently had a touch that didn't feel like a kick in the soul. Lena. He had touched her for less than a second. He hadn't even meant to touch her, and didn't remember consciously deciding to do it. But for that split second, the energy inside him felt like it flowed out of his body into hers. Her touch eased the terrible, energized feeling. In fact, that brief touch had boggled his judgment. Had he really followed her all the way here and wasted all that time for information about how to get into Texas, or did he just want to touch her again?

"Excuse me." Someone tapped him on the shoulder, and the touch shot through him like he'd stuck his finger in an outlet. Warren flinched.

Lena's security guard stood behind him, looking especially surly. Warren had pushed his luck too long. At least she sent regular security instead of the FBI or something. This man couldn't do much more than kick him out of the hotel, and maybe rough him up a little, but the guy stood at least half a foot shorter than Warren, so he probably wouldn't try.

"Would you follow me, please?" he asked.

Warren didn't want to attract attention, so he would go quietly. "Hang on, let me settle my tab."

Warren put some of his last bills on the bar while the security guard glared.

Warren followed the guard, but they didn't head toward the main entrance like he expected; they headed toward the elevator. Once inside, the guard pushed the button for the seventh floor.

"Are you taking me up to see her?" Warren asked. He didn't try to conceal the surprise in his voice.

The guard grunted something Warren couldn't understand. He led Warren to Lena's door and knocked.

Lena opened the door.

He felt her pleasant energy—an inviting contrast to the guard. The guard's energy reminded him of nails on a chalkboard. Lena's energy reminded him of warm water or the sound an acoustic guitar. She wore blue jeans and a body-hugging, gray T-shirt. Hours spent outdoors had made her hair pleasantly messy.

"All right, then," the guard said darkly.

"Come in," Lena said to Warren. He closed the door behind himself and couldn't help smiling like an idiot.

"You know, my boyfriend hired that guard, not me. I had to threaten to tell the President that you got past him in Oklahoma City if he didn't let me see you. I don't appreciate blackmailing people. So, I hope you had a good reason for needing to see me again."

"I told you I would find you again."

"It's been only a week. I haven't returned to D.C. It's not like the President and I have girl talk on the phone every night."

"What about the TFC? Can you get me into Texas?"

"I asked around about how the investigators got into Texas. Apparently they just flew in. The TFC never got approval from the government, they just did it. The head of the TFC told the President their plans and asked her to have the border guards not shoot their plane. He said they'd go in either way. The President ordered them not to shoot down the plane. She probably knew better. It would just add fire to the movement if they were martyrs. She also probably thought the investigators wouldn't find anything, anyway."

"How do I do that?"

"Did you hear what I said? They told the President their plans so no one would shoot down the planes. You'd have to do the same. And I assume you don't have a plane? And no, I don't magically have access to one, so don't ask. Just because I have connections doesn't mean I can do impossible things."

All the energy drained from his body, mystical and otherwise. His only idea had failed. He felt like his knees might buckle, and he sat down on the foot of Lena's bed.

"Excuse me," she said. "What do you think you're doing?"

He pulled himself back up. "I'm sorry. I'm just . . . tired."

Lena cocked her eyebrow and studied him. If someone offered Warren a million dollars to guess what went on her head in that moment, he wouldn't even know where to begin.

"You can sit down for a moment," she said. "But you should know, I have a gun this time."

"Okay . . . . So you're going to shoot me?"

"Not if I don't have to."

"Well, if you do shoot me, aim for the head. Wildes are like zombies, we only go down if you destroy our brains."

"Really?"

"No." He sat back down, and then put his head in his hands. "At least, I don't think so. I haven't tested it."

This could not have gone worse. He knew nothing new about how to get into Texas to look for Isaac, plus, he actually liked this girl, and he felt about as suave as an eleven-year-old at his first school dance. And she wanted to shoot him.

"Are you okay?" she asked.

Warren realized he rocked back and forth slightly, like a crazy person.

"Yeah, I'm fine."

"Are you sure? You look like you're going through withdrawal or something."

"It's nothing like that. I'm just upset."

"Tell me the truth, is this about him?" she asked.

"Is what about who?"

"Will Cole. Is that why you chose me? Am I part of some kind of revenge plot?"

"I have no idea what you're talking about."

"You do know that I'm dating Will Cole?"

"Yeah, I get updates on your personal life from the headlines on the magazines at the checkout counter. But other than your supposed access to the President, why would I care if you're dating Will Cole?"

Well, aside from the fact that I'd rather you date me.

"Perhaps because his father killed everyone in your family and ended the reign of the Wildes. Because your families have been mortal enemies for years."

"I'm not your boyfriend's 'mortal enemy'," he said. "I don't even know the guy."

"Well, that's fine for you. But Will might not see it that way."

"What does he have against me? He doesn't know me, either." Warren stood up without thinking about it and Lena stepped back a few paces. Then, apparently not feeling threatened, she stepped a few paces closer.

"Listen, I'm just some guy," Warren said. "Quit acting like I'm all important and scandalous. I don't have anything against your boyfriend. I don't care what his father did, and I don't care about whoever my father is or what he did."

"You don't know who your father is?"

"No."

"Not to sound like my history teacher or anything, but those who don't learn their history are doomed to repeat it. Not wanting to be who you are doesn't change anything." She pointed her finger at him. "And for the record, I'm not convinced that you're telling the truth about that. You could be saying what you think I want to hear."

"I can assure you, I'm not saying what I think you want to hear, because I don't have a clue what that might be."

Lena looked like she suppressed a smile. "I don't know. The Wildes are known for being charming and cunning. This whole sad, pathetic, please-take-care-of-me-because-I'm-slow-and-simple thing may be an act."

"Uh . . . no, it's not. It's quite real. But thank you for telling me exactly what you think of me. That felt great."

"Advocating for the TFC was easy before I found out you were alive," she continued.

Warren realized by *you*, she meant Wildes in general, and didn't like that she considered him a generic Wilde man.

"We just wanted to offer democratic government to the people of Texas, not usurp Wilde rule. That's not a fight I meant to take on. But the facts remain the same. The people of Texas deserve freedom." She held her head up high, but seemed to blink too much, like she expected him to hit her in the face.

"Great. Yes. I would love for Texas to be free and the Wildes to be out of power once and for all. It would take a lot of pressure off of me."

She looked at him like some exotic animal she had just discovered.

"I know your guard is standing outside the door," he continued. "If I try anything funny, just yell and I'm arrested. Or you can shoot me, whatever. Can you just humor me for a few minutes and pretend like I'm not trying to trick you? You know a lot about all this stuff. Tell me what to do. How do I save my brother?"

"I don't know," she said. She looked at Warren's feet thoughtfully. "We can talk, I suppose, see if we can come up with anything."

Lena should have kicked him out long ago. In fact, she should have had Vance detain him the first time he came into her hotel room and then called the police, or the FBI, or at least Will. She just couldn't bring herself to say no to Warren. Again she worried that he used some kind of Jedi mind trick on her. Either that, or God really wanted to screw with her life.

They ended up sitting next to each other on the bed . . . on top of the covers with a few feet between, of course . . . because they couldn't stand on opposite sides of the room while they talked, and she had no chairs. She told herself that she kept him talking so she could find holes in his story. Or to understand the enemy. Maybe, if he thought she trusted him, he'd relax and start to give things away. But her cheeks felt too hot and the corners of mouth had grown sore from smiling . . . smiling a little too much.

They sat side by side, leaning over a map of North America. They discussed . . . or Lena told him . . . which parts of the border might have the least security.

"The worst place you could try to cross would be Oklahoma. There are whole towns whose economies are based on jobs securing the border. Crossing into the impact zone from any of the Commonwealths would better. Louisiana or Arkansas would be—"

She stopped. They had leaned closer to each other and their bare arms touched. She stared down at the place where their skin met. Like when they touched before, some kind of heat flowed into her skin, like she had plugged her arm into a socket. When she pulled away, it took an extra tug, like the current running between them had a magnetizing effect.

Warren watched her reaction.

"What is that?" she asked.

"You can feel it?"

She laid her hands on his forearm and nodded.

"What does it feel like to you?" he asked.

"Uh . . . ." Her life force, or whatever made her feel happy, depressed, scared, hungry, everything—he amplified it. And right now, happiness swelled inside her like warmth. She pictured it running through her like yellow light. The sensation reminded her of something else she couldn't quite pinpoint—something familiar.

Warren sighed deeply, like he'd just eased into a hot bath. "That feels nice, you touching me. Does it hurt you?"

"No. It doesn't hurt. What the hell is *it*?"

"Wildes have extra energy in them. Don't ask me to explain more than that, because I don't know much more than that."

Lena couldn't help but wonder what it would feel like if they had more skin touching . . . a lot more . . . and the way she felt around him made it hard to care about the consequences. She guessed he thought something similar, and they stared at each other for a few seconds. She broke the stillness by scooting close to him and leaning her head on his shoulder in a manner she hoped would imply she wanted closeness and nothing more. He put his arm around her shoulder and held her. They fell asleep together.

CHAPTER FOURTEEN

Warren watched Lena sleep. They didn't change positions all night. Warren stayed a perfect gentleman, which means he only *thought* about touching her breasts while she slept, and didn't actually do it. For once, he cared more about not scaring the woman off than looking for an opening to touch her breasts. In fact, in the space of twelve hours, he had fallen more for this girl than any he'd ever dated . . . by a wide margin. And he couldn't have picked a worse time or a worse girl. He didn't know if he could handle heartbreak on top of everything else. At least for now, he finally felt sane. Their complementary energies had made his life bearable, at least for the night. He had woken up an hour ago and watched an old movie about the Texas Revolution, when Lena stirred next to him.

"I'm sorry, did the TV wake you?" he asked.

"It's okay. How long have you been up?"

"An hour maybe. You sleep okay?"

"Yes. You?"

"Better than I have in a long time," he said. An awkward silence passed between them. He cleared his throat, "I took your advice. I do think I should learn more about the history of the Texas Empire."

Lena looked at the screen.

"So you're watching movies about Texas history?" she asked, laughing.

"Don't laugh. It's more efficient than reading."

"I guess," she said. "You know, a lot of it is bullshit. If the movie was made in the Texas Empire, then the Wildes are heroes. If the movie was made in the U.S., then the Wildes are villains. Which is this one?"

"*Alamo Rose*. It's an *old* movie. Nineteen-fifties, maybe. I can't tell who made it. The Texas Empire, probably."

"That is supposed to be a good one. Won an Oscar, I think. I've never seen it, though. What is it about?"

"It's a love story," he said.

"I thought it was about the Alamo."

"Yeah. But it's about Matthias Wilde, the dictator . . . or hero . . . whichever, who took control of the Republic of Texas after the Texas Revolution from Mexico. He rode for days to the Alamo to defend Rose from the attack. She would become the first Queen later, but at the time she was engaged to Elijah Holloway. Then, when he got there, Wilde led the Texans to victory in one of the greatest David beats Goliath stories of all time. Somehow he managed to fend off thousands of Mexican soldiers even while grossly outmatched."

"That's how the legend got started," Lena said. "The legend that Wildes have supernatural powers. At least, I always thought it was a legend."

Warren shrugged. "I don't think I have any powers greater than feeling like shit all the time. Wilde doesn't have superpowers in the movie."

"They say Texas won the Battle of the Alamo because most of the Mexican soldiers retreated after Matthias entered the battle," Lena explained. "They called him The Soul Eater. They said bullets wouldn't take him down and the soldiers who approached him died before they even touched him. They just dropped dead, like he sucked their life out."

"Legend," Warren said. "I promise you, I cannot do that."

"That's good to know."

"In the movie, Wilde just inspires everyone to fight harder," Warren said. "Holloway was the General who was supposed to lead the battle at the Alamo, but he got wounded and never made it there. So Wilde took over. Then, stole Holloway's woman. Then, stole the Texas Presidency after the Revolution. Holloway had been leading the revolution and was a shoo-in for President. But Wilde won everyone's vote after what he did at the Alamo. But the way they spin it, this is all a very good thing. An epic love story between Matthias and Rose."

"Have you ever seen *The Last President?*" Lena asked.

"No," Warren said.

"It's a controversial movie made by Texas Empire revolutionaries, the ones who wanted to overthrow the Wildes. The revolutionaries rally behind Elijah Holloway as a symbol. They consider him a hero who loved Rose and loved Texas, and fought like hell for both. All the way up until the King's henchmen killed him."

"Did that really happen?"

"I don't know. But they say that if Wilde had never gone to the Alamo to save Rose, Holloway probably would have become President. The revolutionaries talk about how Holloway would have ruled a democratic nation. The truth is, though, that Holloway was pro-annexation, so he would have pushed for annexation and Texas would have become a part of the United States."

"So, the Texas Empire would have never existed at all?" Warren asked.

"Probably not. The U.S. would have taken the West."

"That's so weird," Warren said.

"Yeah. If a Wilde hadn't led the battle of the Alamo, we would live in the *state* of Texas and you would be a normal guy."

"Sounds nice."

Warren heard a tentative knock at the door. He jumped out of bed.

"Did you call room service?" Lena asked.

As soon as she broke away from him, the energy crashed into him like a dam had broken. He guessed the amplifier had moved closer all night, but Lena's closeness masked the feeling. He had no warning. Now the King's soldiers would take him, with poor Lena in a very wrong place at the wrong time. Energy exploded out of his pores. He felt darkness coming on. He had to fight it. He couldn't pass out and let them just walk in and drag them both out, him limp and lifeless while Lena kicked and screamed.

Lena's concerned face swam in his vision until a strange image replaced it. He saw blue lightning over the Alamo as it appeared on the day of the famous battle. He felt the soldiers dying around him, their souls extinguishing, while the storm above him seemed to suck their lives into it, a raging electric monster that gave off a charge like heat off a volcano. He felt grief. Rage. He even smelled the place. Blood. Dirt. Gunpowder. The stench of his own unwashed body. He remembered Lena and the knock and the door, and said, "I don't belong here."

"You don't belong where?" Lena asked.

The movie about the Alamo, combined with the surge of resurging energy, must have tapped into a memory. Well, not *his* memory. He returned to the room that smelled like clean linen, but the grief and rage of the battle scene lingered. He reached out to Lena and grabbed her, hoping her body would help him keep his tenuous hold on reality.

"It's them. I can feel it," he said.

"What?"

"It's them."

"It's probably my boss. Or Vance."

"No." His gaze darted around the room wildly. With his energy, he couldn't hide, but Lena could. She didn't have a built-in tracking device like he did. He went to the window to examine it.

"For god's sake, Warren, that's a seventh-story window. Get away from there."

"Lena, you don't understand. I can *feel* them."

Lena looked through the peephole.

"Warren, calm down. It's just Vance. I'll get rid of him. Relax."

Lena cracked open the door.

"Hey," he said. "So, I just got a call from downstairs. Your boyfriend is coming up."

"My boyfriend?"

"You know, *Will Cole*." He said Will's name loudly and slowly, as if speaking to a deaf and stupid girl.

"I know who my boyfriend is."

"That's good."

"When is he coming?"

The elevator dinged.

"Now, I guess."

Lena glared at Vance, then slammed the door in his face.

"He's lying." Warren said. His mother said he would feel the closeness of the amplifier and now he sensed them closing in.

"Don't just stand there! Hide," Lena said.

"He is lying. I can feel the energy like my brother did. They found me. *You* should hide. It's too late for me."

Lena looked at him with furrowed eyebrows, then looked at the closet as he heard another knock on the door, more confident this time.

"Lena. Hide now."

"Warren, you have to trust me. I promise you that it really is Will. Go in the closet."

"That won't help anything."

Another knock.

"Now," she said.

Warren threw the ironing board out of the closet in a deafening clatter. She practically screamed at him with her eyes. He backed into the closet and closed the door.

Lena opened the door, and Will stood with his hands in his pockets, circles under his eyes.

"Are you okay?" he asked.

"Of course," she said, too breathlessly.

He raised his eyebrows and her throat clenched. "I just heard a loud noise."

"I ran into the ironing board on my way to the door."

He scanned the room, still looking wary.

"What is it?"

"I don't know . . . ," He shrugged one shoulder, kissed her gently, and then pulled her against his chest. His grip felt vice-like.

"I missed you," he said.

If she had any suspicious smell or anything, he didn't seem to notice.

"I'm surprised to see you. Happy . . . but surprised. Is something wrong?"

"I'm okay." He let go of her, then rubbed his forehead.

"You look like you still feel bad."

"Better. It's still there, but not as strong."

He fell back on the bed, and his head lolled to the side, as if he couldn't keep it up any longer. She had to get Will out. She couldn't stand the tension, waiting for them to find each other.

"Will you take me to breakfast? I am in the mood for chocolate chip pancakes." Lena grabbed his hand to pull him back up. Instead, he pulled her on to the bed. He climbed on top of her and kissed her. Even his gentle touch felt restraining. She just wanted to get out of that room. A familiar current of energy ran into her torso. She jerked away from him, startled.

"What?"

"Nothing. I just . . . felt something weird."

He got off the bed and grabbed her arms to pull her up. "You know, I do, too. Let's get out of here. Something is . . . off."

"Yes," she agreed, too quickly. "Let me check out and we'll go somewhere."

While packing, Lena kept throwing in odd comments about how she never had time to unpack in hotel rooms . . . so basically he didn't need to go in the closet. Will reached down to help her pick up clothes.

"No!" Lena shouted. She didn't want him finding Warren's shoes. "Just relax and watch TV."

The old movie had taken a violent turn and a man beat Matthias Wilde with a club. No need to put ideas in his head. Lena grabbed the remote and started pressing numbers randomly. A sixty-something woman came on the screen modeling a pair of tacky earrings. "Here. Home Shopping Network."

After Will and Lena left, the more time passed, the more the sensation of the amplifier faded. Warren felt almost normal again, or as normal as he felt these days. Now that his mind had simmered down, he realized that what he felt as Will approached differed from what he felt around the amplifying device. The amplifier made the energy inside Warren grow brighter. It enhanced his emotions and made other energies seem brighter, too, because he could perceive them better, but in reality, they stayed the same. This time the energy hadn't come from inside him; it had come from Will. He blamed his intense reaction on the energy because it came on strong after the shield of Lena fell, and because he also feared the soldiers would capture them. In truth, the energy didn't feel as strong this time as it had before. True, he'd had the weird vision, but he didn't pass out, which he considered an improvement.

Warren drank two Bud Lights from the mini-bar and crushed the cans with loud and unnecessary vigor. Raised in Portland, he strongly preferred microbrews, but he wanted to drink two watery, ten-dollar beers to spite . . . whom? Because Lena left? Because she left with Will? He didn't like Will, although he couldn't say why exactly, other than the fact that he had taken Lena away. A touch of jealously seemed reasonable, but he detested Will more than the situation warranted. He briefly considered that maybe his DNA made him hate Will. He knew as much about genetics as he knew about fly-fishing—in other words, almost nothing—but that didn't sound possible.

Ever since they had left, Warren couldn't get Isaac out of his head. He missed him deep in his gut. But he couldn't remember what triggered the memory. It happened every now and then. Something small, like the smell of coffee, a song on the radio he knew his brother liked, even sometimes his own damn reflection, triggered a wave of miserable worry and loss.

A realization hit him that felt like worms in his stomach. Something did trigger his memory of Isaac. Will. Will reminded him of Isaac, like he might have if they wore the same cologne. He had trouble putting his finger on it. Similar energy, perhaps? Something about Will reminded him of how it felt to be around Isaac. Until now, he didn't realize he had felt Isaac's extra energy radiating off him all these years, but something deep inside him remembered. And he felt the same energy radiating off Will, a man he hated for no particular reason, and it didn't make any freaking sense at all.

CHAPTER FIFTEEN

ena suggested they go to breakfast at a restaurant called Tootie's, which had earned fame in Nashville for serving steak as a side dish. The waitress recognized Will, and the owner came out to welcome them personally to his restaurant.

They got lots of looks from people. A few came up and asked for pictures, but Lena didn't feel camera-ready, and the comfort food felt less than comforting in Lena's nervous stomach. Of all the guys in the world, why in the hell had she just spent the night, albeit fully clothed, with a member of the Texas royalty? And why did he have to remind her of an adorable little lost puppy? She made a small dent in her biscuits and gravy before giving up on eating and focusing on her cup of black coffee instead. Will lined his arteries with fried steak and waffles and didn't notice her not eating.

"I'm sorry I've been so out of it lately," he said. "I feel like I haven't even looked at you properly in a while."

Lena smiled as sweetly as she could. He caught her in a good, long moment of pure eye contact, which he probably meant to demonstrate his intention to give her more attention, but Lena just felt X-rayed.

"Would you excuse me? I need to use the ladies room," Lena said. Will stood as Lena got up. She had to get away from his eyes for just a moment. She wandered to the back of the restaurant, toward the restroom, taking her time.

She walked past the counter, and her stomach flew into her throat. *He* had followed them there. Warren sat at the counter wearing sunglasses, drinking a cup of coffee. He swiveled his barstool to face her.

"I need to talk to you," he said.

Lena felt like giving him a good, hard slap in the face for approaching her in public, but that would surely cause more than one camera to flash. She turned to check that Will couldn't see them. He couldn't. Secret Service kept their eye on Will and not her. But plenty of people in there knew her face, and most of them probably had cameras in their phones. She imagined everyone in the restaurant stopping and holding up their phones in unison and aiming them in her direction. She did the only thing she could think of. She ignored him completely.

She kept her eyes focused on the blinking neon restroom sign and made her way into the one for *Gals*. She found a comfortably furnished single room, a good thing, since she might need to spend the rest of her life inside. She tried to close the door but it jammed on something.

Warren's hand grasped the outside knob.

"That was rude," he said.

"And ambushing a woman in the restroom is gentleman-like?"

He pulled open the door and let himself in, her white-knuckled grasp of the inside knob apparently not much an obstruction. He closed the door behind them and locked it.

"What is the matter with you?" she asked.

"I didn't know if I'd get a chance to talk to you again. You need to know something."

"What?"

"Your boyfriend." He said *boyfriend* like a dirty word. "You know how I thought the Wildes were coming when he was on his way up?"

"Yeah, so?"

"I was right, Lena. He is one of them . . . us."

"That's insane." Lena shook her head and chuckled. "He's a Cole. He's *blond*."

"I can't explain it, but I know what I felt. The energy came off *him*. I'm sure of it. The feeling increased as he got closer and went away when he left."

Warren's icy blue gaze bore into her. Lena shuddered. She had seen those eyes . . . that gaze . . . moments ago. She stepped back from him, alarmed. Will and Warren's eyes looked almost identical.

They also *felt* alike. She realized she had felt the charge coming from Will on a few occasions but hadn't understood it. She felt tingly around her boyfriend sometimes, which seemed normal. Now that she saw it, it seemed impossible she hadn't noticed before.

"Oh, my God. I think you're right."

"Good. You need to stay away from him."

"Why?"

"Don't you understand what this means?"

"Not even a little bit."

"Okay, I'm not sure what it means either. But he is clearly some kind of spy or assassin, trying to bring down the United States from the inside. You have to get away from him."

Warren looked like he might break something. Lena didn't know if she should try to comfort him or back away.

"Warren, I don't think—"

"There is something seriously dangerous about someone with evil in him from both the Wildes and General Cole," Warren said.

"Are you listening to yourself? If he's a Wilde, he can't really be General Cole's son."

"Just . . . come with me."

"No."

"Lena, this is not a joke."

"I'm not laughing. You say you don't want to be involved, but you're a Wilde and you want to abduct Will Cole's girlfriend. That is not smart."

"I'm not abducting you and I am not a Wilde. My last name is King."

Lena pushed past him and unlocked the door with fumbling hands.

He didn't stop her.

"Don't follow me." She couldn't tell if he did follow her because she raced back to the table without a backward glance. She threw herself into her chair and shook as she put her napkin in her lap.

"Lena," Will said, "What's wrong?" He actually stood up and came over to her. He touched her upper arm gingerly. "What happened?"

She looked at her arm and saw a faint red hand print. It didn't hurt. Warren couldn't have really grabbed her that hard. Maybe his charge left a mark. She heard the scraping of chairs as Secret Service agents broke from their inconspicuous posts to investigate.

"Can we just go?" she asked.

"Lena—"

"Will." She looked him in the eyes. "Let's just go. Now."

"Okay." He helped her out of her chair.

She had eyes only for the exit. Will put his arm over her shoulder and led her out.

"What's wrong?" asked one of the guards.

"She wants to leave," Will said.

"Why?"

Will shrugged, and Lena didn't feel like explaining. Plenty of people expected the son of the President to date a crazy, spoiled brat, so she might as well take advantage and act like it when the situation called for it.

When they walked onto the gravel parking lot, Will turned to his guards. "Could you just give us a second?"

They nodded, and Will took her by the hand and pulled her to the far edge of the parking lot, away from the guards.

"Seriously, what's the matter?" He tucked a strand of hair behind her ear. "Tell me."

She considered blaming some kind of imaginary female illness when she noticed Will's eyes glaze over. He gazed at a spot on the ground and looked like he might throw up. Then, he clutched at his chest.

"Will?"

He lowered himself onto the ground gingerly, like he couldn't stand a moment longer.

"Hey, talk to me. What's the matter?" She shook his shoulder. A heart attack? He had just eaten several days' worth of saturated fat, but eighteen-year-olds didn't often have heart attacks.

She turned to run back to the guards. A large black vehicle blocked her path. The vehicle ground its brakes and the tires dug into the gravel after turning off the main road at too high a speed. It reminded her of a Hummer, but she had never seen that model before. Before she even had time to panic, the doors opened and two soldiers in black suits emerged, moving quickly. One grabbed Lena and the other grabbed Will and pushed them into the vehicle.

The charge hit Warren so suddenly he stumbled on a parking spot bumper and face-planted into the gravel. The pain from his cheek and hands scraping the gravel blossomed through his body in a tingly wave, no doubt the effect of the energy and not the minor fall. His heart pummeled his chest irregularly. He wanted to stay put. Maybe roll under a mini-van and curl into a ball.

But the amplifier felt close, like someone had just sent a pulse of energy across the parking lot. He didn't want them to find him lying there curled into the fetal position. If his gangly, geeky, little brother put up a fight, so could he. He grabbed onto the side mirror of the mini-van and pulled himself to a standing position. He slid along the side of the van, with at least one hand holding him up so he wouldn't face-plant again. He peeked around the rear to see if he could spot them.

He did. The giant black vehicle that had almost snatched him before pulled into the parking lot . . . snatched Will and Lena instead. Then, it pulled back onto the main road. It all took less than ten seconds. *What the hell?* The energy from the pulse lifted a little and he moved faster, running toward his Camry so he could follow the vehicle before it disappeared around the bend. Maybe the poor little rich boy *wasn't* part of a plot. From what Warren could tell, they found Will the same way they had found Isaac and almost found him. Will gave off the signature energy. Warren just couldn't figure out why. But he didn't have time to think about it, he had to act now. They might take Will to wherever they took Isaac. He could save Isaac *and* Lena if he managed to follow that vehicle.

As he opened the door to his Camry, he paused. The big black vehicle sped back toward the restaurant. It skidded to a stop in the gravel and Will and Lena tumbled out. The vehicle turned back onto the main road before the people inside had fully closed the doors.

Warren didn't even think about it. He ran over to Lena and took her hands to pull her up. He brushed dirt off her back and looked her over, inspecting her for injuries. Lena looked at him like her eyes had frozen in the wide-open position. Warren didn't even notice how loud the parking lot had been until it got quiet. Scrambling footsteps on the gravel, a man shouting orders, a monster SUV peeling out of the parking lot. And then, nothing.

Four members of the President's Secret Service huddled around Will, about three feet away from where Warren picked gravel bits out of the scrape on Lena's palm. They froze there for a span of several seconds in stunned silence as a voice on the other line of the lead agent's phone said, "Hello? Did I lose you?"

CHAPTER SIXTEEN

arren reminded the Secret Service agents that he had broken no laws, but that didn't seem to matter. They flew him to Washington, D.C. for questioning and put him in a cell. Being a Wilde and doing something dumb like touching all over Lena Lowell in front of four Secret Service agents must count as a federal crime. On top of that, he had managed to drift even farther from Waterloo and saving Isaac.

Warren looked at his watch. 6:30 a.m. Or, in other words, only five minutes since he had checked his watch last. Maybe soon they'd bring him breakfast. He wondered what type of food they served to prisoners. Imagining possible breakfast options served as a good distraction, and he started making a mental list of every breakfast food he could think of.

He couldn't remember any part of his life that sucked more than the past nineteen hours. Not because they had tortured him or anything else he'd imagined as the Secret Service van took him away, but because they left him alone with his thoughts for most of that time. Just waiting. With nothing as much as a candy wrapper to read for distraction and the magnitude of what had just happened weighing on him, dark thoughts rolled unchecked through his brain, like a series of violent films with who or what the hell knew running the projector.

"Is quiche considered a breakfast food, or is it just for brunch?" Warren called to the guard.

"Stop trying to talk to me," the guard called back wearily.

"You know, I don't think I've ever actually had quiche. I'm sure it's good, I would just never think to order it, you know? Whenever I eat breakfast out, I always get pancakes, or at that diner in Eugene, I get the waffles with strawberries. I mean, if they have pancakes, why would you order anything else? What do they serve here?"

"Not pancakes."

"Eggs? Toast? Or just some kind of gruel?"

"Shut up or it's nothing."

Warren considered for a moment. "I'd rather talk than eat. Is a fritter a breakfast food? I think I'm thinking of a frittata. Do you know what that is?"

A phone rang and Warren heard the guard speaking.

"Really? All right, then. Yes, sir." The guard made swift, scrambling noises. Warren heard the crinkle of wrappers and something thudding into the trash, then a series of beeps and the sound of the heavy door opening.

"Good morning, Senator," said the guard.

"And to you, my good man," responded a voice that sounded vaguely familiar to Warren. "Would you mind waiting outside, so I can speak to Mr. King in private?"

"Of course, sir. Press the intercom button when you're done."

Warren heard the beeps and the sound of the door again. A man came into view of Warren's cell, and he recognized him right away from his copious campaign ads from last year's election.

Senator Brighton smiled at Warren. "Look at you, fresh and bold as an American morning."

"Thanks," Warren said. "But I was going more for the lazy, sticky afternoon look."

The Senator looked at him quizzically but didn't seem too fazed.

"I am Samuel Brighton. You can call me Sam."

"Hello. I guess you know my name."

"I sure do. Would you mind terribly if I came into your cell for a chat?"

Warren shrugged. Sam Brighton didn't frighten him. At least on television, he always seemed fatherly. Perhaps the appearance of the Senator just broke the monotony, but Warren felt better now, like Sam would fix everything. Thankfully, the amplifier must have stayed down south. The smell of stale cigar smoke emanated from Brighton, but no noxious energies.

"Have a seat, son," the Senator said and Warren sat next to him on the hard bed.

"I've done my homework on you. Good student. Nothing on your criminal record except a minor in possession of alcohol charge and a couple of speeding tickets. But, nothing wrong with having a little fun now and then." He winked. "All in all, you seem like a fine, upstanding young citizen, am I right?"

"I try to be."

"So tell me, how did you get tied up in all this mess?"

Warren considered the man for a moment. He had wanted the government's help in finding Isaac. He didn't know much about the Senator, but he had power, maybe he could help. Perhaps his mixed-up, charged self had accidentally done the right thing by running in front of those guards.

Warren told Sam his story—about Isaac and the amplifier and how he'd run from the Wildes. Sam listened with a crease in his brow, his face still and impassive. Sam also asked how Warren escaped the bomb and how many other Wildes had survived. Warren told him the truth . . . he had no idea.

Sam just nodded.

"If what you're saying is true, you sound like a loyal American," Sam said. "And you don't see eye to eye with the others of your kind."

"You could say that."

"There is only one problem with your story," he said. "According to you, those men were after you. But they grabbed Will Cole. Now, why would they do that?"

Warren hesitated. He had had some time to think about Will's little problem. It sucked enough for Warren find out about his ancestry, but for Will Cole . . . yikes. Not to mention for the President. If her son was a Wilde . . . well . . . they all knew how babies were made. That intimidating little woman with the blonde bun and American flag pin who led the free world had one hell of a secret.

"They made a mistake," Warren said. "They meant to take *me* out of that parking lot. That's why they brought him back like that."

"I'm not saying that Texas Empire soldiers win any prizes for their intellect, but wouldn't you think they could tell the difference between you and Will Cole?"

Warren didn't want to rat out Will if he could help it. But he had never mastered the art of a good lie. He tried his best.

"They moved really fast and didn't look at him too closely," Warren said. "And they may not have even been looking for me specifically. They're looking for Wildes. They caught on to my signature but didn't narrow it down well enough. I know Will doesn't look like me, but like I said, they weren't necessarily looking for me. It could be anyone with Wilde DNA. They couldn't see me because I fell down. They thought the energy came from Will. They messed up."

Sam didn't respond right away.

Warren started to get nervous. He could tell that something he said upset the Senator, but he tried to hide it. His already ruddy face became redder and his breathing became irregular.

After a guard served Warren breakfast, a surprisingly delicious bowl of oatmeal laced with brown sugar and raisins, Warren finally fell asleep. Or rather, he passed out. His body overthrew the mad leadership of his brain and shut the whole operation down without notice.

He awoke when he heard a loud metallic bang. The adrenaline kicked in and he returned to full-on consciousness. A different guard, the day guard he supposed, had struck his nightstick against the bars of the cell to wake him up. Another man, so obviously Secret Service he could have walked out of a bad action flick, glanced at the other guard with disdain. The Secret Service guy looked like he considered himself a fifty-dollar steak and the guard a ninety-nine cent junior cheeseburger. Warren thought he looked like the kind of guy who had authorization to torture people.

"Mr. King, please come with me," said Secret Service in the toneless, all-business voice Warren had expected.

"Where am I going?" Warren asked. He pictured a small room with no windows or cameras . . . or witnesses.

"That is classified."

"Classified? Aren't I about to see where we're going?" Warren wanted to laugh, although it probably would have come out sounding hysterical.

The Secret Service guy said nothing but gave the briefest look toward the guard. Warren caught on that the *security guard* couldn't know. Also not good. He didn't want to go anywhere classified even to security guards.

But Warren couldn't do much to alter his fate. They might waterboard him and he didn't even know what waterboarding meant. The man cuffed Warren's hands and walked behind him, directing him with an occasional, "Turn left," or "Turn right."

They appeared to be in a nice office building. Everyone wore badges and looked official, but they had time, in their serious and important business, to stop and gawk at Warren, like seeing a little green man they'd taken from a secret UFO crash.

They went down an elevator to a deserted floor with narrow hallways. The Secret Service guy led Warren to a door, opened it, and directed Warren inside.

Warren entered a small room with no windows, and no cameras Warren could see, but it looked more like a meeting room than a torture chamber. At the head of a small conference table sat the President of the United States.

Holy shit.

"Have a seat," the President said to Warren in a somber tone that reminded him of meeting with the principal.

To Warren's astonishment, the Secret Service guy closed the door and left the two of them alone. They didn't worry about him assassinating her? Of course they had taken anything from him that could serve as a weapon in any way, including his belt, and cuffed his hands. It must mean she didn't think he had any super-powers, at least, not any that would allow him to break out of handcuffs or suck out her soul with his mind.

She looked smaller in person than on television. She also looked older in person, but her skin had held up pretty well for a woman close to fifty who probably had the most stressful job in the world. He found her attractive for a woman of her age. Perhaps that came from her power. She gave off one of the strongest auras of confidence he had ever witnessed. She didn't appear frightened of him, or even concerned in any way. She stared at him for a while, studying him. He wondered if she could read minds. Good luck to her. *He* barely knew what he was thinking.

When the silence had gotten so unbearable that he considered telling raunchy jokes to the President to fill space, she finally spoke. "Are you always this reckless, or was yesterday a special case?"

Maybe he might still get waterboarded.

"I'm sorry, Ma'am, I don't know what you mean."

"You ran out in front of four Secret Service guards, just to help your girlfriend stand up."

"She's not my girlfriend."

"There are people who have gone through a lot of trouble to keep you alive. Please respect that."

"Yes, Ma'am . . . what do you mean?"

"What is your opinion of the Texas monarchy?" she asked, apparently too important to stop and explain things.

He felt like a complicated issue deserved a complicated answer, and he hadn't prepared for this pop quiz.

"They're bad?" He must have sounded like he had the IQ of a gnat.

She smiled slightly. "Bad?"

"Yes. Yes, they are." He started to come back to himself. "They kidnapped my brother, and they're coming after me, too. I know what I look like, but I'm not on their side."

"You know, even if they have taken your brother against his will, they won't kill him. They took him to protect him. To preserve the bloodline. That's why they want you, too, although something tells me they're not trying as hard to get you."

"What does that mean?" That actually offended him. Those idiot royals thought he wasn't good enough to capture? Did they have some kind of IQ requirement Warren didn't meet?

"When they do bring you to the palace at Waterloo, you may find that it's not objectionable."

"When?" Warren said. "Don't you mean if?"

She didn't respond. "Do you intend to seek the throne?"

"No."

She raised her eyebrows. "Why not?"

"Why would I? It sounds like a lot of work and people would always be trying to kill me. Why in the hell would I want that?"

She actually laughed.

"Perhaps you are smarter than you appear." She looked down at her hands and her jaw tightened. She took a deep breath. "Tomorrow, the military is taking custody of you. They believe that you wish to assassinate the Cole family."

"I don't."

"I did not suspect that you did. However, my Cabinet is against you. I know what you're thinking. I am the President. But I am not always in charge. I do, however, have access to resources to help you avoid military custody. I assure you, that is not something that you want."

Warren didn't need convincing.

"Secret Service will transport you to another facility tomorrow. You will escape from their custody in transit."

"I can't escape from the Secret Service."

"You can if they let you go. But the news will say that you used your abilities to overtake them and flee."

"You mean my super strength and ability to fly?"

She smiled slightly. "The public is so frightened of the Wildes' legendary preternatural abilities that they will believe it without specifics."

"Why are you helping me? I mean . . . I'm not trying to be ungrateful."

"If the American government keeps you in custody with no cause and no trial, Saul Wilde may consider that an act of war. I don't want war. Many of the others around me are itching for a reason to engage what's left of the Texas Empire and wipe the Wildes out once and for all, when they are weak and so few. But war is not in the best interest of the country or my family." She paused. "And perhaps, one day you'll remember that you owe me a very large favor."

That last part had an ominous feel to it, but Warren didn't see any reason to argue. He did owe her a favor and frankly didn't think he had much to offer, favor-wise, anyway.

"I'll owe you two very large favors if you help my brother Isaac as well."

She pursed her lips. "I can tell you with reasonable confidence that they will treat him well and will not harm him. I will speak to the King about his trespass onto U.S. territory and acquisition of American citizens."

"You will speak to him about it? I'm sorry, Madam President, but that doesn't sound like much. I want Isaac home. And I want to go home, too, back to my normal life."

"You can't ever go back home to your normal life." She said the words with a surprising tenderness, a motherly tone surfacing above her presidential demeanor. "I can't help you with that. It's not possible. I don't have any reason to trust Saul Wilde, but my instinct tells me that he doesn't want war any more than I do. At this point in history, the United States is far stronger than the Texas Empire. War would hurt his country and his family far more than it would hurt mine. Thus, I do have some power over him. But I don't know what weapons he might possess or how quick he would be on the trigger. So I can't demand Isaac back. He would not comply, and it would hurt diplomatic relations, or worse."

"You don't know that he wouldn't comply. You said yourself that you have power over him, that he doesn't want war. How come keeping me prisoner is considered an act of war, but him imprisoning Isaac isn't?"

"Because you have great value to him. I value you as I value all American citizens, but you're not special to me. I won't endanger millions of people for you."

Warren opened his mouth to argue, but she continued.

"In his rational mind, the King doesn't want war. But historically, the Wildes have not been rational, especially when it comes to protecting their bloodline. And his is dwindling . . . because of the actions of *my* husband."

It sounded strange when she referred to General Cole as simply *her husband*. They had divorced before the trial and Warren couldn't remember hearing her call him that in public.

"He's desperate," the President continued. "Lions don't usually hunt humans, but if you starve them and whip them, they will not think twice about mauling you to death."

Warren didn't really understand her metaphor. But he knew it meant she wouldn't help him get Isaac back. He felt a little bit like a starved lion himself at the moment.

"What if you're wrong? My mother told me that Saul Wilde is seeking out other Wildes because he wants to eliminate competition for the throne. If that's true, it would make the most sense to kill Isaac and me."

The President nodded thoughtfully, like she agreed with his point, and the tiny nod made his chest seize. He did not want to have a good point. He wanted to be dead wrong.

CHAPTER SEVENTEEN

ecret Service agents questioned Lena for six hours about her *relationship* with Warren King, then sent her home to her D.C. apartment and asked her not to leave town.

Lena's cell phone had rung about twenty times the next morning, but she had so little interest in answering, she had almost forgotten what the sound meant. Eventually she would have to get out of bed and live her now much-less-promising life. Her phone sat on a cardboard box that served as a nightstand. Her combined dislike of unpacking and her inability to afford an apartment full of furniture worked together nicely. She picked up the phone without leaving her cocoon of blankets.

"Lena? It's Marjorie." Her boss.

"I'm sorry. I told Shelly what had happened. They took me to D.C. I didn't have a choice. They won't let me leave town. They have a black van outside my apartment and everything."

Marjorie paused, and Lena could hear the bad news sitting silently in that pause. "I'm calling because the Board voted to let you go."

Lena's stomach clenched.

"I want you to know that I'm against it," Marjorie said. "I don't believe what they're saying about you."

116

"Like what?"

She paused again. "You haven't seen the news?"

"No."

"They caught the whole incident on video. They say you led Will out of the restaurant and away from his guard so some Texas radicals could pick him up. And that you were seen being intimate with a Wilde man."

"None of that is true. It's all a misunderstanding."

"I told you, I don't believe it. But the Board doesn't want you associated with the TFC. It's bad for our image."

"Marjorie . . . please, don't do this. I can explain everything." Lena felt tears coming on, but she kept them back. She wouldn't cry on the phone with her boss.

"Lena, don't feel too badly." Marjorie lowered her voice. "I shouldn't tell you this, but the TFC is going under. If they weren't forcing me to fire you, I'd have let you go in a few weeks anyway. Our backers are pulling out. They're afraid of the King. It's over."

"So all the work we did. It was for nothing."

"I'm sorry."

"No. This can't end like that. I'll keep working for freedom myself."

"I hope you do. Goodbye, Lena."

Lena hung up the phone without saying goodbye back, then flung it across the room. It just didn't make any sense. Lena believed in fate. She escaped the bomb against all odds. She lived, when so many others didn't. God wouldn't let that happen without a reason. She had a purpose on this Earth, and she thought that purpose meant working for the TFC. If she didn't make her life matter . . . then, her parents' death wouldn't matter, either.

She picked up the remote, but couldn't bring herself to turn on the TV. She wanted to know what happened to Warren, but on the other hand, she might not want to know. He had to be the stupidest man alive for doing what he had done. How had the Texas Empire lasted as long as it did with people like him in charge? She wanted to see him to make sure they hadn't killed him, but she also wanted to hit him square in the face.

Lena heard a knock at the door.

She looked out the peephole. She expected a reporter, but saw Will. Her stomach twisted into knots. Her boss fired her about a minute ago. Now she would get dumped by her boyfriend too.

She opened the door.

Will walked into her apartment without invitation. He had an ugly bruise on his jaw where the Texas soldier had hit him.

The soldiers had taken only about a minute to realize they had screwed up. They had thrown her into the back of a van with Will. Will tried to kick the door back open and got punched in the face for it.

The soldier who hit him gave Will a good hard look, then said, "Shit. Is he who I think he is?"

The soldier holding Lena said, "It's motherfucking Will Cole."

Then, the driver said, "What are you waiting for? If that's Will Cole, shoot him in the head."

The one who hit Will said, "Wait, how did this happen? Wasn't he giving off the energy signature? Matt, you said it was him."

"I thought he was," said Matt, the one holding Lena.

The one holding Will pulled out his gun and pressed it to Will's temple.

"Don't shoot him," Matt said. "That's not anywhere near our orders. Do you want to start a war?"

"He deserves it," the driver said.

"He's a kid," Matt said.

"Fuck this," said the soldier with the gun. "Abort. Turn the car around."

And they did. Before she knew it, Lena's hands scraped gravel back in the parking lot, then Warren pulled her to her feet.

"Why didn't you answer your phone?" Will shouted. She had never heard him raise his voice before and the contrast frightened her.

"I'm sorry."

"I thought they had already taken you."

"What?"

He went into her bedroom and Lena followed. He pulled the suitcase out of her closet and opened it on the bed.

"Pack," he commanded.

"Why?"

He ignored her and ripped an armful of shirts off their hangers and threw them in the bag. "I suggest you start helping me," he said.

She grabbed his arms and made him face her.

"Will, stop. I don't understand what you're doing. We don't live together. You can't kick me out of my own apartment."

"You really messed up," he said.

"I didn't do anything. Please let me explain. There is nothing between me and that guy. The news is sensationalizing everything."

"He spent the night in your room," Will said.

"How did you know that?"

"Your security guard 'fessed up."

"Nothing happened. It wasn't like that."

"So you just painted each others' nails and had a slumber party?"

"Will—"

He cut her off. "It doesn't even matter. This isn't about you cheating on me."

"I didn't."

"You're going to be arrested any minute." He squeezed her arms back and shook her a little. "You *really* messed up. They've decided to try you for treason. My mother gave me the heads-up. They will arrest you any minute now."

"If I run, I look guilty. I haven't committed treason, and the evidence will prove that."

He laughed humorlessly. "You think it works that way? The only reason my mother wants to help you is because they're going to torture you. Maybe worse. There are corrupt people high in the government. And I don't want you to be tortured or killed . . . call me a romantic."

"Torture me? I don't think so."

He shook her again, harder this time.

"Remember who you're talking to. The Coles and the Brightons are corrupt. You really believe the story that my father went rogue? The pressure got to him and he just went nuts and launched that bomb all by himself? Don't get me wrong, he did it, but he wasn't alone. He was just the scapegoat. The one they executed to pretend like they cared. The people who helped bomb Texas are still in power. They were willing to kill millions of people in their war against the Wildes. Don't think they won't kill you."

"What are you saying? You know other people who were involved in the bombing? You know their names and you have never said anything?" A burst of rage joined her whirlwind of emotions. "People who killed my parents are still walking around running the country, and you're just okay with that?"

Will finally slowed down. He put down a pair of running shoes he had pulled from her closet.

"I shouldn't have said all that. I don't have proof. I'm sorry. I just want you to understand the seriousness of the situation. I want you to run." He put a piece of folded paper in her hand. "I have instructions for you. A way to get out of the city."

"So you're telling me goodbye?"

Will looked at her with indifference. Like they hadn't dated for the past year. Like they hadn't lost their virginity together on the bed in front of them. Like he barely even knew her name. He said nothing.

"I didn't sleep with Warren," Lena said. "After a year together, you have to at least let me tell you what happened before you dump me. You owe me that."

"He was still in your room when I came over, wasn't he? I recognized him later when we *met* at the restaurant. Where was he, hiding under the bed?"

"I hid him because of who he is and who you are. Not because of anything else. There was no sex . . . no anything. Wait, what do you mean, you recognized him? Did you *feel* him?"

He said nothing.

"Wherever I'm going, you should come with me," Lena said. "I mean . . . do you know why they grabbed you? Why they thought you were who they were looking for?"

"And I assume you think you do."

"You must be a Wilde."

Will laughed coldly. "I know who my parents are. And it's not just because I look exactly like them. There were no mistakes when I was born, Lena. My dad's brother was born with cystic fibrosis. It runs in our family. So my parents didn't have me the old-fashioned way. They used in vitro so the embryos could be checked for the genetic disorder before they were implanted. They had my whole family tree mapped out to determine the risk. I'm related to the Kennedys, the Brightons, even the British royal family. But no Wildes."

"You're related to Victory?"

"No. Well, not really. We're fifth cousins or something."

"But—"

"Goodbye, Lena."

"No."

"Just read the paper and do what it says."

"Will . . . ."

He left the apartment without looking back.

CHAPTER EIGHTEEN

The black Secret Service SUV pulled into an alley in a very sketchy part of D.C., and the driver instructed Warren to get out. Portland had bad areas . . . Warren had grown up in one . . . but this alley looked like a crime scene waiting to happen, and it smelled like urine.

"Now what?" Warren eyed a pile of rags that resembled a sleeping or dead human. They hadn't even given him his belt back.

"This is the end of our instructions."

"Can I have my wallet? At least give me money for a train ticket."

"What do you need a train for? Use your superhuman powers."

Great. *Now* Secret Service had a sense of humor. The driver pulled away, still smirking. Warren figured that, although they had to follow the President's orders, they still hated him for his DNA and wanted him to know it. Well, he had been a straight, white man for eighteen years, so he figured the world owed him a little discrimination. Although he could handle it better if he really did have superhuman powers. He thought about Lena. In reality, he wouldn't have wanted her within ten miles of that alley, but he found himself suddenly wanting her there. He probably wouldn't see her again.

With the crunch of broken glass, a car pulled into the alley.

Warren's adrenaline kicked in, and he looked around for things that could serve as weapons. He settled on a loose brick and held it up ready to throw. He didn't have any super-powers, but he had thrown a mean fastball when he pitched in high school.

A man stepped out of the driver's seat, and Warren threw the brick as soon as he saw the man's face. He had never seen the man before, but Warren didn't need to know him. Tall, black hair, blue eyes, a Wilde if he ever saw one. The man ducked, and the brick hit the top of the car, leaving an impressive dent.

"You little shit," the man said. He pulled a gun on Warren. Gun beat brick. "What is the matter with you? I'm here to help you."

"At gunpoint?"

"If need be."

Warren's thoughts felt red and cloudy, but through the haze, he noticed that this man didn't fit with the soldiers who tried to take him on the road. He looked forty or maybe fifty, wore khakis and a polo shirt, and drove a Prius. He had no Texas accent. With his height, don't-fuck-with-me stare, and of course the gun, he did look frightening, but he looked more like a professor than a soldier. Also, although Warren did feel the pressure of the man's energy, the amplifier wasn't on. This man found him the old-fashioned way. Someone told him he could find Warren here.

"Get in the car," the man said.

"And if I don't?" asked.

"Do you not understand what guns do?"

"You're one of them."

"So are you."

They stared each other down for a moment.

"You won't shoot me," Warren said. "You wouldn't chance killing another Wilde when we're so few."

The man laughed. The laugh had a strained sound like he hadn't used his laughing muscles in a while. "Wow. That's a good one. Just get in the car."

Warren stood his ground.

"Think about your options, boy. You can get in my nice air-conditioned car, and I will help you escape the people who wish to harm you. Or you can stay out here, get shot, and try to find a way out of D.C., bleeding, with no money, and that face."

Warren knew he would have to get in the car, but if it had to happen, he would prefer the man to drag him in kicking and screaming. He didn't want to go willingly. Although he guessed the gun made it count as unwilling.

"You know, I'll be taking you to where Lena is."

The sound of her name hit him like a punch in the gut.

He squinted at Warren smugly, like he had known that line would work.

"What have you done with her?"

The man rolled his eyes. "I am helping her, dumbass. Just like you."

That didn't convince Warren, but with no alternative other than a gunshot wound, he got in the car.

The man drove for a while without saying anything, but he kept glancing over at Warren. After about twenty minutes, the man said, "Do you need to use the restroom or anything? I don't want to stop after I get on the freeway."

"Where are we going?"

"Boston."

"What for?"

"I live there."

"Are you going to tell me who you are or what you're going to do to me?" Warren asked.

"Jack Craven. And I already told you what I'm going to do with you. Keep you safe from the Wildes and the United States government. At least, as long as I can. I'm no miracle worker."

"Why are you helping me?"

"How about, *thanks*?"

Warren glared out the window.

"So, you're in school, right?" the man said. "What are you studying?"

"I'm undeclared," Warren said coldly.

"Undeclared? What field do you want to go into?"

"I don't know. That's what undeclared means."

"Don't you have any interests?"

"Yes. I like collecting stamps and competitive eating," Warren said sarcastically.

"You don't take yourself very seriously, do you?"

"Why do you care about career goals? You sound like my—" Warren felt sick. After all his years of picturing someone awesome, he would hate this man to be *him*. "You're not my father or anything, are you?"

Jack laughed. "No, I have no interest in spreading my curse. My DNA dies with me."

They ended up at one of those East Coast-type houses, much taller than wide and smooshed in with the other houses in matching red brick. In this neighborhood, the homes had flags in their yards and signs supporting either Cole or Brighton. Apparently these people had continued campaigning, even though the American people elected President Cole well over a year ago. Jack's house didn't have any flags or signs, or any other sign of loyalties or affiliations, not even a name on the mailbox.

Warren followed Jack to the front door, which had a sign that read, *No solicitors.*

Only one word could describe the inside of his house. Sparse. He had clean beige carpeting, bare white walls, and a light gray couch. Warren didn't see a single photo or decorative touch.

Jack must have gone out of his way to personify blandness. One could not achieve blandness this severe by accident. He had wanted to make it very clear to anyone who entered that he didn't care about any people, hobbies, sports teams, universities, or political parties.

Lena ran down the stairs. Warren felt like a weight lifted from his chest. The man had told the truth. She ran up to him and paused before him, with her hands out in front of her. It looked like she planned to either hug him or throttle him, and by the blazing look on her face, he didn't know which to expect.

Lena punched him in the arm as hard as she could.

"Ow." He rubbed the spot where she hit him.

"You ruined my life."

"What happened?"

She punched him in the arm again.

"*You* happened. Now that they know I know you, the United States government thinks I'm a spy. I had to run to avoid being arrested and tortured for information, maybe even executed for treason."

"I didn't . . . what?"

"Oh, and the TFC fired me, and Will broke up with me."

"Come," Jack commanded, clearly unmoved by Lena's predicament.

They followed him around the corner into a large room overflowing with books and papers in stacks. This room would have driven Isaac crazy. Although Isaac might overlook Jack's lack of organization to get a chance to talk to a man who could keep up with him intellectually. Even the titles of most of the books made little sense to Warren. From what he could tell, the books focused on human genetics, biology, and anatomy. He saw titles like, *Theory of Translocations in Autosomal Chromosomes* and *Human Recombinant DNA Technology*.

"Are you a doctor or something?" Warren asked.

"Yes," Jack said.

Maps covered his desk. The largest map showed the entire continent of North America, updated with fresh, new Commonwealths to replace the old Texas Empire and one gray Texas

Territory-shaped hole marked *Uninhabited Area*. A web of multi-colored lines followed seemingly endless, different routes traced with colored pencil . . . routes to the Texas Territory.

"Hell, yes." Warren said. Jack seemed to have his wits about him. If anyone could get in to Texas, he could. "Are you taking me to Waterloo? Are you helping me save Isaac? Did the President send you to help me? How do you know the President?"

Jack regarded Warren like a particularly large and annoying gnat.

"No," Jack said.

"No to which questions?" Warren asked.

Jack didn't respond, and Lena said, "He's helping us escape the U.S. government. And for you, the Texas government, too. He needs to take you where the sensors can't find you."

Lena lowered her voice, although Jack could certainly still hear her. "The President *did* send him to help us. At least, that's the impression I got. I think she's on our side, but she doesn't want people to know it."

Warren looked back at the hopeless maze of possible routes. "Wouldn't the sensors work pretty much anywhere?"

"Well, sort of. But Jack says the energy coming off you is more obvious here. You need to go somewhere where it blends in better."

"I don't get it," he said.

"I don't know, ask him." Lena gestured to Jack who looked at his computer screen and at least pretended not to listen.

"You know what, don't even worry about it," Warren said to Jack. "Get Lena somewhere safe. I'm done screwing around. I'm going to Waterloo to find my brother."

"If you don't want the King to snatch you, you'll do as I say," Jack said. "We're going to go as far as we need to and that's it. One of their old outer territories may be enough, somewhere along the border. Louisiana, perhaps. Do you know how to drive a stick shift?" Jack asked them both.

"I think so," Warren said.

"I don't have a driver's license," Lena said.

"You don't have a driver's license?" Warren asked.

"I live in D.C. and I grew up in foster care. It's not like I got a car for my sixteenth birthday," Lena said defensively.

"How come we give off energy?" Warren asked. He planned to try and limit his questions to one per breath.

Jack gave Warren a heavy look, like Warren had interrupted his lecture on microbiology to ask him where he bought his pants.

"It's complicated."

"I'm not an idiot. Explain it to me."

"It's written into our genetic code," Jack said. "It's not the hocus-pocus that some of our kind believe. We're not special. We're broken. We have a mutated gene that causes us to generate too much bioelectricity. It's the same bioelectricity that everyone has in their bodies to send messages through the brain and nervous system." He gestured toward Lena as if to give an example of a normal human. "Wildes often call it Blue Energy."

"What does it do? Do we have any powers?"

"I told you. No. Some posit that it makes Wildes more intelligent, which I might believe. Messages travel through our brains more quickly."

That explained Isaac pretty well.

"It's an energy source," Jack continued. "We have more than we need to survive, so some have even suggested milking our energy from us like we're cattle. I'm actually a fan of that one. Serves the royals right for letting corporations pollute our planet. Make them a renewable energy source."

"Or they could just use solar or something," Warren said. He recycled, and switched to LED light bulbs for good old Mother Earth, but even a Portland boy had his limits.

"Why do you think the sensors can't find us in Texas?" Warren asked. "That doesn't make sense."

"If you're running from someone, you don't turn down an empty alleyway, you run into a crowd," Jack said.

"You're saying Texas is more crowded than the U.S.?" Warren asked. He wouldn't call Texas uninhabited territory like the map said, but he doubted he'd find a bustling metropolis.

"Yes. But not with people," Jack said. "The kind of energy that comes from Wildes doesn't dissipate. It gets transferred into the atmosphere. After years of Wildes living in Texas, the level of energy has steadily increased. It's wreaking havoc on the climate. What I'm saying is that when they turn on their amplifier, the energy coming from a Wilde in D.C. will stick out. The energy coming from a Wilde near Texas will blend better with the energy in the air. Still can probably find us, but it's not as easy."

"Why are you helping me?" Warren asked.

Jack shook his head. "This isn't just about you. Look at me. I'm running, too."

Lena touched Warren's elbow.

"What about Will?" she whispered.

Jack looked down at his maps again, and didn't seem to care to listen.

"What about him?"

"If he's a Wilde, he's probably the only one left in D.C. They'll find him easily."

"If the President wants to help us, then you can bet she's helping her own son. She'll find a way to protect him."

"What if she doesn't know?" Lena asked. "Will doesn't believe it."

"How could she not know?" Warren asked.

"I haven't told anyone aside from Will," Lena said. "Did you say anything about it when they questioned you?"

"No."

"Why not?"

"The same reason you didn't, I assume." Warren shrugged. "I told you plenty of times. I have nothing against the guy. I'm not going to ruin his life just because I can."

Jack broke out of his problem-solving frenzy. They had captured his undivided attention. "So, you think Will Cole is a Wilde?"

"No," Lena said.

Jack gave the faintest hint of a smile. "Warren, why don't you go up to one of the bedrooms and get settled? We won't leave until tomorrow morning."

"I'll show you," Lena said.

He followed her up the stairs and watched her intently from behind. Might as well look; she would never let him touch her again. He actually cared about this woman, and he had gotten her fired, dumped, and nearly gotten her tortured and executed. He didn't know how to come back from that.

"He has three bedrooms up here and he sleeps in the bedroom downstairs," Lena said. "I already took the biggest one."

Warren wandered into the next bedroom down from Lena's and stood by the bed, feeling very aware he had no possessions. At least he could borrow clothes from Jack, although he didn't look forward to learning more about that man's taste in clothes.

"I don't know how to tell you how sorry I am," Warren said. "I wasn't thinking."

"No kidding."

"You're the last person I would want to hurt. I'm sorry."

"I don't forgive you."

"I'll make it up to you. You're in danger because of me. I'll protect you. I won't let anyone hurt you."

She laughed.

"I'm serious," Warren said.

"I don't know if you can protect me, but at least you can reach things on high shelves. That's got to come in handy."

He didn't appreciate her tone, but after all he had done, she earned the right.

"So did you notice?" Lena nodded vaguely down the hall to reference Jack. "He already knew."

"What?"

"Jack already knew Will is a Wilde."

"What makes you think that?"

"The tone in his voice. He was surprised, but not nearly surprised enough. I think he was just surprised *we* knew."

"Maybe," Warren said.

"Do you think he could be Will's real father?" Lena asked in a whisper. No one else could possibly hear her, but the scandal in the statement warranted a whisper anyway. "I mean, we think Will is a Wilde. And Jack knows the President."

"I don't know," Warren said. "Jack specifically told me he didn't have any kids."

"If he had a secret affair with the President of the United States, he probably wouldn't tell you."

"You know, it could be true," Warren said. "He doesn't have much personal stuff, but he missed something."

"He did?"

"He has his college degrees in his office," Warren said. "The earliest one was an undergraduate degree in genetics from MIT—twenty-eight years ago."

"So?"

"He's not a survivor of the bombing. He already lived here."

"What does that mean?" Lena asked.

"I don't know. But it's kind of weird, don't you think? Why would a Wilde change his name and move to Boston, of all places, *before* the bomb hit?"

"So he was here on the East Coast when Will was conceived," Lena said. "I wonder where the Coles lived then."

"You really think the President would have cheated on her husband with a Wilde? I'm not a fan of General Cole, but still, that's cold."

"Can I ask you a question?"

"Okay."

"Were you born in the Texas Empire?"

He sighed. He didn't want to talk about this. He sat down on the bed. "Yes. We left after the bomb."

"Do you remember it? Did you live in a palace?"

"I don't have many memories from before the bomb. I *might* remember my real mom. I think she had long black hair, which makes it hard to know when the memories of my real mom stop and my adopted mom begin. I had a room with a lot of toys. Blue carpet . . . I don't know why I remember that. I guess when you're small, you spend a lot of time on the floor."

"I remember so much. I remember what my house looked like. I remember the trees outside. I remember my dog. How old are you?"

"Eighteen."

"That's the same as me. Why can't you remember more?"

"I don't know. I think the bomb might have messed up my memories."

Lena sat down next to him. "What do you mean?

"Sometimes I remember some things, but it's like a bad dream. Now that I know what the charge feels like, I think I felt that as a kid, after the bomb. I felt that way all the time while we were leaving Texas. It felt awful."

Lena realized too late she had leaned close to him while he talked and her heart beat faster. She feared what he might say next and she didn't want him to go on. Then, she realized some of the fear she felt didn't come from her; it seeped through his skin. *He* didn't want to go on. Warren stared at the floor, his eyes glassy. He didn't seem to notice she had practically fallen into his lap.

"You don't have to say anything," Lena said. "It's weird what you remember and what you don't. I remember I had a doll named Molly. My uncle handed me over to the missionaries to be smuggled out. I couldn't take much and he told me I could take one toy. I took Molly. I carried her all across Texas. I held on to her for dear life at the shelter in Little Rock. I took her with me on the bus when they transferred me to Washington, D.C. Then . . . ." Tears ebbed out of her eyes and she wiped them away, embarrassed. An eighteen-year-old shouldn't cry about a doll. "I left her on the bus. She was my only possession. The only thing I had that my parents gave me. I brought her all that way and I left her on the bus when I got to D.C."

Some tears made it through and slid down her cheeks. She tried to laugh. "Isn't that ironic?"

Warren kissed her. For ten seconds—or perhaps ten minutes, she lost track of time—her mind emptied to a beautiful quiet. No one had ever kissed her like that. Their lips matched like pieces of a puzzle snapped into one. In the peaceful stillness of her mind, she felt his energy building in her lips and riding the current of her blood. The energy poured through her body into her abdomen, where it seemed to intensify with a momentum impossible to stop. She pulled away from him with a jerk, like pulling a magnet off metal.

"I am still mad at you," she said. She kept her eyes away from him to avoid temptation.

She heard him sigh deeply and the covers of the bed rustle as he shifted away from her.

"Okay," he said.

CHAPTER NINETEEN

ictory researched suicide methods on the Internet. All her life, she had taken success seriously. She believed one should approach every endeavor with preparation, diligence, and attention to detail. Death was no exception. She couldn't make a mistake. No one could call it a cry for help. The first attempt would be the last attempt.

The bright computer screen hurt her eyes and her whole body shook. The sickness returned. She persevered until the light from the monitor became so intense she had to back away, so far that she could no longer read the writing. She shut down the computer. She usually cleared her browsing history after a search like that, but couldn't bear the energy of the computer long enough. She wrote the letters CBH, for *clear browsing history*, on a sticky note and crawled under the covers in her all-white canopy bed.

Her father would return home soon. Well, the man who had raised her. She knew now that he could not be her real father. A Wilde man had raped her mother or she had had an affair with one. Perhaps they had inseminated her in some other unnatural way. Victory didn't know her mother well, as she currently lived in Italy spending her alimony on shoes and other vanities. However, it seemed unbelievable that even a stupid, pointless person like her mother would have an affair with a Wilde man. Her mother may not have really loved her father, but she hated the Wildes, and didn't have the wits about her for an elaborate deception. But one way or another, it happened.

She heard footsteps on the stairs and her father's presence agitated the darkness that cursed her body. Her father's energy felt like chewing on Styrofoam. Not all people felt quite so unpleasant, but she assumed the darkness inside her sensed the closeness of a being who wished to destroy it. When he appeared in the doorway, she couldn't help but wince. The darkness grew stronger. She couldn't stand to look at him. The energy radiated off him with so much intensity, she felt like her skin might blister.

"What's wrong?" he asked.

For some reason, looking at his reflection in the mirror didn't hurt as much. She looked at him in her vanity. He held a large black box that looked like some kind of electrical equipment from twenty years ago, like the CPU of an old computer.

"I'm fine. Just a headache."

"You don't eat enough," he said.

"That's probably what it is." She braced herself and turned to look at him. She looked in his direction and used an imagery exercise to dull the intensity of his energy. She looked at the spot between his eyes and visualized him as a mannequin, an empty vessel, and pretended his voice came over the phone from across the country somewhere, instead of right in front of her. It worked well enough that she could keep herself from passing out.

"I picked up some takeout from that Indian place."

"Sounds good. Thank you."

She followed him down the stairs, several paces behind. He didn't seem to notice. Their relationship had always been distant, in emotional and physical terms.

Her father sat at the head of the table and Victory chose a spot three chairs away from him. He furrowed his brow and looked at her, but didn't say anything about it. She could always count on her father not to question her about odd behavior. If he thought the answer to a question might include some kind of womanly emotional talk or anything unconventional, he didn't ask it.

He placed the black box on the table. When her father moved away from the box, she could still feel his unpleasant presence, but it lessened; the *box* made her want to go upstairs and find some pills to take right away.

"Can I move this thing?" she asked.

"Don't you want to know what it is?"

She shrugged and turned her eyes down to her saag paneer. She moved a few pieces of cheese around her plate and wondered how she would consume them. Her agitation couldn't handle food right now.

"That," he pointed to the box, "is a sophisticated piece of military technology we stole from the Texas Empire."

She raised an eyebrow to fake interest.

"Highly classified. In fact, you and I are the only ones to see it in a long time. I never let the military scientists get their grubby hands on it."

"Because your possession of it implicates you in the bombing."

"Such a clever girl." Out of the mouth of someone else's father, that might have sounded like praise. But from him, it sounded mocking. He continued, more sincerely, "I need you to help me figure out how to use it. You're so good with these kinds of things. And I can trust you, can't I?"

"Of course. I'm not sure if I can help though. I am not an electrician." It also didn't help that she wanted nothing more than to set it on fire and throw it off the third-floor balcony

"It doesn't need to be fixed. I just need to know how to work it. I have never used one, myself."

"What is it supposed to do?"

He smiled and leaned forward in his chair, as if to speak with her more privately in his empty twelve-thousand-square-foot mansion.

"It's like one of those whistles only dogs can hear. Turn it on, and you and I can't feel a thing, but it makes Wildes go crazy."

Her fingernails felt like they vibrated. That box had ruined her life. Ruined Will's life. She should just kill her father, and then dispose of the machine. God . . . what was she thinking? The darkness made her want to do terrible things.

"What's its purpose? Torture?" Victory managed to keep her tone level.

"You remember how I told you about how Wildes give off a certain type of electricity?"

Yeah, she did. During that talk, she had determined the root of her aberration.

"Turn this on," he continued, "and their energy levels increase and you can track them across a significant distance. Bastards got their own damn homing device. And they go bat-shit crazy. It's fucking hilarious."

So, he had seen it used on someone before. She wondered mildly who, and when he had gotten the chance.

"I just need to figure out how to turn the damn thing on," he said.

Victory dropped her fork on the table with a clatter. Bits of spinach scattered on the tablecloth.

Sam chuckled. "Got greasy fingers?"

"It's not on?" Victory asked.

"What?"

"The device, it's currently off?" If that box made her want to peel off her own skin when in the off position, she would have a serious problem.

"That's what I said."

"What do you want to do with it, anyway? Will it affect the Wildes all the way in Texas?"

"I doubt it, although it may be fun to bring out if Saul ever comes back to get his cock sucked by the President again."

"You think she's being intimate with him?"

He laughed. "You have no sense of humor, child. I don't mean it literally. Although she probably would do it, the fucking cunt. At least that's one benefit of having a woman for president. Diplomacy can include sucking cock."

Victory wrinkled her nose at him, but he didn't seem to notice. It didn't matter what he thought anymore. She had intended to become President one day. But whether she killed herself or not, that wouldn't happen now.

"What do you want to use it for?" she asked again.

"Oh . . . just test it out. Why don't you invite your friend Will over and we'll turn it on together and see what happens?"

Victory felt her organs turn to ice.

"I think the fewer people who know about it the better," she said cautiously. "We shouldn't include Will."

"His father would want him to see it."

"Will is pro-Texas. It's too risky."

Her father leaned in again. "You seem rather opposed to Will helping us with our little science project. Any particular reason you would like to share with me?"

"No."

"Invite him over tomorrow. He's a puppy around you. He'll come running with his tongue hanging out."

CHAPTER TWENTY

arren and his new sidekicks, Jack and Lena, drove twenty-four hours straight to the Louisiana Territory. Of course, Lena probably considered Warren *her* sidekick, and Jack regarded both of them with about the same tenderness he showed his luggage. And Jack did most of the driving. Jack allowed Warren to drive for only five hours so he could sleep, but he may not have even done that if Lena hadn't threatened to grab the wheel and pull the car over herself if he didn't stop and rest.

The Louisiana Territory liked to make an entrance. A hundred miles' worth of billboards lined the highway, luring Americans to Louisiana's fine casinos, racetracks, gun merchants, parlors—aka whorehouses, and apothecaries—aka places where they sell drugs. Warren figured the United States had outlawed at least the last two things now that Louisiana had become a state again, but the new state government surely had more pressing matters than taking down billboards.

Warren occasionally listened in history class and he knew that in the final hours of the Civil War, when the South was falling, Texas helped cinch a Northern victory by convincing the slave states along their border, Louisiana and Arkansas, to join the Texas Empire as territories instead of re-joining the Union. The Texas Empire abolished slavery in 1897 anyway, but Louisiana and Arkansas stayed a part of the Empire until it fell.

Even after the massive build-up from the signs, Louisiana did not disappoint. The government had posted notices at the border reminding Americans that prostitution and the sale and purchase of controlled substances were illegal and offenders would be prosecuted. The signs seemed to have little effect. The area around the Louisiana border reminded Warren of Pleasure Island from *Pinocchio,* although he hadn't seen as many parlors in the Disney movie. In addition to the many opportunities to do terrible things not lawful in the United States, he saw ample miniature golf courses, go-cart tracks, carnival rides, wax museums, drive-in daiquiri bars, places to buy fried Twinkies, and anything else known as a tourist trap. Warren didn't say it out loud, but part of him wanted to jump out at his first chance, buy a fried Twinkie and a daiquiri and run over to that go-cart track.

It didn't take a genius to get why those businesses congregated around the border. This highway connected the Texas Empire to the east coast of the United States, and everyone who lived in the eastern United States who wanted to be very, very bad with few consequences came here. Apparently, they wouldn't drive many miles past the border station before they wanted to get out and party, so supply had met demand.

The more obviously illegal places, like Madame Minnie's Saloon and Parlor, had done minor things to seem like legal businesses. For example, the largest sign for Madame Minnie's looked brand new and used the term *dance hall,* but many of the smaller signs still said *parlor.* Another place, called Order of the Garter, advertised *jazz and women,* which Warren supposed left the commodities up to interpretation.

Once they got deeper into Louisiana, the land become much less colorful but rather beautiful and humble. They drove over swamps on roads possibly sponsored by the Hungry Alligator Lobby. He marveled at homes built on stilts right in the middle of the swamp.

The residents had small fan boats tied to the steps, instead of cars parked in driveways. He couldn't imagine why anyone would look at that mosquito-infested swamp and say, "Yes. I wish to live here," but apparently, that's exactly what they did. He wondered if they did it just to prove they could.

The trio *finally* stopped at a motel that looked like it belonged in a bad horror flick. But Warren wanted out of the car so badly, he had started to think the swamp looked like a perfect place to stop and make camp. Anywhere but that damn excessively clean and well-kept Prius. Warren's trusty Camry remained at the diner in Nashville, or probably now in an impound lot. He had lost his family, his identity, and even his goddam car.

Jack got one room, which seemed like two too few.

"I'm not made of money," he said, which Warren took as code for, *I am a rich Boston doctor with oodles of cash, but I'm cheap and mean.*

"The lady can have the bed and we'll sleep on camp beds," Jack continued. "Or does sleeping on the floor offend your royal sensibilities?"

"I'm not royal," Warren said. "And I don't have any sensibilities."

Jack chuckled. "Then, you'll love this place."

"Only days after the FBI began investigating Lena Lowell for espionage and conspiracy, the Texas Freedom Campaign has closed its doors. A spokesperson for the nonprofit states that although the TFC claims no knowledge of Miss Lowell's true intentions, their backers began pulling funds."

After about ten hours of uninterrupted sleep, Warren and Lena sat on the mottled orange carpet in front of the TV. The motel room smelled of mold and cigarettes, with an inexplicable hint of gasoline. Warren eyed Lena cautiously as she bit her nails. The animal-like anger in her eyes made her look like she might eat her own hand. He suppressed his instinct to put his arm around her and say something comforting. Best to try and look invisible.

"Texas isn't going to be free and it's my fault. Rather, it's your fault," she said. "I would say you did this on purpose, but you're not that clever."

Warren didn't appreciate her calling him stupid or blaming him for major shifts in history, but he didn't say anything.

"Everything happens for a reason," she said. "Texas was destroyed so that the Wildes would be destroyed and their territories could finally enjoy democracy. Millions died so that millions more could have better lives for hundreds of years into the future. It happened for a reason. But now, it looks like the Wildes are going to take control again and everything will be exactly like it was before the bomb. They all died for no reason at all."

Lena looked like she held her breath. Maybe she held back tears or more shouting. Warren laid his hand on top of hers, the most he had dared touch her since he had kissed her.

"I was supposed to help Texas," she continued. "That's why I lived. I have to earn my salvation. I have to deserve it. Otherwise, why was I saved?"

"The fate of Texas hasn't been decided yet," Warren said. "You haven't lost."

The TV buzzed with static and Warren shuddered. The energy had blown through the room like a prickly wind. Lena flinched away from his hand and Warren guessed she had felt it, too, through his skin.

"What was that?" she asked.

My own personal hell, Warren thought.

"It's probably because we're so close to the Texas territory," Lena assured him. "Like Jack said, the energy is stronger the closer you get to Waterloo."

The prickly sensation crawled up his shoulder and he shrugged involuntarily.

"Yeah, you're probably right. It's just because we're close," he said.

"I can't believe I'm trying to hide with people who have built-in GPS trackers," Lena said. "No one could find me on my own."

Warren gave her a sideways grin. "Yeah, I'm sure you'd get really far with your face plastered all over the news twenty-four hours a day."

Warren stood up and peeked through the blinds.

A thunderstorm brewed on the horizon . . . not a normal thunderstorm. Deep black clouds towered above the Earth, pulsing with lighting flashes that looked almost blue. Warren's heart skipped a beat as he saw a dark-haired man appear at the top of the stairwell outside the room. He breathed a sigh of relief when he saw Jack. Jack opened the door, letting in mosquitoes and the earthy smell of the impending storm, and handed them greasy-looking brown bags.

Lena pulled back the foil and sniffed.

"Just eat it," Jack said before she could comment.

"What's the deal with those clouds?" Warren asked Jack.

"Thunderstorm," Jack said simply.

Jack moved next to Warren and peered out at the storm as if he puzzled over a complex mathematical equation. He opened the window. The air that blew in had already grown colder. Jack put his hand out the window and waved it around like he searched for a lost object in water.

"Does it feel different to you?" Jack asked Warren.

Warren nodded. Jack looked back at the sky and looked . . . scared. And that scared Warren. Jack didn't seem to have any emotions ever, about anything, so if he seemed worried about this, Warren must have reason to worry, too.

"Dear god," Jack said. "That son of a bitch did it."

"Who did what?" Warren asked.

"Never you mind," Jack said.

"I think I can feel it, too," Lena said. "The wind feels prickly. Is that normal?"

Jack continued to stare at the storm.

"Severe weather is more common in Texas because of the Blue Energy in the air impacting the climate," Jack said. "But *that* is not normal."

The more Warren looked at the storm, the more terrified he felt. He couldn't say why, but this one evoked a feeling in him that would have fit more with seeing black smoke towering over his home or a mushroom cloud. The storm meant something bad. The core of the storm looked like a hole in the sky where deep space peeked through. The bluish-purple edges of the cloud reminded Warren of a bruise. Lighting hit the ground . . . blue lightning. It didn't hit in single strikes, but spanned large portions of countryside in a web of spindly fingers.

"When I was a kid, I remember my mom telling me that the Wildes created the storms," Lena said. "I always pictured a guy in a cloud shooting lightning out of his hands, like Zeus."

"A children's tale, meant for children," Jack said. "But many adult Americans still think that."

"Let's get back on the road," Warren said. "Maybe we can stay ahead of the storm."

"Back on the road?" Jack asked. "To where?"

For a smart man, he had some dense spots in his brain.

"Waterloo," Warren said.

Jack laughed. "I think we're plenty close. If the energy in the air causes *that*," he pointed to the storm, "it will screw up their sensors. We don't need to go farther."

"That's awesome," Warren said. "I can sneak up on the palace then."

Jack raised an eyebrow and studied Warren. "What are you talking about?"

"Have you not listened to anything I've said? I need to find my brother."

Jack pursed his lips and squinted, either a thoughtful look or a sneer. "Don't worry about your brother. I'm sure he's fine. Just worry about yourself."

"So we plan to live in this hotel forever?" Warren asked. "Hide out and keep our heads down until we die?"

"You think that's what I want to do?" Jack asked. "I can't imagine anything more objectionable."

"I'll go to Waterloo with you," Lena said.

"You will?"

"I'm not the type of person who just sits around waiting for things to happen," Lena said. "I'd rather act and hope for the best. You want to help your brother, that's a noble cause. I could use a new cause. And maybe while I'm there, I'll punch the King in the face for trying to kidnap me."

"That all sounds well thought out," Jack said.

"She's not serious about the punching thing," Warren said . . . at least, he didn't think so.

"Listen, I'm not going to say that I'm the best person to give life advice, but I have learned one thing," Jack said. "Don't try to act like a hero if you're not one. You'll just make things worse."

Lena woke up suddenly. She felt someone touching her hair. She swatted the hand away and turned over to see Warren standing by the edge of the bed.

He winced when he saw her reaction.

"I'm sorry. This probably makes me seem really creepy, doesn't it?" he whispered.

Warren glanced toward Jack sleeping in a camp bed.

"It's nothing weird, I promise."

"What are you doing?" she whispered back. When she saw the duffle bag he had over his shoulder, she figured it out. "You want to ditch him?" she asked.

"I didn't mean to wake you up. I was just . . . saying goodbye. Maybe it was a little creepy to touch your hair, sorry. Listen, I don't think you should come. This is my problem. It has nothing to do with you. Like you said, I already ruined your life once. I feel bad about leaving you here with him. But when I think about my choices . . . I think if he wanted to murder us, he would have already done it.

You're safer just staying put. He's got money. He knows things. His face isn't all over the news."

Lena reached up to pull Warren's duffle bag off his shoulder and tell him to go back to bed, and she accidentally brushed his arm. A blast of unease flared through her body, way worse than anything she had felt off him before.

"You're scared," she said.

"What?" He looked at his arm, as if realizing what she meant. "Oh. Hell yes, I'm scared. But that's not what you felt. It's another storm. It's close."

Now that he mentioned it, she felt it, too; the air had a heavy, electrified quality. She felt like if she swept her hand through the air quickly, her fingers might make sparks.

"There's no point in waiting," he said. "I need to go while he's asleep and I might as well try and avoid the storm."

"You could drive right into it."

"So what if I do? A little thunder and lightning never killed anybody."

"Sure it has. Floods. Getting hit by lightning. Wind blowing trees into houses. And that's not even considering hurricanes and tornadoes."

"I wasn't being literal."

She grabbed his hand. She used all her willpower to keep from dropping it. The anxiety flowed off him so thickly, it hurt. Her ribs vibrated. She released him.

"When I touch you, do I feel what you feel?" she asked.

"I have no idea. What does it feel like to you?"

"Right now? You feel like panic."

"I don't want you feeling my emotions. They're mine to tell you about or not. You don't just get to tap in whenever you want." He took a jagged breath. "It's not as bad as you think. I'm getting used to it."

Lena leaned over and snatched Jack's keys off the bedside table before Warren could stop her. "You're in no state to drive. I'll do it."

Warren had snuck out of the house a few times in high school, so he had some practice closing doors quietly. But the heavy door still made a loud, squeaky click when it closed. Warren didn't stop to worry about it and he raced down the stairwell with Lena at his heels. The energy from the storm made him want to run. He had the adrenaline level of someone running from a chainsaw murderer. He felt like if he stayed still, the electricity in him would make him catch fire.

He smelled the rain in the air, and the night sky brightened with a flash of blue lightning.

"Warren, wait," Lena said. "Slow down."

With great effort, he switched from a jog to a brisk walk.

"I want to go to Waterloo, too," she said between hard breaths. "But can you tell me why you want to leave during a storm?"

"I can't stay still," he said. "I'll go crazy. We need to move."

"So we're not leaving in spite of the storm, you want to leave because of it. It's making you antsy."

"I can't sleep. I can't sit still. It's as good a time as any." He reached the car and pounded on the roof on the driver's side. "If you're not going to get in, give me the keys."

"I don't get it. How come you're acting like you're on meth and Jack can sleep through the storm? Shouldn't it bother him, too?"

She had an unfortunately good point. Warren realized he hadn't really looked carefully at Jack's camp bed. He had just seen a bundle of covers.

"What the hell are you two doing?" Sure enough, Jack came from in between two cars. He held a lit cigarette.

"You smoke?" Lena asked.

"I quit fifteen years ago. I thought it might help. It doesn't." He crushed the cigarette under his shoe. "Should have known better than to try and calm my nerves with a stimulant."

"Lena, please," Warren said. He felt the storm inching closer. Under the cover of night, he couldn't see the clouds, just the fireworks display of blue flashes; each one seemed to echo as an irregular pulse in his heart.

"Tell me you're not stealing my car," Jack said. He pulled his gun out from inside his jacket.

"He's not going to shoot us," Warren said. "Please, let's go."

Lena didn't look so sure. She dropped the keys on the ground and put her hands up. She still wore the gray cotton shorts and *Free Texas* T-shirt she had slept in, and untied running shoes without socks.

"He's not going to shoot us," Warren said again.

"Warren, we don't have to leave now. If you don't want to stay still, then don't. I'll run laps with you around the motel if you want. We can race up and down the stairs."

Warren didn't hesitate any longer. He grabbed the keys she dropped, threw himself into the driver's seat, and turned the ignition.

"Stop," Lena said.

"Get in if you want," Warren said.

She ducked down behind the car to shield herself from bullets and crawled into the back seat.

Jack didn't shoot. Warren saw him watch them drive away with the look of someone who just got sucker punched. Warren felt a little ball of guilt harden in his stomach, but ignored it. He looked for the big *W* on the interstate sign that meant west. He didn't know where to go exactly, but west seemed like the right direction.

Lena didn't say anything in the back seat. He had known her long enough to know she usually liked to ask questions and give suggestions. He glanced back at her in the rearview mirror and she looked back at him with an unreadable expression. He turned his gaze back to the road, then felt her breath on the back of his neck. She reached her hands over the seat and rubbed his shoulders. Her gentle touch hurt his tight muscles. Correctly reading his tension, she stopped kneading his muscles and moved her hands across his shoulders and neck with gentle pressure. She siphoned out his extra adrenaline with her fingertips. It felt like she unraveled tight strings around his muscles, one by one.

She moved her hands up his jawline and through his hair. She grazed her nails up the base of his scalp and let her hands linger on his temples. He pulled the car onto the shoulder.

"What are you doing?" she asked.

"That's very distracting."

"I'm sorry."

"I'm not complaining. You don't have to stop."

"Just let me drive. At least until the storm is over."

He didn't like this idea, but mostly because it meant she intended to stop touching him.

"Please."

He felt the hiss of the *s* in *please* graze against his earlobe. It made him forget what she asked for and he said the only word his brain could manufacture.

"Yes."

She got out and opened the driver's side door.

"Scoot over," she said.

He scooted grudgingly. "You said you didn't have a driver's license."

"Just because I'm not licensed to drive doesn't mean I *can't* drive. Any idiot can drive a car."

"If you say so."

"What do we do when we get to the Texas territory border? It's fenced off."

Warren didn't respond.

"You were so *take charge* for a minute there that I forgot that you didn't have any sort of plan," Lena said. "Well, I think you still have a few hundred miles to think about it. We hadn't even made it to Baton Rouge yet."

He couldn't stop staring at her. He wanted a reason to touch her, but since his touch made her feel anxious instead of the other way around, he couldn't use the same excuse she had. If she was his girlfriend, he could hold her hand, brush her hair away from her face . . . or run his hand up her inner thigh.

Fortunately, the relief he had felt with her hands on him remained and even the slight release of tension relaxed his body enough finally to sleep. When he closed his eyes, he crashed hard.

Warren woke up from a nightmare. An image of an old rusty car with all the windows broken in shook him awake. He felt terrified without knowing why. A man sat in the driver's seat. He had a white dinner plate for a face with broken black holes instead of eyes and a mouth. Warren froze and couldn't run.

Why would he dream that? How could his subconscious come up with something so creepy and random?

The fear from the dream stayed with him when he woke up, but he could immediately tell the fear came from the air around him, too. He thought they would make it past the storm, but the charge in the air had increased. Even his lips vibrated with energy.

Outside he saw a dusty, purplish-green hue to the sky that didn't fit with his idea of what any hour of the day should look like. Thunder rumbled and rippled the water in the cup holder. He didn't see Lena.

The electrified air hit him hard when he thrust open his door. It bothered him to breathe the air. He didn't want that energy in his lungs or near his heart. He still managed to expel a deep breath when he saw Lena, safe and accounted for. By the looks of it, the car had broken down. She had pulled the car off the road and had had the foresight to park the car behind a patch of brush. She had the hood open and stared at it as if trying to read Japanese.

"Why didn't you wake me up?" Warren asked.

"I thought you might as well sleep while you could."

"What's wrong with the car?"

"I think the battery is dead."

"Let me take a look. If I could keep my old car running, I think I can handle this shiny new one. And if I can't, we'll just attach some jumper cables to me and see what happens."

"Very funny."

Warren started by trying the ignition. It just clicked, and, nothing happened, consistent with a dead battery.

"I don't think it's the car," Lena said.

"What do you mean?"

"When the car started to act funny, so did the lights outside. We passed a gas station and all its lights started to flicker and go dead. I saw a couple of other cars pull onto the shoulder. It's not just us."

Rain started. Through the trees, Warren saw that deep black had seeped across half the sky, like the sky had split into day and night all at once.

Lena turned to Warren. "I'm sure that the storm will suck, but like when the amplifier is on, the feeling will go away after the storm passes. Once it's over, you'll be fine. Hopefully, the car will start again, too. Let's just get in and wait for it to be over."

"It's going to blow right over us. And we can't go anywhere." Warren couldn't hide the panic in his voice.

"Like you said, a little thunder and lightning never killed anybody."

"And you disagreed with me."

"Okay, so maybe that wasn't very reassuring of me." She held out her hand. "You've got me, anyway."

That one reassured him. He took her hand and she led him into the backseat. She pulled his arms around her and wiggled her body close, to manage as much skin contact as possible. If anything, it distracted him from the storm for a moment.

"It's not real," she said. "It's just the storm. You're not really scared."

Not real? What? The storm? The energy? Very real winds caused the trees to shake, like even the forest panicked in the sight of the very real storm. But he knew what she meant. The energy triggered a false flight-or-fight response. He had nothing to fight and nothing to run from.

He felt sweat drip down his neck, and the back of his shirt stuck to his skin. He knew she could feel him sweating on her and could probably feel his pulse drumming against her skin where his wrist laid against her palm.

Rain pummeled against the window so hard that he thought there might be hail too. The trees continued to flail.

When the storm passed over them, it reminded him of falling asleep. But not in the warm, cuddly, way. He entered that middle place right before sleep when thoughts turned into dreams. Random images started to float into his consciousness without him summoning them. However, his subconscious didn't send the thoughts. They came from the storm. He picked up frequencies like a radio—some marred with static and hard to understand, others crystal clear.

A barrage of unfamiliar emotions enveloped him. He couldn't pinpoint exactly which emotion he felt, like a palate of colors mixed so that they became a brownish non-color. His heart raced and adrenaline pumped through him. The feeling could go with anger, fear, lust, even joy. Those emotions felt oddly the same to him now, slightly different flavors of one force inside him—life.

Images popped into his head. Other people's memories. A little black-haired, blue-eyed girl with pigtails laughing as he pushed her on a swing. He loved her. His daughter. Then, he walked through darkness; he smelled mud, and possibly blood. He heart beat in his throat. He knew within minutes he would die. Then, a beautiful view over green rolling hills from a limestone balcony. It smelled like recent rain. A woman sitting next to him wearing a gown that belonged to a hundred years ago. His wife. Then, brown eyes looking at him in terror. A woman covered in blood and dirt. He planned to rape her. Then, a Wilde woman who looked like a doll floated into the scene and the rape scene washed away around her feet like water. She smiled.

"Who are you?" she asked, her voice alight with mischievous curiosity. Unlike the other images, she didn't seem like long-lost memory. She spoke directly to him.

Lena heard the rain hitting the trees before she saw the massive drops smack the windshield. The sky turned a shade of deep violet Lena had never seen before. Or had she? Some terrible memory stirred deep within her. Suddenly, she could clearly see the sky above Texas after the blast. Even in the daytime, the sky looked black with blasts of blue lightning. She had forgotten it completely until that moment. The memory caused her body to seize up and she struggled to breathe. Did the memory or the storm or Warren's energy cause her to feel that way? She focused on her breathing to stave off hyperventilation. The windows streaked with water, distorting her view of the trees. Something seemed off outside. She saw flashes and movement, as if lightning stalked through the trees like an animal.

When she saw the distorted image of a man outside the window, she thought could be seeing things. However, when he knocked on the window, Lena realized he was no illusion. The door opened. A young man in a simple black uniform embroidered with the flag of the Texas Empire stared in at them.

Someone else outside said, "The sensor is still not working, but this is around the place we caught the signature before."

Lena could tell when the man had shifted his eyes to Warren because his expression changed significantly.

"It's them," he said quietly, almost to himself. Then, he shouted, "Target identified. Swarm!"

Another soldier opened the other door and stabbed a syringe into Warren's neck. She felt his arms slacken around her. Then, she felt a sting in her own neck, and then darkness.

CHAPTER TWENTY-ONE

arren didn't know where he was. Actually, he couldn't quite remember *who* he was. Thoughts that didn't belong to him had crowded his sleep. He had to grasp for his identity like he fished for a lost object he dropped in a puddle. *Warren King. Warren King.*

His eyelids felt stuck closed with magnets. Through heavy blinks, he registered bright sunlight. His whole body vibrated with jerks and bumps. Riding a roller coaster? That didn't make sense. He experimented with moving his arms, then his legs. They felt about twice as heavy as usual.

He realized he had dropped something else in the puddle. Or someone. *Lena.* He still couldn't quite see but he thought he smelled her. He moved his head toward the smell and felt her hair against his face. Her hair smelled like chocolate and coconuts.

"Warren?" He could hear her voice now. "Are you awake."

A sudden lurch dug his seatbelt into his neck and he coughed. It shocked him a little more awake, but opening his eyes fully made his temples erupt with one of the worst headaches of his life.

"Ugh," he said.

They rode in a large vehicle that smelled like carpet shampoo intermingled with cigarettes, and cool air graced his face from an air conditioning vent. They sat upright on a bench seat in the back. Lena sat to his right and he felt the warmth of another body on his left. He turned his head slowly.

An unconscious Jack sat to his left. These assholes caught a nice net of fish today. They must have picked up Jack before they snatched Warren and Lena. Or after, hell, he didn't know how much time had passed since they stuck him with that needle.

Things gradually came into focus. None of them appeared hurt or restrained, except for seat belts. But they couldn't reach the closest door, and a Texas soldier sat in a seat facing them with a gun in his lap. He didn't look much older than Warren, and had hair and eyes the exact same shade of chestnut. He gave Warren the creeps, but he couldn't say why exactly. But the man didn't seem to blink enough and his manicured fingernails looked wrong on a Texas soldier, although maybe Warren stereotyped.

The soldier leaned toward Warren with his shiny, unblinking eyes. "Your Highness, may I get anything for you?"

"What?" Warren asked. "No. Don't call me that."

The man looked back up to the front, as if waiting for an instruction.

"It's okay," said the man in the front. "Call him whatever he wants."

"What would you like me to call you?" the unblinking soldier asked Warren.

"Uh . . . Warren."

"Can I bring you anything, Mr. Warren?"

"I don't want anything," he said automatically. He realized his mouth felt sticky and tasted like rotten milk. "Water."

A bottle of cold water appeared in his hand at impressive speed. He drank half of it without coming up for breath.

"Aren't you going to ask her, too?" Warren asked, nodding toward Lena.

"Oh, yes, sir," the soldier said. "Can I bring you anything, miss?"

"No. I don't need anything you have," Lena spat back.

"That's not true," the soldier said seriously. "Humans need food and water. If humans go even short periods without water, they may experience irritability, headache, and constipation."

Lena looked at Warren. "What a strange thing to say. What's the matter with him?"

"And let me know if you need to urinate or empty your bowels," the soldier said.

The two soldiers in the front laughed.

"Vir, don't say it like that," said the man in the front passenger seat.

"I'm sorry, sir. How should I phrase it next time?"

"Just ask them if they need a pit stop. You know what, just go sit up front. I'll watch 'em."

The soldier from up front made his way to the back and took Vir's place. He wiped his hand on his already-dirty black uniform, and then held it out to shake Warren and Lena's hands in turn. He looked more like what Warren had expected. His freckled, sun-beaten skin made him look old, so Warren couldn't pinpoint his age, maybe late thirties or forties. He smiled at them genially, with crooked teeth.

"My name is Bill. Driving the vehicle is Trevor. You already met Vir. We are soldiers of the King's army. I do apologize for needing to transport you against your will today." He spoke like a local guiding a sightseeing tour. "It's still six hours to Waterloo. I hope that we will all be good friends, but if you try to run or try to hurt me or any of my boys here, I will shoot you."

He showed them his gun and continued his speech. "It *is* a tranquilizer gun. But there is really no need to waste my tranquilizers. Your friend here shot at me when I picked him up, so I pumped him full of tranquilizers and now he's all drooling on his fancy clothes. He was a nice catch, just walking down the side of the highway in his college-boy shoes."

Walking down the side of the highway? Did he actually try and follow them on foot? Warren figured he would have just shrugged and gone back to the motel. Then, maybe the next day, he would have bought a new car in town or even called his insurance company to make a claim. Then, he'd go on his way.

"When we stop and re-fuel, you can get out to take care of your business and stretch your legs. But remember, this isn't your cotton candy world. Stay close to the road. Don't go into the forest. If you see any movement in the forest, or if other cars come along the road, get back in the vehicle immediately. Any questions?"

"Oh, I've got questions," Warren said. "First, where do you get off? What makes you think you're above the law and can do whatever you want? And where the fuck are you taking us and why?"

"Listen, I'm just following orders, sir. It's no use yelling at me."

"Where is my brother? Is he okay?"

"Who is your brother?"

"Isaac King."

"Didn't pick him up. But we're not the only collection team."

"You can't kidnap American citizens. We have rights," Warren said.

"You know you ain't in such a bad way right now," he said. "Lots of people with nothing would be thanking God right now if they were in your shoes. Never have to want for a damn thing."

"So what are you saying exactly?" Lena asked. "What does the King want with him?"

"What does the King want with *her*?" Warren said, gesturing toward Lena. "Let her go. She's not a Wilde."

"Spouses and partners come, too. Orders."

"Why?" Warren asked. "You know, it doesn't matter why. She's not my spouse or partner. I don't even know her. You made a mistake. Let her go."

"That's a nice try," he said. "It's still a ways until we make a stop. In the meantime, Vir will get you anything you need. And forgive him for his people skills. He's new."

"To the planet?" Lena asked.

Bill laughed. "I like you," he said to Lena. "No. He's what we call a Beta. A recent advancement of the Texas Empire, and you know how the King likes to keep all the cool toys to himself."

"I'm sorry, he's a what?" Warren asked.

"A Beta. It means 'second'. Second to man. They're made, not born. Part organic, part mechanical. Good for doing things that men don't want to do. But damn if he ain't smart and sweet as a little puppy."

"He's a robot?" Lena asked.

"Hey now, watch your language, little lady. He may not be a person, but he's no object, either. Betas aren't here just to serve you and me. They're here so that our culture and blood might be able to survive if you try and massacre us again."

"Don't yell at her," Warren said.

"I don't understand why you're mad," Lena said.

"I guess you didn't know. Lesson one—don't use the r-word. It's not nice."

Warren glanced out the window. "Where are we?"

"Just passed through the border. We're in the great territory of Texas."

Inside the Texas territory, deep cracks filled the roads where storms had washed away the asphalt, so the ride reminded Warren of falling down a flight of stairs. He didn't see much point in driving on the roads at all, but the road cut through a pine forest so dense he couldn't see more than a few feet in, so they didn't have a choice. However, after some miles passed, the large trees dropped off suddenly and new growth dominated the landscape. Probably the edge of where the bomb hit. He watched the landscape with the rapt attention of someone who had just landed on an alien planet.

Warren had pictured the impact zone as a post-apocalyptic wasteland with as much life as the surface of the moon. But instead he saw gas stations, markets, working farms, and plenty of homes, most of which looked newly constructed. However, he saw patches of older buildings and tall trees, too. The explosion seemed to reach out fingers from its core, instead of creating a single circle of destruction. The bomb left some areas untouched.

They passed by several oil refineries, gleaming with lights and flames, and emanating disgusting smells. Amazing. Either they built these refineries recently or the rigs never fell. When they passed near Galveston, once Texas's second largest city, Warren actually glimpsed some leftover skyscrapers on the horizon.

Although he saw plenty of signs of civilization, he didn't see signs of government. Most of the roads that split from the highway looked like dirt. He saw some highway signs, but based on their state of repair and apparent accuracy, Warren guessed they had been there since before the bomb.

The vehicle they rode in seemed new, but the other cars on the road looked more than fourteen years old. He saw people riding horses or in carriages pulled by horses and others on bicycles. The telephone poles also looked like relics from another day, and he doubted electricity ran through the wires. He saw windmills dotting the horizon in some places and guessed if anyone had electricity, they had to generate it themselves. He had trouble wrapping his mind around a world where he saw people who rode horses and didn't have electricity on the same day that he met a robot . . . or Beta.

The lack of government also meant a lack of police or firemen. Fires burning unchecked left large black patches in the landscape. One wildfire currently hugged a part of the highway, and the soldiers had to take a detour.

Jack groaned, rubbed his temples, and blinked like the light blinded him. He squinted at Warren and Lena.

"I'm sorry," Warren said. For stealing his car. For his current predicament. Just sorry in general.

"They caught you," Jack said, master of the obvious.

"Yep."

Jack rubbed his fingers into his eyelids so hard it must have hurt.

"Why were you walking down the road?" Warren asked.

"I was looking for you, you little shit."

"On foot?"

"I had a hunch that the storm would disable the car. I hoped you wouldn't make it very far."

"Yeah, we got past the first storm, but the second one killed the battery."

He nodded slowly, like his head weighed fifty pounds.

"Why did you try and find us?" Warren asked.

"Why wouldn't I?"

"Because you don't like us."

"I never said that. But I'm not helping you because you're so likable. I'm just trying to do . . . the right thing."

Warren didn't know what to do with that statement. He didn't believe Jack simply made Warren and Lena his good deed for the day. Still, something in what he said rang true.

Lena had needed to pee for a long time, so when they pulled into a gas station, she busted to get out. No neon sign listed the prices. Just gas pumps and a trailer home tucked into a thicket of trees. The apparent owner of the station waved them toward the pumps with his gun. Lena said she needed to use the restroom, and Bill agreed to accompany her.

They walked past Trevor talking to the owner. Trevor, an attractive young black man with hair shaved close to his head, had a low voice and understated manner, so although she had heard him talk up in the front seat, she couldn't make out his words. She couldn't make out his conversation with the owner, either. She heard only the thickly accented voice of the owner suggesting prices while Trevor responded in low tones. Trevor had a pile of gold coins in his hand. The sight of them sparked a long-forgotten memory. The Texas Empire used gold coins as their official currency, although they only plated the high value pieces with real gold. The gold lust of some of first Texas Empire settlers to the West had stuck.

Bill led Lena to the woods, which she didn't mind too much. In fact, she preferred the outdoors to a stinky, unsanitary, indoor bathroom. Bill allowed her to walk out of his sight while she did her business. When she emerged from her selected bush and saw Bill, she froze. He pointed a gun at her. Was this how she would die? Executed right after squatting to pee? Perhaps the King had changed his mind about the spouses and partners rule and had ordered her dead.

"Walk . . . toward me . . . slowly." Bill spoke in a barely audible whisper.

She realized Bill didn't look at her. Whatever he aimed his gun at stood behind her.

She turned around automatically. She saw something so unexpected and strange she didn't think to run.

A man unlike any other she had ever seen stood nearly within arm's reach. He looked seven feet tall, at least, no exaggeration. He looked like he could push a steam engine with his bare hands. He wore nothing but a tattered pair of blue jeans that looked like he'd never washed them. In many ways, he reminded her of a Wilde. He had black hair, however unkempt, but instead of blue eyes, his glimmered with a startling shade of bright violet. He grunted like an animal and carried himself like a bear trapped in a man's body. The creature didn't look at Lena, or even Bill; he looked at Jack and Warren.

"Put down your gun," Jack called.

"No, don't," Warren said. "He's dangerous. Lena, get away from it."

"Don't make any sudden movements," Bill said. "Running won't help, he'll pounce on you like you're a doe."

"No, he won't," Jack said. "Not if he's not threatened. Lower your weapon."

Lena didn't know what to do with all of these conflicting instructions. She backed away from the creature slowly, with her hands raised in surrender.

"Lower your weapon," Jack said again.

Bill shot at the creature with the tranquilizer gun. The dart hit the creature in the neck, but didn't take him down. He pulled out the dart and advanced on Bill.

Vir ran at the creature with surprising speed and stood between it and Bill.

"No, stand down," Bill said.

"I am a soldier," Vir said.

The creature must have mistaken Vir for a regular human man because he didn't block the massive punch Vir landed squarely in his neck. The creature struggled to breathe, and Vir jumped on his back and attempted to tackle him to the ground. Even though Vir looked like an average-sized man, for a moment Lena thought Vir had the upper hand against the massive creature. But the creature wrestled Vir into a dangerous position. He held Vir's body upside down and slammed his head into the ground. Vir's neck bent the wrong way.

"No!" Bill cried and he pulled another gun out of his holster, presumably one that shot real bullets.

Trevor also aimed his gun at the creature.

Lena felt frozen. She wanted to do something, but didn't know what. She couldn't even run off to call 9-1-1. In the fallen Texas Empire, they didn't have 9-1-1.

Then, Jack did something crazy. He stood facing the creature, blocking their shots.

"Get out of the way," Bill said.

But Jack didn't even turn to look at him.

"Non nocet," Jack said. "Amicus." Jack patted his chest.

What? Lena didn't think she had heard that language before.

The creature raised his eyebrows, a much more human expression than the snarling one he had before. Lena could see the man behind the monster.

"Tu quis es?" the creature asked in the same unknown language.

"Nomen Jack. Filium ducis . . . Praetor. Uiuus?"

"Yes," the creature said.

For some unknowable reason, Jack smiled.

"Eius parum humanum?" the creature asked, and he also smiled. He held his hand out down by his knee like he patted the head of an invisible tiny person.

"Yes," Jack said.

"Non nocet," the creature said, and he dashed back into the forest.

"What the hell are you doing?" the gas station owner yelled. "Don't fire guns near my pumps."

Bill put his gun down and knelt by Vir's body. Lena crouched next to him. Again, she felt helpless. She could perform CPR . . . on a human.

"He might be okay," Bill said. He held Vir's hand and stroked his hair. Vir's eyes had gone glassy, like a doll's. "We'll just take him back. They can fix him, don't you think?"

Bill looked up at Trevor for a response, but Trevor didn't answer. He looked at Jack.

"How did you talk to it?" he asked.

"Just like you talk to anyone."

"They can't speak."

"As you can see, that's not true. They just don't speak English. At least, most of them can't."

Bill struggled to sling Vir over his shoulder. He breathed heavily and his eyebrows knitted together in worry.

Warren picked up Vir's feet.

"Grab him under his arms," Warren said.

"He's heavier than he looks," Bill explained. But between the two of them, they carried Vir to the vehicle. Lena opened the door for them and helped them lift Vir inside.

Warren had so many questions, his tongue itched, but he waited until Trevor and Bill climbed into the front seat and the jerky sounds of the road covered their voices. But Jack spoke first.

"You said he was dangerous," Jack said to Warren. "Why? Do you know what he is?"

"Caebellum."

Jack nodded with the satisfied sense of a teacher listening to a student answer a question correctly.

"What's Caebellum?" Lena asked.

"A race of super soldiers engineered to kill Wildes," Warren said.

"What?" Lena asked.

Warren hated to ignore her question, but he had too many of his own.

Even when Lena spoke, Jack kept his eyes on Warren.

"What language was that?" Warren asked.

"A dialect of Latin," Jack said. "Texas Empire scientists genetically engineered the Caebellum to be soldiers and nothing else. The scientists left the parts of the brain the soldiers didn't need to hunt down and kill Wildes purposely underdeveloped. Including language. But soldiers must follow orders, so the military taught them Latin—a language that no one else speaks. That way, they couldn't communicate with those they killed. Communication breeds sympathy, understanding. It's harder to kill someone when he's pleading for his life and you can understand his words. Their underdeveloped brains make it difficult for them to learn other languages, so most of them speak only Latin."

Warren's mother had often used nonsense words, which Warren now realized hadn't been nonsense at all. He never suspected she knew Latin when she barely had a command of English . . . but of course she hadn't, English was her second language. Warren wondered if Isaac had ever figured this out. Didn't he take Latin in high school? If he had, he would have noticed and he would have said something . . . right?

"You said a word I've heard before," Warren said.

164

"Did I?" Jack asked.

"What is 'filius'?

"It means son," Jack said. He hesitated, and then asked, "Your mother called you that?"

"How do you know that?"

"I may not be your father, but I am your uncle," Jack said.

"My uncle," Warren repeated. "So you must know who my parents are?"

"I misspoke. I'm not your uncle by blood. But I am your mother's brother. And by your mother, I mean Tutela, the woman who raised you. Tell me, does she still go by Tutela, or did she pick a more common name?"

"Ella," Warren said.

"Ella," Jack repeated with a smile.

"Just stop," Warren said. "You're not making sense. When you talked to that guy, you said 'filius' when you introduced yourself. You introduced yourself as someone's son, presumably someone he knew. You're not trying to say you're one of them? It's clear that you're not."

"No," Jack said. "Of course not. My real father was a Wilde, and a cruel man. My mother fell in love with a Caebellum man, took me, and ran away with him."

"She fell in love . . . with something like that?"

"Yes. He was the leader of the Caebellum and unique. His name was Praetor. The designers of the race created him to lead the others into battle. As such, the engineers gave him greater intellect than the others. He could speak English fluently and had enough intelligence to make critical judgments in the heat of battle. He had many characteristics of the Caebellum, but he was human enough to make a good husband to my mother, better than my *civilized* father. However, my mother had Wilde blood, and the royals considered her marriage to a Caebellum a gross insult to her people.

"When I was eight-years old, the Wildes executed my mother for joining the Caebellum tribe. When I saw what they did to her, I ran so they wouldn't take me. I stayed with the Caebellum and Praetor raised me like a son. I helped him care for my half-sister, Tutela, who was still an infant when my mother died. But I couldn't stay forever. I'm human. I wanted to go to school. But I couldn't go back to Waterloo. I moved to the place most unlike Waterloo that I could think of, Boston."

"So my mother is only half Caebellum?"

"Yes. Half Caebellum, half Wilde, the perfect mix of blood so that she's hated by everyone." Jack laughed, although Warren didn't find it funny. "But that's why she can function in society. That, and the fact that her Caebellum father was Praetor and not one of the rank and file."

"And she pretended to be our mother because . . . ?"

"Because you needed one. She smuggled you out of Texas. In desperate times, every child becomes your child. What would you do if you saw small children alone and in need, in the aftermath of a bomb?"

"What does *quiescatis* mean?" Warren asked. "It's like shut up, isn't it? She shouted that one."

"Be quiet," Jack said.

"Somnum?"

"Go to sleep."

"Mea alumna?"

"My child."

"Amo te?"

"I love you."

Hearing his mother's nonsense translated felt so strange. His throat felt hot and tight and he knew he should stop talking so his voice wouldn't crack. He missed his mother.

CHAPTER TWENTY-TWO

hey drove late into the night. The energy had grown as thick in the air as the humidity, and Warren thought he'd have a better chance composing an opera in Russian than getting some sleep. He thought about Isaac. He hadn't intended to find him by getting captured and thrown into a cell with him, but at least he'd be with him.

He held Lena's hand and she didn't stop him, but she also didn't say anything. She stared out the window with intense attention, like she could actually see something besides pure blackness. The absence of electricity made the night rather absolute.

Jack glanced at Lena, then back toward the soldiers, and then looked Warren in the eyes. "We're almost there. Can you feel the difference?"

Warren nodded. Even with everything going on, Warren knew some of his anxiety didn't come from within. It seeped into his skin from the air around him.

"How can they feel like this all the time?" Warren asked.

"Something was in that bomb," Jack said. "It didn't used to be this bad." He stared at Warren intently. "They might kill me."

"You think they're going to kill us?" Warren asked. His stomach clenched. He thought about Isaac, who'd disappeared almost a month ago.

"I didn't say *us*," Jack said. "I said *me*."

"Why just you?"

"In case they do kill me, I need you to know something first."

Lena turned away from the window and listened.

Jack glanced at Lena, as if deciding whether or not to trust her, and then locked eyes with Warren again. He lowered his voice to a whisper.

"I misled you when I told you the story of how Tutela became your mother. She did it out of the goodness of her heart, certainly, but that's not the only reason. I asked her to take you."

"Why?"

"I knew what Cole was planning. I knew about the bomb."

"You knew—" Lena started but Jack interrupted.

"Let me talk," he said firmly. "No matter how much I hate the Wilde family for killing my mother, in the end, I . . . I couldn't let them all die. Maybe something in my blood made me do it. Some self-preservation instinct. I told my father . . . my Caebellum father . . . what would happen. I asked him to take his clan back to Waterloo and kidnap you and your brother, Isaac, and take you out of range."

"You saved me," Warren said. "Why didn't you tell me this sooner?"

Jack didn't answer.

"And why did you just save *us*?" Warren asked. "You let everyone else die."

"It's your fault my parents died," Lena said. "That *millions* of people died."

Warren guessed that if she had a gun right then, she would have shot Jack between the eyes.

"I know," Jack said, finally looking at Lena. "It is my fault. When they execute me, I'll deserve it. I could apologize to you, but it wouldn't be enough."

Lena stared at him, her chest moving up and down with short, angry breaths.

"I know it doesn't change anything, but I didn't know the bomb would have such a large strike range. My plan included only an attack on the palace. I didn't want to kill innocents. I didn't want to kill your parents." Jack looked at Lena. Obviously, Jack had wanted to kill *Warren's* parents.

"How many others did you save?" Warren asked. "Not just me and Isaac?"

"That's what I want to tell you. The entire royal family did die in the bomb, that is, all of the actual monarchs in Waterloo at the time could not have survived that hit. I believe that the other Wilde descendants Saul has found are the children of estranged Wildes living outside of Waterloo at the time of the blast. People like me, or descendants of bastard Wildes from extramarital affairs. Saul can't be closely related to the King. I don't even know what his relation is. I don't remember him from when I lived in Waterloo, but I suppose he is too young for me to remember. I don't know how he and his wife survived the bomb, but regardless, they lead Texas purely based on the fact that they are the only Wildes anywhere near Waterloo.

"I saved only you and your brother. I didn't have time to do much. I chose children to save, because you were still innocent. You had done nothing to deserve death. Even then, I couldn't save all the Wilde children." He paused for a moment, and then continued. "I chose you and Isaac because you are the sons of Antony and Cassandra Wilde, the reigning King and Queen when the bomb hit."

Lena gasped.

"You're saying . . . you *do* know who my real parents were?" Warren asked. "What were they like?"

Jack leaned closer to Warren and his voice increased in intensity. "Warren, listen to what I'm saying. You are King Antony Wilde's older son."

"That can't be right. My name is Warren King, not Wilde."

Jack laughed in exasperation. "Your *name* is Antony Wilde II. I changed your name when I made you a fake birth certificate. King. Please excuse my lack of creativity."

Warren just stared at him.

"Warren, don't you understand what he's saying?" Lena said softly. "You're the King of the Texas Empire."

Warren stared at her and slowly shook his head from side to side.

"No," he whispered. "I'm not interested in being King."

"I didn't ask you if you were interested in being King," Jack said. "I am saying that you *are* King. Right now."

CHAPTER TWENTY-THREE

ictory lovingly slid her finger down a page of miniscule, slanted handwriting, faded with time. Her father had given her these notes to use to turn on the amplifier. He hadn't even known which parts of the notes related to the amplifying device, so he gave her all of them, a thick folder of loose, yellow, notebook paper covered in writing, numbers, and diagrams about a variety of topics. Her father did not write these notes, and neither did William Cole. Whoever wrote them had an intellect that challenged even Victory. Between the genius of the writer, the tiny, messy writing, and the fading ink, she barely understood the notes. Oddly, it felt wonderful. She felt truly challenged for the first time she could remember.

She hadn't needed to read the notes to figure out how to turn on the amplifier. It took her about thirty seconds before she found a clearly labeled switch hidden behind a panel. But she did not feel rushed to turn it on and have her father discover the truth about her and Will. However, her interest in the notes extended beyond delaying the inevitable. She had found something else, something that gave her hope for the first time since she'd learned of her defect. And her brain lit up, not like it did with the amplifier, but in that beautiful way when a new idea coursed through it and all the pieces of the puzzle snapped together. She had found the instructions for building a weapon.

She picked up her phone and dialed.

"I can't talk now," her father said as soon as he picked up. "I'm on my way to the Senate floor."

"I know why you want me to turn the amplifier on Will," she said. He didn't respond.

"I know he's a Wilde," she said.

"How do you know that?" he whispered.

"The notes explain everything. It explains his *illness*. It's the only thing that makes sense. Dad . . . I can fix him. Please give me a chance."

"What do you mean?"

"Don't kill him."

"Shut your mouth," he said in a harsh whisper. "I'm in the middle of the Capitol."

"The virus. I can create it."

Will stood on the porch of the Brighton mansion and waited for someone to answer the doorbell. He dripped all over the stoop. A heavy rain had fallen all afternoon, and he'd walked from the train station in order to stay off the radar of his guard. The guards at the gate of the mansion would probably call in his whereabouts, but it had at least given him an hour or so alone.

Victory opened the door and looked at him like a stray dog that would shake water all over the rug if she let him in.

"I asked you not to come here," she said.

"Yes, but you never explained why. You'd think that with our shared affliction, we should stick together."

"Shh!" She pulled him inside. "Don't say things like that."

"No one knows what it means."

"Well, my father's not here. So wipe your feet and come upstairs."

"Upstairs?" Her father didn't allow boys upstairs, but he guessed that rule might have expired, since she was twenty now.

"If my father comes home unexpectedly, I don't want you wandering around in plain sight."

"Why do you live here anyway? I thought you hated your father."

"I don't hate him. He's my father," she said.

He followed her upstairs and into a bedroom fit for a princess. The color white dominated the room—the carpet, the canopy bed, the drapes over her window seat, all white. It smelled like gardenias. Even in his imagination, her bedroom hadn't compared to this. So beautiful. So much like her.

She opened the door to her bathroom. "Go and clean yourself up."

He followed her instruction. She had mysterious bottles and gadgets that did mysterious woman things organized neatly in her palatial bathroom. He dried himself with a plush towel and took off his shoes. For a moment, he thought his wet clothes might serve as an excuse to strip down to just the towel, but didn't want to risk getting thrown out of the house. He tossed the towel in the hamper and noticed a black lace bra slung across the side. Will pictured Victory standing here in that bra . . . and then taking it off. He found himself completely aroused in about five seconds flat and hoped she wouldn't notice.

When he came out of the bathroom, he saw Victory on her bed, holding a silver tray with two drinks. She put the tray on her bedside table and gestured for him to sit next to her. Somewhere in the back of his brain, Will realized something odd about this. First, she didn't even want him in the house, and now she had brought him up to her bedroom and planned to serve him a drink. But 99.9% of him really didn't care why. He sat down next to her.

"I wanted to apologize for being such a bitch to you," she said. "You know, always."

"You're not a bitch. You're just . . . aloof."

"When you told me before how you felt about me, I didn't react like I should have."

Will's throat tightened up. He didn't want to think about that conversation. But then, she put her hand on his leg and he realized this conversation would end differently.

"You know, better than anyone, that I've been a mess lately, not thinking clearly, acting inappropriately. I wanted to make sure you knew that I do love you."

Will opened his mouth to say something, but couldn't form words.

"And maybe one day, if we both make it through this, we can be together. I would like that."

He saw his opening. He took her head in his hands and kissed her. He wanted to just throw her on the bed and rip her clothes off, but he knew he had to take it slow. He just focused on her lips, warm and soft, actually kissing him back.

She pulled away and handed him a glass. "Do you like Scotch?" she asked.

"Not really," Will said, at the moment not liking anything placed between them.

"You should learn to like it if you want to be a politician in this town."

Will shrugged and drank.

"Have you heard anything more about Lena?" Victory asked.

"No. But my mom keeps telling me she's okay."

"I hope so."

"Me, too." Will felt like the Scotch made him drunk too quickly. He had trouble keeping his head up. He realized Victory had given him more than just Scotch. He looked at her in horror. "Victory."

"I'm sorry," she said.

The edges of his vision turned gray, and then black.

CHAPTER TWENTY-FOUR

aterloo did not have many electric lights. Warren could see as many stars in the sky as they probably saw in the eighteen-thirties when some idiot came up with the idea for the Texas Empire. He hadn't seen so many stars in his life. For the first time, he really understood constellations. Orion really did look like a hunter, with the extra stars.

Funny how the mind worked. He thought about stars while the soldiers walked him and the others down a wide, pink granite promenade full of cracks, which glittered in the moonlight. One of the cracks had a small tree poking through. Warren didn't see the elegant, domed palace of limestone and granite he had seen in photos. Even the famous ancient oaks around the palace had disappeared. He felt foolish for wondering about them. He stood at ground zero. The bomb had leveled everything.

As they came closer, he saw a structure rising from the earth, covered in scaffolding. In the moonlight, the scaffolding looked like the dead skeleton of the palace, but he knew it wasn't a skeleton of the old palace—but the beginning of the new one. The palace at Waterloo was famous for how many times the government had rebuilt it. War, storms, fires would bring it down and they would just build it again . . . and again, and again. He had to admire their determination.

They stopped in front of a small granite building, about the size of a garden shed, but decorated like the King's house. It had a domed roof and carvings covering the sides. The darkness made it hard to see, but he thought he made out the image of the Alamo. A large bronze star covered another side. Warren couldn't imagine what could fit inside that room that would justify its design, except for maybe a tomb. *Please god, do not let it be a tomb.*

Fortunately, he guessed wrong. Trevor, and three other soldiers who had joined him, led them into the building, which housed nothing more than a tiny waiting area and gold elevator doors. Trevor pushed the button and the doors opened.

"Where are we?" Warren asked.

"The palace," Trevor said.

The inside of the elevator reminded Warren of one in a nice hotel. He had never stayed in a nice hotel, but he had delivered pizzas to some. Mirrors with gold trim lined the walls, making the car only slightly less claustrophobic, and what smelled like new carpet covered the floor. The elevator had buttons for twenty levels with fingerprint plates by levels 15-20 instead of buttons. Trevor pushed the button for level 14.

The elevator moved down. Warren glanced at Lena and Jack. They both looked about as comfortable as people should while taken deep underground in a mysterious elevator. Jack had his eyes cast down to the floor. If that man ever did pray, Warren would bet he prayed now. Although for some reason, he didn't imagine Jack as the praying type.

The doors opened and what Warren saw momentarily distracted him from his current predicament. He entered a huge chamber that again reminded Warren of a high-end luxury hotel. The same polished white stone covered the floors and walls. Instead of one large chandelier, crystals hung in elaborate patterns and made the ceiling look like a frozen rain shower. At the end of the chamber,

Warren saw a staircase with red carpeting. The room distracted him so much he didn't notice at first that only he and Trevor had exited the elevator.

"Hey! Wait!" Lena cried as the doors closed.

"Stop!" Warren cried, too, but the doors closed. "Where are they taking them?" Warren demanded of Trevor.

"Don't worry. They're just meeting with you first," Trevor said.

"Don't worry? That's very helpful. No one better hurt her or . . . ." Warren didn't really know what to threaten. For the first time, he considered actually trying to claim his throne. If he had to do it to save Lena and Isaac, he would, but the thought still made his stomach hurt. What would taking the throne actually entail, anyway? Would he just go up to Saul and say, "Hey, dude, you're in my seat"? Even if he wanted to be King, he doubted Saul would simply let Warren take the throne. Warren didn't think he had it in him to kill a man, even if he had to.

"If she's not a threat, they won't hurt her," Trevor said.

Not very comforting. *Threat* sounded like a subjective term and she had worked for a group that wanted to make Texas free and had dated the son of the man who had destroyed the Texas Empire and killed everyone in the King's family.

Warren followed Trevor up the carpeted staircase. Saul Wilde, from the television, and another woman who looked liked a Wilde stood up when he made it to the top of the stairs. He couldn't pinpoint their ages. Something in the way they carried themselves gave them the appearance of maturity, at least in their forties, but their faces had few lines.

They said Texans liked things big, and this room personified that, even for its above-average-sized inhabitants. The room rivaled the size of a train station; the leather couches could seat small cars; the chandelier took up the whole ceiling; and his freshman dorm room could fit into the fireplace.

The woman smiled and in a few strides, threw herself into his arms without so much as a *how do you do.*

He tried to shake her away, but she just squeezed him harder. He watched her male counterpart examine him with a lot less warmth. Her energy felt weird, not like the other Wildes he had known. It felt . . . cleaner and colder, like water, or a crisp fall morning, or as if someone had filtered out all of the emotions.

"I'm Sabine Wilde," she said, after she finished her hug.

She was too nice, too pretty, and her furniture was too big. He couldn't remember ever trusting anyone less. Saul didn't introduce himself and neither did Warren. They didn't need to.

"Welcome home," Saul said in a toneless voice.

"This is not my home," Warren said.

"Fair enough."

"Where is Isaac?"

"He's here," Sabine said. "I'll take you down to see him if you like."

"Why have you brought us here?" Warren asked Saul. Sabine seemed friendlier, but Warren didn't appreciate Sabine treating him like a long-lost pal. Saul acted more genuine. Warren wanted to know what *he* had to say.

"Think of yourself as an insurance policy," Saul said. "There aren't many of us left. All the members of our dynasty must be protected. It's no longer safe for you outside these walls."

"You can't keep us here against our will."

"Yes, we can," Saul said.

"It's illegal. I am an American."

"No, you're not. You're a Wilde. And the only laws that apply to you are mine."

"So, it's not the King who makes the laws?" Warren asked. As soon as the words left his mouth, he regretted them. He should learn to play his cards closer to his chest. Warren thought he could feel Saul get angry. The energy in the room seemed to intensify slightly.

Saul didn't say anything for what seemed like a very long time, and then finally said, "Would you shake my hand?"

Never did such a simple request sound so menacing.

Saul held out his hand to Warren. It seemed like an odd thing to refuse, but who knew what Saul could do by just touching his hand.

Warren held out his hand, about to take Saul's when Sabine grabbed Saul's wrist.

"Saul," she said. "Let me take him downstairs."

"Let go of me," he said. "I don't need you to do that."

Sabine put both her hands on his arm. She breathed deeply and looked pained.

"I said let go," Saul said. "Now."

She released his arm, and then turned to Warren.

"Let me show you downstairs," she said.

Warren didn't argue, and fortunately, Saul didn't either. Warren followed Sabine back into the elevator.

"What did you do to him?" Warren asked. He didn't really expect her to answer, and she didn't. Instead she grabbed his arm for a demonstration.

Her hand sucked out anxiety somewhat like Lena's did, but much more efficiently. She only sucked out a small measure of his tension, but enough that he felt the muscles in his back relax. And it took all of two seconds. She could take all of the world's spa and masseuse businesses down if she wanted to. She let him go and took a shaky deep breath.

"Thanks," he said.

She smiled.

"You must take it on yourself when you do that." Warren said. "The energy. It doesn't just disappear. You experience it yourself, don't you?"

"I can handle it," she said.

The elevator doors opened to a room that contained everything Warren had ever wanted in his entire life . . . including Isaac.

CHAPTER TWENTY-FIVE

am home. Out through the window, the sky is on fire. A ball of flame falls and sets a nearby trailer ablaze. The fire spreads across the brown grass hungrily and another trailer lights up, then another. I want to scream for Mommy and Daddy to wake up, but I can't move or speak. The fire rushes toward me.

Lena jerked awake. The smell of burning grass lingered in her nostrils. She had soaked the sheets with sweat. She punched her down pillow. Apparently, she didn't wear imprisonment well. Her sentence had lasted only thirty-two hours so far and she already felt like ripping the paint off the walls. At least her prison looked like a nice hotel room, complete with 1500 thread count linens and rose-scented soap in the bathroom.

Lena heard a knock at the door. She expected to find the Beta who brought her food holding a breakfast tray, but instead, she opened the door to find the Wilde woman she had watched walk through the capitol rotunda from the catwalk. The woman smiled in the most unthreatening way possible, but Lena still couldn't subdue her sense of panic. The woman had a larger-than-life quality that intimidated Lena. She didn't want to look at her directly.

"I'm Sabine Wilde."

Sabine held out her hand, and Lena shook it, not too surprised that the woman's touch made her fingertips tingle. Lena felt Sabine's energy electrifying the air around her, much stronger than Warren's. She thought she could hear the charge around her, like a crackling hum.

"Are you comfortable?" Sabine had a hypnotizing voice, with a touch of Texas, perfect for a relaxation tape.

"No."

"I'm sorry to hear that. What can I do to make your stay more comfortable?" She cocked her head in concern, as if she really thought Lena needed more pillows.

"Let me go."

"Not just yet."

"Is Warren okay?"

"Yes."

"Where is he? Can I see him?"

"Soon. Would you join me in the sitting room?"

Lena followed her out of the bedroom into the small sitting room. Sabine gestured toward the sofa and Lena sat. Sabine sat across from her in an armchair.

"My husband will join us shortly. So tell me, dear . . . where did you come from?"

"What do you mean?"

"You were born in Texas, correct?"

"Washington-on-the-Brazos."

"Ah."

Lena thought about asking about the state of her hometown, but didn't really want to hear the answer.

Saul Wilde appeared behind Sabine. He held his hand out to her, formally, and reminded her of Will when he played the role of politician. While preparing to greet him, she had a moment of panic . . . did he expect her to call him *Your Majesty* and curtsey or bow? But she supposed it didn't matter, because she sure as hell wouldn't do either.

"Miss Lowell, my name is Saul Wilde. It is a pleasure to meet you."

He didn't call himself King. She hesitated, in anticipation of the bizarre sensation before touching him. If he noticed the hesitation, it didn't seem to bother him.

Instead of sitting in the other armchair as she had expected, Saul sat on the sofa and gestured for her to sit back down next to him. When she sat, he moved close enough to her the hairs on her arm stood on end. She couldn't help but lean away from him slightly.

"This will feel uncomfortable, but it won't hurt you. Can you pull your hair off your shoulders?"

Sabine smiled at her reassuringly. "It's all right."

"What are you going to do?"

"I can't explain it. I have to show you."

Before she could react, he pulled the sleeve off of her shoulder and placed his hand on her bare skin. She wanted to pull away, but his hand seemed to lock onto her like a magnet. It burned. All other senses failed her. She felt only that hand.

Lena had always believed in the soul. But only on faith, until that moment. She felt hers now. He touched it. She had pictured the soul as a point of light near the heart, but it ran like electricity through her entire body and mingled with the energy outside her skin. It felt like he gently tugged on parts of her soul. She didn't feel pain, but she could hardly bear the intimacy.

When he pulled away, she trembled. When her sight returned, she saw his glowing blue eyes.

He looked at her thoughtfully. "I don't know. There are a lot of mixed intentions."

"What did you do to me?" She felt like he had thumbed through her most private thoughts like his own personal library. She wanted to take a shower.

"I wanted to get a feel for you. Determine whether or not you are a threat," Saul said.

"So, you read my mind?"

"No. It's more like reading your energy."

"Can Warren do that?" Lena asked, her curiosity temporarily overtaking her sense of violation.

"No," Saul said.

Lena waited for him to explain why, but he didn't.

He turned to Sabine. "There is a good amount of beneficence. But there is a lot of anger, and a lot of fear. She doesn't like us. And she's hiding something. She has quite a bit of guilt."

"Stop that," Lena said.

"Considering her situation, you would expect her to have some negative feelings toward us. And fear. The guilt could be about anything. Didn't she cheat on her boyfriend?" Sabine said.

"No, I didn't."

Sabine widened her eyes at her slightly, as if she wanted to Lena to read her thoughts.

"You don't have to lie about it," she said. "It's not a crime, and we certainly don't care about the feelings of William Cole, Jr."

Lena realized Sabine wanted to defend her.

"So, what do you think about what we discussed?" Sabine asked Saul.

He continued to stare at Lena. Then, he nodded slightly, and then left the room.

Sabine clapped her hands together, to declare the matter settled. "Well, let's move you downstairs, then."

Lena stared at her blankly.

"Saul wanted to examine you before he decided what to do with you."

The statement seemed ominous to Lena, but Sabine's chipper attitude gave her the impression she must have passed the test. If *downstairs* meant an execution room or dungeon, Sabine's tone didn't match the implication.

"Is downstairs good?" Lena asked, just to make sure.

Sabine laughed. When she laughed, she seemed to sparkle. "I hope you will think so, yes. I figured it would be hospitable of me to let you stay with your boyfriend."

"Warren? No, he's not my boyfriend."

Sabine's face darkened. For some reason, Sabine seemed to want them together.

"But I would like to see him," Lena added.

"You make such an adorable couple," she said, her smile returning.

Lena followed Sabine into a lobby-type sitting area with over-large, black leather couches and wooden floors, a cross between a ski lodge and a castle. A chandelier took up most of the ceiling. Realistic afternoon light trickled through the fake trees outside the faux windows. A large plasma television took up most of one wall and a well-stocked bar encompassed another. A bartender stood behind the bar staring at the empty room eagerly like he could stand there for all eternity just waiting for the ecstatic experience of serving a drink. Probably a Beta.

As they went deeper into the room, Lena saw a dark-haired man sprawled across a couch in front of the television playing a first-person shooter game.

"Warren," she called out. The man turned, and Lena saw a stranger's face glance back at her with a look of tragic boredom.

"No," he said and turned back to his game.

"Lena, meet David. He was our first find, living in the New Mexico territory." Sabine spoke of him like a rare coin from her collection.

"Hi," Lena said.

David raised one finger, in either a lazy wave or a shush, and kept his eyes glued to his game. Lena put him on her mental no-good list.

"Follow me to Warren's room," Sabine said.

Lena followed her down a wide hallway with more wooden floors. An assortment of paintings lined the walls. She spotted a painting that she had seen before, a painting of a white sofa with a woman's hand draped over the back. The couch obstructed the rest of her body from view and the artist had arranged everything in the painting to mystically draw your attention to her hand. If she remembered correctly, one of the Wilde men painted the famous canvas, titled *Portrait of My Mother*, many years ago. His mother had poisoned herself when he was a child, and the painting depicted how he found her body. She assumed this was the original, and priceless.

Warren lay on a couch so expensive it actually smelled like money, and stared at the fake tree outside his window.

"Do you think they change the leaves for the seasons?" Warren asked his brother. "Will they bring in brown ones in fall, and then take them off in winter? Maybe add flowers in the spring?"

"I don't know," Isaac said, "I guess we'll find out."

"No, we won't," Warren said.

Isaac didn't answer and turned back to his stack of papers and books. Ever since Warren had arrived, Isaac had studied his books in Warren's room. Watching Warren sulk must facilitate his thinking process. He looked the same as he had when Warren last saw him. A nerdish version of Warren, or what might happen if he stopped going to the gym and never went out in the sun. The nerd look suited Isaac, though.

"What are you looking at, anyway?" Warren asked.

"Textbooks about Beta engineering. It's fascinating."

"Does this mean you're going to start building a person?"

"I have time."

Warren wondered what would happen if he used his time trashing his room like a drug-addled rock star. They had filled his room with amenities not useful or necessary by any definition, the worst of which being a snow-cone machine and a trampoline. Warren knew his brother didn't care about any of the stuff either, but they had found his price . . . knowledge. As for the other two in their spectacular prison, David's price—video games and weed. Oh yeah, a real winner. And the odd little Wilde girl, Calliope, just appeared happy to live indoors and eat three meals a day. They hadn't found Warren's price yet. Warren didn't know his price either, and hoped he didn't have one, but it certainly wasn't a snow-cone machine.

"You're angry," Isaac said.

Warren didn't respond.

"I know you're not happy to be here," Isaac said. "But I'm happy you're here. I worried about you. I saw you on the news being arrested in Tennessee."

Warren got up from the couch. "You worried about me? Damn it, Isaac, I worried about you. I thought you were dead or hurt or who the hell knows what. But you're fine!"

"And that makes you mad, that I'm fine?"

"You know what I mean," Warren said.

"Not really."

Warren heard a knock at the door. He ignored it and fell back onto the couch.

Isaac got up to answer the door.

"It's for you, Warren," Isaac said.

Lena walked into the room and Warren jumped up to meet her. He didn't think twice about hugging her so tightly he pulled her off the floor. She smelled wonderful. Like sunshine and rain and grass, and all the other things he didn't have down here . . . or she smelled like shampoo, but either way, it worked for him. He put her back down and inspected her.

"You look okay. Are you okay?" he asked.

"I guess so," she said. "I'm not hurt."

"They wouldn't give me a straight answer about you," Warren said. "They just said you were fine and that I'd see you soon. I thought . . . they lied."

"I know. They said the same thing about you."

He hugged her again.

"I hate it here," Warren growled into her ear. "We have to get out."

"Warren doesn't take to imprisonment well," Isaac said. "When our mom sent him to his room, he'd lie on the bed and kick his feet against the wall until she gave in. He could do it for hours."

"Thank you for that," Warren said. "If you couldn't guess, this is my brother, Isaac."

Lena shook his hand. "It's great to meet you."

"Yeah, you, too," he said. "I've heard a lot about you."

"You, too," Lena said.

"Yep," Warren said. "We can live happily ever after . . . underground forever."

"So we really are prisoners?" Lena asked. "It's confusing. I expected a dungeon or something."

"If we're not allowed to leave, we're prisoners," Warren said.

"They might let you leave," Isaac said to Lena. "But not us. Since we're the last of their kind, they want to protect us."

"I'll tell you what's really happening," Warren said. "Saul wants to kill us so that he can officially become King. But Sabine wants us alive to preserve the bloodline. Marriage is about compromise, right? Alive, but imprisoned."

"Is this your room?" Lena asked Warren.

"Yes."

"It's really . . . big," she said.

"I think the word you're looking for is *excessive*."

"That word works, too. I think it's bigger than my entire apartment building," Lena said. She moved over to the sitting area and inspected the couches. "This is sort of awkward. But this is my room, too, now."

"What do you mean?"

"The woman, Sabine, thinks we're a couple," Lena said. "She would get mad every time I told her that we weren't. I just gave up."

Warren tried not to look too happy about it. Maybe Sabine did have his best interests at heart, at least one of his interests. "Why does she care if we're a couple?"

"Hmm," Isaac said thoughtfully.

"What?" Warren asked.

"Well . . . Lena is a woman of child-bearing age who is not related to you," Isaac said.

"Wow, what an enthusiastic endorsement," Lena said.

Isaac's ears turned pink. "Like Warren said, she wants to preserve the bloodline. I'm just saying that in the bathroom there are probably seven types of aftershave and no condoms."

"You're saying that she's trying to get me to breed like I'm an endangered polar bear at the zoo?" Warren asked.

"Gross," Lena said.

He'd prefer it if Lena didn't consider sleeping with him *gross*, but in this special case, he had to agree with her.

Warren noticed Calliope hovering in the doorway watching them.

"Callie, you can come in if you want," Isaac said.

Calliope kept her eyes on the floor as she came in and stood next to Isaac. Calliope had the expected look of a Wilde, but in miniature. She stood almost a head shorter than Lena. A combination of unusually large eyes along with flawless white skin and childlike features made her look like some kind of creepy antique doll. She told them she was fifteen-years old, but Warren thought she looked younger except for her fully-grown breasts.

"This is Lena Lowell," Isaac said.

"Texas Freedom Campaign spokesperson. Will Cole's girlfriend," Calliope said like she answered trivia questions on a game show.

"Um . . . yes. That's me. Was me."

"Lena, meet Calliope," Isaac said. "We usually call her Callie."

"Calliope? What an interesting name," Lena said to Callie. "Isn't that what you call the organ that goes with a traveling circus?"

Callie shrugged. "I saw it in a book. I thought it was pretty."

"You named yourself? Your parents didn't name you?" Lena asked.

Isaac shook his head, and Lena understood not to ask questions because she changed gears quickly.

"Well, it's very pretty," Lena said. "It's nice to meet you."

"Traitor. Assassin. Rose Wilde wannabe."

"Excuse me?" Lena said.

"Don't get mad," Isaac said. "She just reciting things she heard on the news. She doesn't mean anything by it."

"I'd like to leave now," Callie said.

"Okay, Callie," Isaac said.

"What is wrong with her?" Lena asked after Callie had disappeared out the door.

"Take it easy on her," Isaac said. "She's been through a lot. Sabine told me that they *bought* her from a crime lord known for sex trafficking. She's just a kid. It's awful."

"That is awful," Lena said.

"I forgot I told her I would help her download some music she wanted," Isaac said. "I'll be right back."

"He takes care of her," Warren said after Isaac left. "She sleeps in his room even though she has her own."

"Are they a couple?" Lena asked.

"I don't think so," Warren said. "Besides, I would hope he would pick a woman he is not related to."

"Doesn't stop Saul and Sabine," Lena said. "I wonder how closely related they are."

"Maybe so close they can't have kids," Warren said. "Why else wouldn't they have any? If they care so much about breeding and all."

"Yuck," Lena said.

"I know," Warren said. "Incest. Just another lovely thing about royalty. I bet my parents were brother and sister."

"They weren't," Lena said. "You know . . . since you know who they are now, you don't have to speculate. You can look them up."

Warren shrugged. "I guess."

Just like everyone who knew anything about history, Warren knew a thing or two about his father. Some of the kings of the Texas Empire had been good. Some had been bad. And then, some had been very, very bad. Warren's father fell into the last category. He passed a law that made him a shareholder in every business in the Texas Empire from oil companies to wedding cake decorators, and entitled him to some of the profits. The citizens who wouldn't comply with his excessive government profit-sharing laws had their businesses and homes taken away and had to live in tent camps with no clean water or safe food. He denied government aid to victims of a massive Category Six hurricane so they would learn to build their houses stronger next time. Some say he kidnapped and personally raped the daughter of the President of Mexico over a border dispute. His father had been the final straw, the King who pissed off the U.S. so much they finally just bombed the shit out of the Texas Empire. Warren already knew more than enough about his father.

"Have you told your brother?" Lena asked.

"Told him what?"

"What Jack told you on the drive here," she said.

"No. I'm not going to tell him. As far as I know, he still thinks our mom is our mom and it will stay that way."

"Warren, I'm not sure how to tell you this," Lena said. "But I think he may already know."

"What are you talking about?"

"I've seen him before."

"Who?"

"Isaac," Lena said.

"I don't think so."

"Did he ever do any work for the TFC?"

"No . . . ."

"I saw him at the TFC offices," Lena said. "He met with the president of the TFC. It was him and a girl. She was short and had red hair, looked like a doll."

"Jessica?"

"You know her?"

"You must be wrong. Why would they go there?"

"I am pretty sure it was Isaac. He is memorable. It was around the time they were planning the expedition into the impact zone."

"When exactly?"

"Right before. A few days before the footage."

"That was after he was kidnapped."

"He didn't look kidnapped to me."

CHAPTER TWENTY-SIX

arren looked his brother in the eyes, examining him for signs of lying. He didn't know quite what to look for.

"She's mistaken," Isaac said. "Of course I wasn't at the Texas Freedom Campaign headquarters. I don't think they would let me in there looking like I do."

"Why would she say that?"

"I have no idea. Maybe she's trying to manipulate you."

"Manipulate me how?" Warren asked.

"I don't know what her plan is, but think about this objectively. She's worked for the TFC, she dated Will Cole for a year, for God's sake. How could you possibly trust her?"

"Because my gut tells me I can," Warren said.

"Your gut is not the part of your body you're listening to," Isaac said. "You're a simple man, Warren. And that's dangerous."

"Simple? Screw you. Just because I'm not a certified genius doesn't make me simple. I'm *very* smart. Smart enough to get a college scholarship and kick ass in school."

"I didn't mean that you're stupid. I mean that you are not complicated. You care about simple things and desire simple things. You only ever talk about microbreweries, baseball, and girls."

"I talk about other things."

"It's not an insult. I've always been jealous of you for being simple. You could have just finished college, gotten a decent job, married a pretty girl, and lived happily in your little bubble for the rest of your life, never caring that you were ordinary."

"You don't know as much about me as you think." It actually sounded like an apt description of him, and a satisfying happily-ever-after. But Isaac could shove his correct assessment up his ass.

"I don't want to fight with you, Warren. I really don't. I just want you to look around and think about things. Lena might not be our enemy; I hope she's not. But don't let her take advantage of you because you like her. And don't think she wants what you want. I don't know her from Jane, but I know she doesn't want a simple life. If she did, she would have made different choices. Different choices in men, for starters. I find it a little hard to believe that you and Will Cole were the only two dating options she's had. It's no coincidence."

Warren geared up to disagree with him, even though he sounded right once again, when he heard high-heeled footsteps clicking down the hall. Warren left his room and saw Lena, Calliope, and David already standing in the hallway.

Saul and Sabine approached with a woman walking between them, the President. Next to them, the President looked tiny and aged. She didn't have the same aura of confidence he remembered. Worry hardened in Warren's stomach. The President had no guards with her. She didn't walk through her own Capitol building without Secret Service, but deep in the bowels of the palace of the Texas Empire, she walked surrounded by Wildes without a single guard. Could she be a prisoner? Warren thought he felt a cloud of anxiety coming off the President.

"Madam President," Lena said. "What are you doing here? Are you here to take us home?"

The President looked at her blankly for a moment, then said. "Hello, Lena. No, I am afraid that is not why I'm here."

193

"I know that not seeing him here does not prove anything," Sabine said. "But perhaps it helps. You're free to look around if you like."

"Why don't you ask them as well?" Saul said. "You will see that they have not been coached on their answers."

The President scanned the group of people in the hall, and then looked at Lena and Warren in turn while she asked her question. "Is Will here?"

"What?" Lena asked. "Will? You don't know where he is?"

"He's missing." The President whispered the words as if it hurt her to say them. She didn't look as put-together as she did on TV, and looked even older than before.

"He's not here," Isaac said.

"Don't trust them," Lena said. "This is just where they keep the *good* prisoners. They have people somewhere else, too. We came here with Jack Craven and haven't seen him since. Ask them to show you where they keep him."

Warren had to suppress the urge to tackle her and get her to shut up.

"Unless they already killed him," Lena said.

"Jack Craven is alive and well," Saul said to the President. "We are happy to let you speak with him."

Saul turned to Lena and Warren prepared himself to attack Saul if he needed to, even though he doubted he'd make much of a dent. But Saul didn't do anything more than take on a stern tone.

"Young lady, your friend Mr. Craven is a very dangerous man and therefore is kept under maximum security for the protection of my family, but he has not been harmed."

Warren wondered what Saul meant by his *family*. Did he just mean Sabine or did he actually think of all of them that way.

"I would like to see him," the President said.

CHAPTER TWENTY-SEVEN

fter the President left, Lena pulled Warren aside.

"Do you think Will's here?" she asked. "Can you feel his presence?"

"The extra energy in the air makes it hard. Everything is all jumbled. I can't feel anything from anyone unless they are really close. I guess Jack was right about that."

"It's impressive that she's even giving them the benefit of the doubt," Lena said. "They already tried to kidnap him once. If Senator Brighton had been elected and his daughter was missing, he would bomb first and ask questions later."

"But they also returned him right away," Warren said. "If they had wanted to kidnap him, they would have just kept him then. They proved that they don't want to do that."

"If not them, then who? Who else would kidnap the son of the President? And why?" Lena's skin hummed with her own anxiety and the charge wafting over from Warren didn't help. She wanted to act. To do *something* to help Will.

"She said he was missing, not kidnapped. I think he figured out what he was and got the hell out. Just ran. Maybe went overseas. I would if I were him. I'm sure he's fine."

The television screen grew suddenly brighter, and then dimmed again, in an irregular pulsing. Lena rubbed her eyes.

"Something's wrong with the TV," Lena said.

"Hey," Isaac said. He had entered the room unannounced.

"What do you want?" Warren said.

"I wanted to warn you," Isaac said. "Sometimes the electricity starts to act up before it goes out. They have some powerful storms here, and I'm guessing that one is coming."

"We know about the storms," Warren said. He hung his head like it suddenly weighed a hundred pounds.

"Let me check something," Isaac said. He snapped his fingers and flung them outward. A tiny bolt of blue light webbed from each of his hands.

Lena stood up in surprise. "Whoa."

"You can shoot freaking lightning bolts from your hands?" Warren asked. His tone made it sound like an accusation. Warren snapped his fingers and flung them about wildly. Nothing happened. "How did you do that?"

"I wouldn't call them lightning bolts," Isaac said. "I found that when the energy levels in the air increase, I can disperse my own energy into the air. I can't do it all the time."

"Can you do it again?" Lena asked.

"Hang on. We might not have time for demonstrations now."

Isaac went into one of the closets and pulled out what looked like a blue lunch box. He handed it to Warren.

"Get that going. I need to be with Callie when it hits." Isaac left the room, apparently leaving for his own.

Warren opened the box and pulled out three flashlights, an oil lamp, some candles, and a lighter.

Lena's back felt wet. Sweat beaded on her face and made the hair around her face wet. She didn't usually sweat like this, even on the treadmill. Warren also had damp spots on the back of his shirt. She pulled at her blouse to allow in some air.

"Why is it so gross in here all of a sudden?" she asked.

"The air conditioner must have gone down," Warren said.

"The storm must be close, then. Can you feel it?"

He nodded. "I've felt anxious for about an hour. But I didn't know it was a storm. It's harder to feel the storms coming when the energy is already so high."

"We should probably turn on the lamp before the lights go out," she said. "It will be worse underground—complete dark."

"Shit. I didn't think about that," Warren said. His hands fumbled while he took out the oil lamp and Lena took it from him to do it herself.

The television screen glowed brighter, this time reaching a completely white screen before dimming again. Warren turned it off and unplugged it.

Lena's anxiety increased, probably from a combination of the storm and nerves. Feeling the need to anchor onto something, she linked arms with Warren. A wave of worry and sadness surged through her at this touch. It hit her so suddenly and with so much force, she started to cry. She imagined the energy inside her glowing white hot, like the energy for the TV.

Warren took her into his arms.

"Are you okay?" he asked.

"I think I feel what you feel. It's awful."

"I'll be okay," Warren said. "We'll just stick together, like last time. It will pass."

The emotional surge died down, but she still felt shaky. She breathed deeply to try and steady her nerves. The energy coming off Warren's skin grew stronger. His energy flowed into her now, and she felt her own energy mixing with his like the barrier of flesh between them had disappeared. The lack of boundary made her feel uncomfortably vulnerable.

He must have felt the same way because he sighed, as if pained, and pulled his chest off hers by an inch. However, she had no desire to let go, and apparently, neither did he.

She heard the sigh of many electrical devices shutting down at once and the lights went out. They hadn't turned on any of their light sources and Lena braced herself for an onslaught of darkness. But it didn't come. A dim but warm light bathed the room. She noticed many of the outlets had tiny lights on them, like nightlights.

"They must have some kind of back-up power," Warren said.

"Thank God," Lena said.

Warren kissed her.

The distraction helped, and Lena had no problem kissing him back with interest. She felt the color of the energy moving between them change. The lack of a barrier still felt disarming, but the sensation of the energy warmed like a hot spring. She remembered when she had first felt his energy in the hotel room. The energy matched their emotions. If they could control their emotions, they could control how the energy felt, too.

They did not need to discuss what would happen next. They moved to the bed and Warren began to undress her. As he kissed her breasts and her stomach, Lena realized Blue Energy had undiscovered benefits. The sensation of warmth started between her legs but didn't stop there. The warmth spread out all the way to her fingertips. Wherever he kissed her flesh, heat surged through her nerves in all directions, leaving the whole area where he touched her pulsing. Her sweet spot seemed to cover her whole body, like he could run his finger along the inside of her elbow and she would lose it.

Warren unfastened her jeans and raised his eyebrows questioningly.

"Yes," Lena said.

CHAPTER TWENTY-EIGHT

ill felt himself dying. He didn't know how or why, but he felt his energy growing dimmer. Like a sinking ship, the only thing between him and death were his cupped hands frantically shoveling out water. The terror of knowing his death approached dwarfed the physical pain he felt, which pushed him toward the brink of unconsciousness. Sharp pains shot through the nerves in every part of his body. He might be on fire.

He tried to keep his eyes open long enough to look at his arms to see where the pain came from. Someone held one of his hands.

"Will? Are you awake?" asked a woman.

He tried to speak but could only scream, a piercing, guttural sound that didn't sound like it could possibly come from him.

"He's in pain. Maybe we could give him something for it. Something to knock him out again while the virus works." Victory's voice.

He tried to focus on her, but his eyes hurt, too. The air hitting his eyes when he opened them felt like acid. He should say something to her. Yell at her. Call her nasty names one should never call a woman. He knew he should feel angry, but he didn't feel anything but pain.

He didn't care what had happened to him or why. He wanted to die to make it stop. He dug his fingers into her palm as hard as he could.

He felt pressure against his face. When he tasted blood he realized someone had hit him, but he hurt so much already, he barely noticed it.

"Don't you dare hurt her," said a man.

"Dad! Don't. He didn't mean it. He's in pain."

"He's a dangerous madman. He has the Devil's blood. He'd be happy to kill you now if he could move."

"I think I'm doing it wrong. I must have given him too high a dose. His blood pressure is dropping. What if I'm killing him?" Victory said.

Will felt his internal organs more keenly than usual. They all burned like hot stones. The next pulse of pain might take out his heart. Wetness slid down his neck. He guessed blood at first, but no, he was weeping. He knew the tears meant he wanted to live. He wanted it more than he had ever wanted anything. The thought of one day doing something simple again, like a jog in the park or flipping burgers on a grill, sounded both impossible and wonderful. He cried out again. He still sounded like an animal, but he knew what the cry meant: it meant *fight*.

"God is on our side," said the man. He felt his breath on his face. The man must have leaned in to speak directly to him. "Everything is working in our favor. Everyone thinks the Wildes took you. Mothers are so predictably reckless about their children. She went straight to Waterloo to look for you and took only a small protective detail. They lost radio contact with her a few hours ago."

He laughed. "They can't trace the plane anymore. I'm betting the King shot it down. Right now, the military is preparing to respond in kind. The fighter planes are already on their way. And all this happened because they kidnapped *you*. Isn't it beautiful?"

Will cried out again and the man laughed. Just as the man had said, Will knew if he could move, he would kill him right then and there without thinking twice. He felt Victory grab his hand again.

CHAPTER TWENTY-NINE

ack tried to wedge his body into a corner so he could lay his head on the wall. The cuffs around his wrists cut into his already raw skin as he moved. Between the energy from the storm and the physical discomfort of his cell, he didn't know how much longer he could go on. He wondered if he could kill himself by banging his head into the wall. He knew better, though. The extra energy in Wildes made them resilient and only very decisive attempts at death succeeded. Halfhearted attempts at suicide usually ended in brain damage and an even less enjoyable long life. He would need a gun to do the job and without perfect aim, it might take more than a few bullets.

He thought he felt a presence in the hallway, but the storm confused things. He thought he felt people's energy in his empty cell, too.

The door opened and a soldier entered—a human soldier. A young Hispanic man.

Jack covered his eyes in expectation of blinding light from outside, but it didn't come. Small lights along the wall bathed the corridor in a dim glow. The man un-cuffed his hands and grabbed his arm to help him stand.

"What is happening?" Jack's voice felt strained from lack of use.

"I have orders to have you clean up before you meet with her."

"Who are you talking about?"

"Come," he commanded.

Jack followed him down the hall to a slightly more upscale prison cell. This one had a private bathroom and shower. The soldier instructed him to shower and put on clean clothes. Jack didn't protest. At this point, he couldn't say no to the simple comfort of a shower and clean clothes, no matter what the reason. After he cleaned up, the man took him down to a floor that contained what looked more like hotel rooms than prison cells.

The man led him to a door and opened it for him without comment.

When the door opened, Jack felt a sensation much like a plummet on a roller coaster—alarming and joyful at once. Beyond all reason, Lorelei stood there, barefoot and wrapped in a shawl. It made so little sense to see her there, he half-wondered if he had found his way into the afterlife. Even if such a fairy tale existed, Lorelei wouldn't be where he was going. She had her hair down around her shoulders, which made her look more like the young woman he had once known, than the President of the United States.

"You want me to leave him alone with you?" the soldier asked her.

"If you don't mind."

The man nodded and closed the door behind him.

"You've aged badly," Lorelei said. "Did they torture you?"

"In a fashion."

"I thought they would have killed you," Lorelei said.

"Disappointed?" Jack asked.

"Don't be so cold."

"So you always knew?" he asked.

"I knew my husband hired you as a scientist. I did not know that he hired you to design a bomb. That I figured out after the bomb went off and our military determined that the bomb was custom made, fueled by a type of energy they didn't understand. William didn't have the intelligence or the training to do that part

202

himself. That must have been what you worked on for him, all those years."

"If you knew all this time, why didn't you tell anyone?"

"I had already lost one man I loved. I didn't want to lose another."

Her words caused a pain in his stomach. He wished she wouldn't say things like that. He didn't want to feel anything for her.

"I never agreed to have my technology used for genocide," Jack said. "I would never have agreed to that."

"So designing bombs was nothing more than a hobby for you?" she asked acidly.

"I only wanted to assassinate the King. I designed a precision bomb with special energy properties to disrupt the King's Blue Energy as assurance that he would die even if the bomb failed to kill him in the usual way."

"But that's not what happened," she said.

"I stopped helping William with the plan for the bombing years before the strike. I told him that a Blue Energy bomb wouldn't work. Too unpredictable. I offered to design a different weapon. A biological one, a virus that attacks Wilde DNA. If used properly, it will kill all the Wildes in the strike zone, but leave everyone else unharmed."

"Why didn't you do that, then?"

"Several reasons. For one, I never got the virus to work. I did create a virus that can be deadly to Wildes, but it has to be administered intravenously over the course of several injections. So it wasn't much more effective than any other type of poison and much less effective than a bullet in the head. The best it does is make Wildes weaker, so it's easier to kill them. After years of research, I had to conclude that the virus wouldn't work. And you know what happened after that."

"I do?"

"William found out that you and I were having an affair."

Lorelei turned her face away. "So he stopped funding the research."

"More than that. He tried to kill me. He and the noble now-Senator Sam Brighton pumped me full of my own virus and left me for dead. They must have thought I did die, because I never showed my face to them again."

"Or to me," Lorelei said in a near whisper.

"I wanted to."

"But you didn't have the courage. You just hid away."

"And what would you have had me do? Would you have left William and married me?" As soon as the words left his mouth, Jack wished he hadn't asked. What would it mean if she said, *yes*? "I wonder, sometimes, if I should have come back after . . . your marriage was over. But, I assumed you wouldn't want me."

Jack's honesty startled even himself. The energy agitating his nerves and lack of proper food and sleep made him say things he hadn't even admitted to himself. "When I watch you on television, all I can think about is what it would have been like if you were coming home to me, where you would take down your hair and take off your starched, buttoned-up clothes."

Lorelei moved very close to him and Jack's heart rate increased. Would she kiss him? For once, they actually could kiss. The storm had disabled any cameras or listening devices. However, when she leaned close enough that he could smell the lavender scent of her hair, he could tell her eyes blazed with a different type of emotion.

"Will is missing."

"What?" Another stab of pain in his stomach.

"Did they bring him here?" she asked.

"I am not sure," Jack said.

"Who else would want to hurt him?"

A loud crash shook the room. The glasses hanging from the room's bar rack fell and shattered. Lorelei clung to him. Jack's heart rate increased again.

"Was that the storm?" Lorelei asked.

"I don't know." Honestly, Jack didn't think so. Even these storms wouldn't shake a building like that, and he thought he smelled smoke.

He took Lorelei's hand firmly in his own. "We need to get out of this building."

CHAPTER THIRTY

Warren held Lena and watched her twitch in her sleep. She twitched and squirmed more than when he had watched her sleep before.

The storm raging above made the one they faced in Louisiana look like a summer afternoon rain shower. Dark energy seemed to emanate from everything. The walls, the ceiling, and worst of all, the air. Life and electricity didn't seem to have anything to do with it. Everything seemed alive. He felt like he had to hold on to Lena to keep his energy from blowing away.

He pulled the comforter over their heads to protect them from what he could only describe as phantoms swooping down from the ceiling—singular bundles of energy coming at him randomly like unexplained cold spots in a lake. The air itself tried to run its fingers down his back. The sensations could be a trick of the mind, or maybe not. Either way, he knew he couldn't come out from under the comforter.

Lena shot up in bed and threw the comforter off of her face in a panic.

Warren grabbed it and tried to cover her back up.

"What are you doing?" she asked.

"I . . . ."

"I had a dream with Senator Brighton in it . . . I think that's it."

"What?"

"He figured out Will is a Wilde. You must have given it away when you talked to him. Either that, or someone else who questioned us figured it out. I mean, it doesn't take a genius. They were looking for Wildes, and they took Will. Somebody put two and two together, and I bet it was the Senator. He hates the Wildes more than anyone. Imagine how pissed he would be if he found out that his best friend's son was a Wilde. Maybe the President is still here. I can tell her." She threw off the comforter and crawled out of bed.

"Please . . . you can't get up. You might blow away," Warren said.

She stopped and squinted at him through the darkness. "Warren, what are you talking about? There is no wind. We're inside. Underground even." She crawled back onto the bed and examined him. "Are you all right?"

He grabbed her arm. "Just stay here."

She grimaced and pulled away, like his hands burned her. She appeared to have trouble catching her breath. "No wonder I was having crazy dreams. I can't even describe what's coming off of you. Do you feel okay?"

Warren didn't say anything but however pathetic he looked cowering under the covers must have answered her question.

"I'm so sorry," Lena said. "I hate that you have to feel like this. I wish I could do something to help."

"Stay."

The tiny back-up lights went out, followed by a distant rumble. At first, Warren thought he had lost his body. He couldn't see his hands in front of his face. This was death. Darkness. No body. He had turned into another phantom in the storm. When Lena scrambled across the bed and into his arms, he realized he was still alive. He had to pull himself together.

"It's okay. It's okay," he said in her ear, not sure if he meant to comfort her or himself.

"Let's get the flashlights," she said. "Come with me."

She took him by the hand and pulled him out of bed. Leaving the shelter of the bed didn't lead to anything horrible. Why did he think he couldn't get out from under the comforter? The storm had turned his brain into a hive of bees.

"What happened to the lights?" Lena asked.

"No idea."

Warren heard Lena knocking things around the room. If he hadn't known better, he would have thought a buffalo searched for the flashlights. A bluish, fluorescent light hit him in the eyes. After the darkness, it felt like the headlights of an eighteen-wheeler.

"Sorry," Lena said and pointed the light toward the ceiling instead.

Her chest heaved up and down as if in the middle of a panic attack.

"Are you okay?" he asked.

"I never realized how much I appreciate light bulbs," she said.

"Me neither."

Someone knocked on the door and Lena opened it.

"You found a flashlight," Isaac said. "Thank God. You can help us find ours."

They followed Isaac into the room he shared with Callie. Callie sat in the corner of the room, curled in a ball with her face pressed into her knees. Isaac kneeled next to her and rubbed her back.

"It's okay," Isaac said. "They have light." His voice shook, too.

The last time Warren had heard his brother sound that scared, he had dared Isaac to walk through the cemetery at night when he was eleven.

"Is she okay?" Lena asked.

"What happened to the lights?" Warren asked.

"I don't know," Isaac said. "This hasn't happened before. Something must have happened to the back-up power. Something is going on up there."

David entered the room at a run, with wide, glassy eyes. He sat down and put his head between his knees.

"Thank God you have flashlights," he said between panting breaths. He groaned and looked like he might throw up. "What the hell?"

"We don't know," Isaac said.

"Did you hear the noise, too?" David asked. "I heard a crash when the lights went out, and then another one a few minutes later."

"I think so," Warren said.

"We should get out of here," Lena said.

"How?" Warren asked.

"There is a stairwell in this hallway. We run up the stairs until we're on the ground level. Even if we get caught, we can just say we freaked out in the dark, and wanted to find light. You know that no matter what you do, they won't kill you."

"Then what?" Isaac asked. "We can't exactly catch a train to take us back to the United States. We are right in the middle of, well . . . I don't even know what's out there . . . but there are hundreds of miles of it."

"The President's plane may still be here," Lena said.

"Let's do it," Warren said.

"What?" Isaac said.

"I'm not going anywhere," David said. "Why the hell would I want to? This is the best place I've ever stayed. They got me released from the institution to come here."

"Institution?" Warren asked.

"I'm not crazy," David said defensively. "They just didn't get me. And now I know why. I belong here."

Warren looked at his brother. He could tell Isaac wouldn't budge.

"We may be under attack," Isaac said. "And she's trying to lead us into a trap. We're safe here. It's a bomb shelter, for Christ's sake. If we go up there, we could walk right into an assassination."

"I am here because of you," Warren said. "I have been trying to get to you for a month. I wanted to save you. I didn't go through all that shit just to leave you here."

"What makes you think you know what's best for me?" Isaac asked. "You don't know anything. I have nothing to go back to."

"Nothing to go back to? You have a life. You're sixteen and already in college—with a 4.0 GPA I might add. You have a mother. You have *me*."

"They killed our parents!" Isaac shouted. "They took our country! How can you not care?"

Warren paused. "How long have you known?"

"I figured it out when I was about eight-years old, Warren. And since then, I've learned enough to prove it. I know who we are. I know who *you* are."

"Then why not just let me leave so you can be King." Warren said. "Or better yet, just kill me. Take your godforsaken empire back."

"What?" David asked. "You're supposed to be King?"

"I don't want to kill you," Isaac said. "You're my brother. I love you. Quit acting like I'm not on your side."

"If you want all this, then you're not on my side," Warren said.

"Then whose side are you on?" Isaac asked. "The U.S.? The Coles?"

"No."

"Yeah, that's right," Isaac said. "No one's side but your own. Just care about keeping your life easy and carefree and everyone else can go to hell. Not me. I did something. I *was* at the TFC that day. I came here with their reporters. No one kidnapped me. I went home."

Warren lunged toward Isaac. He must have taken Isaac by surprise, because Warren pinned Isaac down and punched him in the face several times before Isaac did anything to fight back. Warren could almost hear the blood rushing through his head. He didn't want to hurt his brother, no matter what he had done. The storm had messed with his head, and he didn't know if he could stop himself. But he and Isaac were evenly matched. With Warren's slightest hesitation, Isaac knocked Warren off him and managed to get his knee pressed up against Warren's chest and his hands around Warren's neck.

Warren knew Isaac could kill him in that position if he wanted to, and for as much as he'd always loved and trusted his brother, he had no idea whether or not Isaac would do it.

But Isaac didn't kill him, and he hesitated long enough for Warren to break free. Warren pounded his fist into Isaac's face. Somewhere over the sound of his own blood rushing through his skull, he heard Lena screaming his name.

Then Isaac yelled, "No" and tried fling Warren to the side.

Warren turned around for just long enough to see the glint of a hunting knife before David stabbed him.

David's body flew through the air like a giant invisible hand smacked him. After David hit the wall, Warren saw that tiny little Callie had grabbed David and thrown him. A Caebellum. He would have never guessed they could look so unthreatening and small.

Callie kicked David in the head and he lay still. Lena and Isaac converged on Warren. Blood covered both of them. Isaac had blood running from his face and Lena had it on her hands.

"What happened to your hands?" he asked her.

She looked at him, wide-eyed. "Nothing. It's your blood. You've been stabbed."

Isaac ripped Warren's shirt from collar to hem and leaned in to examine his wound.

They both seemed really worried, but Warren could hardly feel it. The storm lit up his nerves like firecrackers, and the pain in his side felt like nothing more than a muscle cramp.

"I don't think it's very deep," Isaac said. "She pulled him off before he really got you."

Callie came over and looked at the wound like it was an unusual insect.

"Thank you," Warren said.

"How the hell did you do that?" Lena asked Callie. "Are all Wildes that strong?"

"I shouldn't have said you were King in front of David," Isaac said. "I'm sorry. I wasn't thinking."

Warren didn't get why Isaac apologized to *him*, since Isaac had the busted face.

"Is he going to be okay?" Lena asked Isaac like Warren couldn't hear.

"I hope so. I think there is an infirmary belowground here somewhere. I don't know if any doctors will be around."

"No, we have to leave now," Warren said. "Lena is right. This is our chance."

He grabbed the flashlight and Lena's hand and pulled her into the hallway. Isaac and Lena both made sounds of protest, but Warren ignored them.

In the hallway, their footsteps and breathing echoed through the silence louder than Warren expected, not to mention the blinding light he wielded in otherwise complete darkness. Anyone could see them coming from a mile away.

"Turn off the light," Isaac said, apparently thinking the same thing. He and Callie followed behind them.

Warren turned off his flashlight, but in the last second, his light hit something that sent an extra surge of adrenaline through his already adrenaline-saturated body. He saw a woman, looking in their direction. In the brief moment, she appeared pale and still as a statue, but he didn't recall seeing a statue in this hallway before. Now, with the light off, it seemed like the woman would come up and grab them any second.

"Turn the light back on," Lena said urgently. Warren could tell by the fear in her voice that Lena had seen the woman, too.

Warren turned it on and aimed the light down the hall. The woman hadn't moved. In fact, Warren saw now she hadn't moved in a while. One of the Betas who worked as a housekeeper had frozen mid-stride carrying a bucket of cleaning supplies. Part organic or not, the storm had affected her as much as the television and lights and now she looked like an exceptionally detailed mannequin, her vacant gaze looking right through them.

"That's creepy," Warren said.

"Oh, no," Isaac said.

"This might actually be possible, if the Betas are shut off," Lena said. "But once we get into the stairwell, let's turn the light off again. They probably have human guards somewhere. We can just hold on the railing and count the flights. We're on level 21, I remember from the elevator. Warren, are you sure you're okay to walk up twenty-one flights of stairs?"

He didn't answer. His heart beat fast and caused blood to soak the makeshift bandage Isaac had made out of his shirt. He barely felt the pain, but knew enough about anatomy to know that the body needed blood to function and he would run low soon.

Once inside the stairwell, they positioned themselves against the railing and turned off the light. Warren had the overwhelming urge to lie down. Stabbed or not, he had trouble remembering why he wanted to walk up a pitch-black stairwell in a storm.

"No," Callie said behind him and dragged Isaac back out of the stairwell. Of course, she had the strength to pull him out easily.

Warren switched on the flashlight and pointed the beam at his brother.

"Callie, he's hurt. I can't let him go alone," Isaac said.

"You said it was dangerous up above," she said. "I won't let you go."

"It's okay," Isaac said.

"It isn't safe," she said. She wrapped her arms around him with her feet firmly planted, and looked like the first five-foot-tall woman who could hold her own as a defensive linesman in the pros.

"We have to go," Lena said to Warren tenderly. "We have to leave them."

Warren looked at his brother, and they stared at each other. Warren couldn't think of anything to say and just turned away and continued up the stairs with Lena. He concentrated on his feet and tried to think of nothing else. Step. Step. Step. Step.

Lena eased the flashlight out of his hand and turned it off.

At ten floors up, a crack and a blue flash came from above.

Lena flinched away from it and teetered dangerously on her step. Warren had to grab her. Did these stairs lead directly outside, or did he see lightning in the stairwell? He felt the energy increase as they approached the surface. In the flash of blue, he saw flyaway strands of Lena's hair standing on end, like she had her hand on that electric ball at the science museum.

Warren moved more quickly now, although his haste irrationally led him into the storm faster. He had the general sense of needing to run *from* something. The darkness made it worse. He felt like something might grab him from behind at any moment. The journey seemed to take hours, but they did inevitably count their way up twenty-one flights. Warren turned the light on again quickly, to orient them, and they found a door with L on it.

"Lobby?" Warren asked.

"I hope so," Lena said.

He pushed open the door and blinked. An orange, flickering light, from candles or fire, broke the pitch darkness. Since he had entered the palace, he had seen no more people than he could count on two hands, so the cacophony of many voices took him off guard.

The room had a high ceiling like an old train station. He saw a security checkpoint, an information desk, and instead of trains, a long line of elevator doors. He guessed they had found the public entry point for the underground palace. About twenty people, many with candles or lamps, stood in little groups. The echo of their voices on the pink granite floor made it sound like a larger crowd. They had a haggard appearance, like many of them lived outdoors. He could smell them from a distance, one-hundred percent flesh and blood denizens of Waterloo.

No one turned to look at Lena and Warren. The people all had their eyes on the massive windows. Some pointed toward the sky.

214

They didn't look like soldiers, but there must be soldiers in the mix, or at least outside the door guarding the palace. The whole escape attempt felt childish now. They had almost reached the fringes of the group when a crack and a blue flash erupted right above the crowd. A man backed into Warren as he retreated from the windows.

"Sorry, didn't see you," the man said.

"It's okay," Warren said.

When the man saw who he had backed into, he jumped back the way he'd come, knocking into several more people. The man stuttered something like an apology, but the words came out as gibberish. The people he'd knocked into turned around and in a ripple of whispers and nudges, the entire room gradually turned to look at Warren.

"Why are they looking at us like that?" he whispered to Lena.

"I think they're looking at you."

"Oh, right."

"Just keep going," she said. "Act like you know what you're doing. We'll be fine."

As soon as he saw the way they looked at him, he knew they would let him pass. They would let him do anything. He could have asked them to take off their socks and hand them over and they would have done it without complaint. Some people bowed their heads. *Creepy.* Part of him wanted to yell at them. Give them a good long lecture about how they shouldn't follow orders from a meathead eighteen-year-old who knew as much about politics as a garden gnome. He didn't understand them. How could they be such sheep? But they had gotten used to having no choice. They feared him, because they feared his father. He couldn't blame them.

Outside, blue flashes illuminated clouds as thick as smoke. Unlike American thunderstorms that stayed in their proper place in the heavens, this storm crawled across the earth. By the light in the room, Warren saw water streaming down the glass like a waterfall gone off course.

They had almost reached the door when a petite black woman about his age approached him. She looked him up and down appraisingly and didn't seem bothered by the fact that he towered over her by a foot and a half. She didn't fear him, which he appreciated.

"Why don't we fight back?" she asked. "Why don't we shoot down the planes?"

"What?" Warren asked.

"I know you have guns that can shoot down planes. My cousin is in the army. Why aren't you doing anything?"

"We've been underground, we don't know what's going on," Lena said. "What's happening outside?"

She huffed. "We're under attack, princess."

"By the U.S.?" Lena asked.

"If you don't know we're in the middle of battle, then how come you're wounded and trying to escape?" the woman asked.

The people around the room had kept a few feet of distance between themselves and the fearless woman, until a sixty-something man with an unkempt blond and gray beard came up and stood next to her.

He spoke calmly to Warren. "There are people still at the camp. Hundreds of them. I hope you don't plan on evacuating without them."

Warren felt like an asshole but also very pissed off. They wanted him to go down with a ship that wasn't his and that he didn't want. Even if he wanted to be King, they couldn't expect him to stop a war on his first day, all while bleeding profusely.

"He's hurt," Lena said. "Step aside."

"I'm not in charge," Warren said, more to himself than anything. "I can't do anything."

"It's okay," Lena said.

"No, it's not," Warren said. He felt lightheaded, and the people looking at him had white, fuzzy edges. Warren turned back toward the stairwell and started walking without looking back. Lena pulled on his arm but even in his low-blood state, he could drag her along without much effort.

"Warren," she said. "What are you going to do?"

"I have absolutely no idea."

"You need to be stitched up. You can't mess around."

He stopped in front of the doorway to the stairwell. "Stay here. Even better, talk to these people and see if you can figure out a way to get more people inside. Send them into the stairwell if you have to."

"Warren . . . ."

He kissed her. It seemed like what the hero would do in the movies. At least it shut her up for a moment. Her rational arguments wouldn't do any good.

"Okay," she said. "I'll do what I can."

He hadn't expected her to follow his orders so easily. He wanted to argue with her. *Don't listen to me. You should me the one telling me what to do.*

But instead, he went back into the stairwell and turned on the flashlight. He would find Saul and demand to know why he didn't shoot at the planes attacking the palace. He counted flights going down to the level where he had seen Saul in what had looked like his home. He didn't have Lena to counteract the violent energy of the storm now. His heart beat way too fast, pummeling against the inside of his chest. And oddly, also pulsing away in other parts of his body, like his thigh and most keenly, in his stab wound.

With the blood loss, he probably should have slipped into unconsciousness a while ago, and he didn't know how he kept moving, but he wouldn't spend too much energy questioning why he didn't die faster. Cold energy swept down on him and made his shoulder feel like ice. He shook it away and tried not to think about that either. Step. Step. Breathe. Step. Step. Breathe.

He gave up on counting flights. He had almost forgotten his own name, and couldn't keep count of anything. He aimed his flashlight at the numbers painted on the doors. It didn't matter if they caught him now. If they caught him and dragged him to Saul, at least he wouldn't have to walk. He made it to the fifteenth level.

The door had a fingerprint plate next to it. Warren pressed his finger to the plate. The door opened but he didn't know if his fingerprint had unlocked the door or if the loss of electricity caused the locks to malfunction.

The door opened into pitch darkness. He waved his flashlight around to make sure he wouldn't walk off a cliff or into a pit of snakes. He tried to shake his brain out of its humming, crazy haze. Random snake rooms and doors leading to cliffs didn't really exist, even in underground palaces.

It looked like the same room as before. Marble floors. Fancy chandeliers. He had the urge to lie down again. He didn't know if he would make it all the way to their living quarters.

"Hey!" he shouted. "Saul! Get your ass over here."

No one came, and he didn't hear anything. He put his hand over his wound to try and keep his remaining blood in his body and walked across giant expanse of marble and up the carpeted stairs. He waved his flashlight around the giant's living room with too-big furniture. Nothing. He supposed he should have given Saul a little more credit. If they were at war, he would be in some kind of command center and not hanging out in his living room relaxing in front of his way too big TV.

He almost turned around to leave when the beam of his flashlight caught something that looked like an arm. Fear started to burn in his stomach. He aimed his flashlight back toward where he thought he saw it. Through a cracked open door, he could see an arm, but not much else. A woman's arm, clutched around something. Almost definitely Sabine's. He thought he recognized her massive wedding ring.

"Sabine?"

He hadn't really expected an answer. If she could answer, she would have already come out to confront him. Or she would have at least moved an inch. He had seen dead bodies on television and movies of course, but they usually looked limp. Her hand grasped tightly whatever she held.

Although he couldn't imagine anything he wanted to do less, he inched toward the doorway to investigate. He opened the door to their bedroom and what he saw caused him to drop his flashlight in a loud clatter.

CHAPTER THIRTY-ONE

Warren scrambled around on his hands and knees looking for the batteries that had fallen out of his flashlight. The total darkness seemed less black because of the white fog around the edges of his vision that warned of impending unconsciousness. About to pass out or not, he had never moved so quickly to put that flashlight back together. He couldn't be alone in the darkness with them. They might come alive and attack any minute.

He turned the flashlight back on. Thank God it still worked. He pointed the flashlight back at Sabine, still and unresponsive. But unlike a corpse, she stood by her husband and held him in a tight embrace. Also frozen, he held her head against his chest tenderly. They reminded him of fossilized humans from a civilization destroyed by a volcano—locked together forever, as they waited for a death they knew would come. Except instead of petrified humans, they looked like expertly crafted wax figures.

Betas.

The storm had deactivated them, like the housekeeper.

All this time, it had been nothing but smoke and mirrors. And now the real people of Waterloo would die because their government was nothing more than a clever magic trick.

He heard something that sounded like breathing and looked at Sabine and Saul closely. Were they alive in there? With a jolt of panic, he realized the sound of breathing came from behind him.

"Why are you still here?"

Startled, Warren almost attacked his brother for the second time in the space of an hour.

Totally unfazed by the bizarre sight in front of him, Isaac approached Warren and examined his wound.

"Your skin feels cold," Isaac said. "I don't know what you think you're doing . . . ."

"What the hell is going on here?" Warren asked.

Isaac looked at Warren for a moment before answering. "Do you know what the life expectancy is for a King of the Texas Empire?"

"Answer *my* question," Warren said.

"Thirty-seven," Isaac said. "I calculated it. More than half have been assassinated. One committed suicide. The others are prone to have heart attacks and other stress conditions early in life. I didn't want that to happen to you."

"What are you saying?"

"I designed these Betas and worked with the Texas Freedom Campaign to have them placed. For the record, the real goal of the Texas Freedom Campaign is to restore the Texas Empire. They've been rebuilding the palace for years."

"Why would any regular people want the Wildes back in power?"

"Don't be so ignorant. They are patriots. They honor their King and they love their country. You've been brainwashed by the U.S. anti-Texas propaganda if you believe Texans aren't up to fighting for their nation. They are a nation of ready-made soldiers who love their country like they love their wives."

"Why did you have to make it seem like you were kidnapped? The broken glass? The *blood?* How could you do that to me and Mom?"

"I'm sorry. So many times, I thought about telling you the truth, but I wanted to involve you as little as possible. I had to make it look real. I had to go the same way the others did. I didn't want them to take you at all. It may have been foolishly optimistic, but I had hoped you would go on living your normal life. But if you were going to go around doing things like stealing Will Cole's girlfriend and wandering around the former Texas territory unarmed, I thought you would be better off down here, safe."

"I wasn't *wandering* around. I was trying to rescue you, you ass." It all sounded so embarrassing now, so childish.

"I know." Isaac paused for a moment and then looked Warren in the eye. "I underestimated you."

Warren looked back at the frozen monarchs. "You really created them?"

"I had plenty of help. I have a friend who is an expert in robotics. Not to mention the help and funding I got from the TFC. But yes, I did. Do you find that hard to believe?"

"I suppose there isn't much you can't do with superhuman intelligence and no sense of right and wrong."

"I have a sense of right and wrong."

"Really? And what category does this fall into?" Warren gestured toward Saul and Sabine. "And what about the fact that we're being attacked by the United States and people are going to die because you thought a life-sized action figure could run a nation."

"They're not action figures. At least, they don't think so. The reason Betas seem so real is because they are. They are a combination of electronics and real human tissue, including human brain matter. Robotics meets bioengineering. They've been in production for the past three decades in the Texas Empire, a government project designed to safeguard Texas values and people by making them even harder to kill. I took the next step and used Wilde DNA to create Betas. It was a mistake."

"No shit."

"I knew plenty about Betas, but not enough about Blue Energy. I didn't know what would happen when I used human tissue infused with Blue Energy to make a Beta. They came to life too fast. Too easily. Betas take years to develop. They were fully sentient within days. And . . . they have memories."

"Memories?"

"They know things I never taught them. They love each other like they've been married for years. They knew my name before I told them."

"Your name? How?"

"I have no idea and I'm not sure I want to know. But it proves we don't know the first thing about Blue Energy. It's like the energy has its own consciousness . . . and its own goals. They stopped following my orders as soon as the fake footage showed in the United States. Once they knew that everyone thought they were King and Queen, they just went with it. I came here by choice, but now I'm a prisoner just like you. As a matter of fact . . . I came up here to kill them." Isaac paused and gave Warren a hard look. "Will you help me?"

"No, I won't. I don't know where you get off asking me if I want to help you commit regicide as casually as you might ask me to help you move a couch."

"I can't do it."

"You're sure they're not already dead?"

"Yes, I'm sure. We've had storms like this before. I just wasn't with them at the time. They returned to normal after it was over. I didn't realize this happened until I saw the housekeeper in the hall."

"I had already decided I wouldn't kill Saul," Warren said. "I'm not going to kill anyone, especially not to become King. Now that I know what he is, I want to kill him even less. You're the one at fault, Dr. Frankenstein."

The floor trembled with another roar from above.

"No more screwing around," Warren said. "Kill your own haunted robots. I have to figure out a way to stop the attack. Any ideas in that freak genius brain of yours?"

"I don't have any tactical training."

"What a coincidence, neither do I," Warren said.

"For the last time, you need to see a doctor."

"Holy shit, that's it," Warren said.

"What's it?"

"There is a doctor here . . . and he's got his girlfriend here, too. The President of the United States."

"What did you say?"

"I bet that's why we're under attack. Communications are down and the President can't talk to her military. All she has to do is call them off."

Warren turned to run back to the stairwell and the sudden movement caused the blood to rush from his brain and he fell. His head hit the footboard of the bed as he went down.

When Warren came to, he found himself outside in the middle of the storm. The dense rain might drown him if he opened his mouth too wide, and he couldn't hear anything except the sound of the rain pummeling the earth. Each blink filled his eyes with water and he couldn't see more than a few feet through the dense thundercloud anyway. Tiny blue currents of light wove through the air and cracked like fireworks. He seemed to float along like a ghost, but then realized Isaac and Jack dragged him by the arms.

Currents of energy ran through Warren's body. Once he got past the discomfort and vulnerability, the intensity of the energy made him feel powerful, indestructible. Instinctively, he knew that's how he had regained consciousness. The energy of the storm kept him alive. The realization comforted and terrified him at the same time. Sometime, the storm would pass.

Maybe soon. The night sky broke through the clouds in places, and the rain let up enough for him to see planes circling the palace. Fire spilled out of the dome. Fires also scattered across the grounds. With a roar and a crash, a plane hit the ground less than a hundred yards away and skidded across the plaza, leaving a wake of flames. He still didn't see anyone or anything actually shooting at the planes and realized that the Empire put up a good fight on accident. The storm shorted the electrical circuits of the planes that flew too low and took them down.

Then, something caught his eye that made his whole body go numb. The clouds parted and the distant skyline of Waterloo appeared on the horizon. The indistinct image shimmered dimly through the rain and distance, but the sparkling lights of the city matched the pictures he had seen of Waterloo at night . . . before the bomb. He knew it couldn't be real. But in that moment he didn't care how or why he saw it. *Beautiful.* It looked like home.

CHAPTER THIRTY-TWO

Warren smelled dogs. He blinked a few times and looked around. He did see a dog, but not a real one. He saw a poster of a dog, which described the danger of heartworms. Somehow, he had woken up in a vet's office.

He lay on an exam table sturdy enough for really big dogs, but Warren's feet still dangled off the end. An IV pinched his arm and blood flowed into his arm from a bag.

Jack and Lena faced away from him watching the news on a small television.

"Are you giving me dog blood?" Warren asked.

They turned around.

"Hey," Lena said. "How do you feel?"

"Seriously. Are you giving me dog blood?"

"It's my blood," Jack said. "You're welcome."

Jack wrapped Warren's arm with a blood pressure cuff and checked his vitals.

"Not bad," he concluded. "You need to drink some water."

Warren had clearly missed a lot of important things. In his last lucid memory, he had passed out in the King's bedroom. The image on the television screen grabbed his attention: *Breaking news: The U.S.*

declares war against the Texas Empire. The headline made his heart hurt. Hell, it made his fingernails hurt.

Jack handed him a paper cup with tepid water.

"You don't want me to lap it out of a bowl?" Warren asked.

"Don't be smart," he said. "You're still famous from that footage in the parking lot in Tennessee and you're still wanted for questioning by the U.S. government. With the climate the way it is, I didn't want to take chances by taking you to a hospital. It's nothing I couldn't handle myself."

"So where are we?"

"The President helped smuggle us back on a plane. We're in Washington, D.C. Congratulations. You have your freedom back."

"What about Isaac?"

"Isaac stayed in Waterloo," Lena said. "I'm sure he's fine. They probably stayed downstairs."

Warren sat up too fast and it felt like someone pulled on all the nerves radiating from his stitches. He grunted.

"Please don't do that." Jack pulled up Warren's shirt to check his stitches.

Warren rolled onto his un-stabbed side and stared at a jar of dog biscuits. Jack patted his shoulder in an odd, too-firm jerk while he checked his wound. Warren guessed that Jack didn't have much practice comforting people.

"Why are we at war?" Warren asked.

"The news sensationalizes," Lena said. "The Empire is so weak, the U.S. could hardly fight with them. What's happened is that they've gone public with Will's kidnapping and blamed the King. It's easy to believe, after the near-kidnapping incident. The U.S. is invading Waterloo. They plan to take control of the palace."

"No," Warren said. "Isaac is still there."

"This is how these things work," Jack said. "The U.S. and the Texas Empire hate each other. They'll look for any reason to attack each other. Not once has it made sense. There's nothing you can do about it."

Warren scowled at him. He arranged his eyebrows into perfect angles.

"That's just not true," Warren said.

Jack gave him an appraising look. "You want to be King?"

"You have to play the cards you're dealt. Even if they suck."

Jack nodded.

"I suppose they don't have a *Being King for Dummies* book?" Warren asked. "Because I don't have a clue. Can you get me in touch with the President?"

"I don't have her cell phone number, if that's what you mean," Jack said.

"They can't be at war because of Will. Saul doesn't really have him, right?" Warren looked at Lena. "Did you tell the President when she smuggled us out? The thing you said about the Senator?"

"I tried to. I tried to get anyone to listen to me. But Jack kept pulling me back."

"Why?" Warren demanded.

"She's still wanted for treason," Jack said. "In the heat of the battle, Lena was low priority, but I didn't want her reminding too many people who she was or making a scene accusing a respected senator of kidnapping."

"What if we just find Will ourselves?" Warren asked. "They'd have to stop the war if Will isn't in Texas."

"In theory," Jack said.

"And you know where he is," Warren said to Lena.

Jack drove them to Senator Brighton's house. Apparently, he knew exactly where the senator lived without so much as a Google search, but Lena didn't ask why. She already knew Jack was neck deep in lies and bullshit. They drove through a neighborhood with the biggest houses Lena had ever seen. High fences and trees obstructed her view, but the ones she did she did see rivaled the

Palace at Waterloo. Some of them even had their own helicopter pads. Apparently, the U.S. had its own kind of royalty.

Jack slowed and parked alongside a high, stone fence with purple flowers spilling over the top.

"The gate is just around the corner," he said.

"What do you think?" Lena asked. "Can you feel him in there?"

"It doesn't work like that," Jack said. "The amplifier is not on here. Even so, we'd have to be closer."

"Hang on," Warren said. "I think I sense something. It's like a bad smell."

Lena sniffed the air. She smelled rhododendrons.

"No," Warren said. "I don't literally mean I can smell it. I can sense it. It's like a really offensive-feeling energy."

"What does that mean?" Lena asked.

"It doesn't feel right, but it's a Wilde," Warren said. "I think he's here. Maybe it means he's hurt or sick."

"Jack, can you feel it, too?" Lena asked.

"Perhaps." Jack's forehead wrinkles looked a little deeper.

"The Senator's not here," Lena said. "We just saw him on the news. There's no way he's hanging out at home with everything going on. If the energy is here, it has to be Will. Maybe even unguarded."

"There is a car in the driveway," Jack said. "Someone's home."

"Must be Victory," Lena said. "Why don't you just let me go? I think she'll talk to me."

"She hit you," Warren said.

"I'm not saying we're gal pals, I just think she's less likely to shoot me than either of you. Besides, she was sorry she hit me. She even sent me this apology card. She wasn't herself. She was . . . ."

"What?" Warren asked.

"Oh my God," Lena said. "She's a Wilde, too. She was all amplified. I felt it. I just didn't realize it at the time. And her eyes. And how smart she is."

Lena opened the car door.

"I don't want you going in by yourself," Warren said.

"What is your plan then?" she asked.

"I'll go in myself," he said.

"That's really stupid," Lena said. "I'll just say I'm visiting Victory. The security guard up there is from a private company. He has no orders to arrest me."

"Take a gun," Jack said.

"No. There has to be a way we can do this without guns," Warren said.

"Well, you're definitely the first King of the Texas Empire to use that sentence," Jack said.

Without staying to argue further, Lena jumped out. Warren opened his door and got out to follow her. He clutched his side. She knew if she just ran for the gate, he couldn't keep up with her.

"Last night, I let you go when you had something you needed to do," Lena said. "You have to do the same."

"This is different."

"No it's not. If you dial down your testosterone and think objectively for a second, you'll see that I am the only one of the three of us who can do this."

"I don't like it," Warren said.

"Just be here when I come out," Lena said. "If I don't come out in thirty minutes, call the police."

She felt him watch her as she skirted along the fence. The smell of rhododendrons grew stronger. Her heart beat uncomfortably fast. Even in the heat, it seemed like she sweat more than normal. She watched the young guard's eyes widen more and more the closer she got. He probably thought he'd won the lottery. He would catch a notorious fugitive just by sitting on his ass.

With as much feigned confidence as she could muster she said, "I'm here to see Victory Brighton. Is she here?"

"Aren't you Lena Lowell?"

"No."

"Oh, really," he said skeptically. "Who are you then?"

"Sarah Harris. I go to school with Victory. We're working on a project together for school."

"Okay then . . . Sarah . . . did you walk here?" He said *Sarah* with a sarcastic tone; clearly he didn't believe her at all.

She hadn't thought about that. He would never believe she walked here. As soon as he got the chance, he would walk around the corner and see Warren and Jack.

"I took a taxi."

"Whatever you say. Hold up your arms and spread your legs."

"What?"

"I need to search you."

The moment the gate shut behind her, Lena saw the guard talking on his radio. Whatever she needed to do, she didn't have much time.

The house had three stories, with columns that went all the way from the porch to the roof. In the middle of the circular, brick drive sat a marble fountain of a naked, muscular man holding a globe.

The guard had called Victory on the intercom, and she waited for Lena on the porch, still in her pajamas. She crossed her arms. Maybe it was the contrast against the majesty of her father's home, or the pajamas, but Victory seemed more plain than usual.

When Lena got closer, she winced. Victory's skin and hair both looked flat and gray. That unknowable power in her that made her irresistible and terrible had gone. Lena heard Victory wheezing slightly. Blue veins showed through the skin on her arms and her eyes made Lena's skin crawl. The red around her irises made it look like she bled from the eyes. Lena could hardly stand to look at her.

"Victory?"

"I don't know what you're doing here," Victory said. "But if you stay, you'll probably be arrested."

"I haven't broken any law."

She smirked.

"What happened to you?" Lena asked.

"Exorcism is never pretty. But I will purge this curse from my body."

"I don't understand."

She said nothing.

"Where is Will?"

Her stern face scrunched up like she smelled something bad, then Lena realized she tried to hold back tears. Did that mean he was already dead? She pushed the thought away.

"Is he here?" Lena asked.

"No."

"You're lying."

"If he was here, I would be with him." She sat down on the stairs. "My father would not hurt William Cole's son. He loved him like a brother." Victory seemed to talk to herself, barely aware of Lena's presence.

My half-baked non-plan for coming here might actually work.

"And you are sure that he loves him more than he hates the Wildes?"

Victory twitched, shaking off the thought like a fly.

Lena sat down beside her and Victory turned away from her slightly. Victory didn't seem to have the energy to lie well, and Lena knew Victory knew where to find him, or at least, she knew something important. With no particular force about her that would threaten Victory in any way, Lena would have to kill her with kindness to get her answers.

"Is there anything I can do to help you?" she asked.

Victory looked at her suspiciously. "What do you mean?"

"You look like you're suffering."

"I'm fine . . . . I will be fine."

Lena put her hand on Victory's, but pulled it away just as quickly. Victory felt amplified, but not in the usual way. Her energy had turned rotten. Lena couldn't quite stifle a gasp.

"Look at me," Lena said.

"What?"

Victory did look at her, and Lena took a good, long look at Victory's eyes. Aside from the redness, she had the same pale blue eyes as Will. Similar enough, she could be Will's sister. Who knew? Maybe she was. Anything seemed possible.

"Why are you being nice to me?" she asked angrily.

"Shouldn't I?"

"You know, Will loves me, not you," Victory said.

The statement hit Lena harder than she expected. Victory might as well have smacked her in the face again. Lena had to fight to stay focused. She couldn't be distracted by whether or not Will wanted her or Victory, his possible sister.

"I think you need to go lie down. Let me help you." Lena took Victory's hand and tried to pull her up, but she didn't seem like she could get up. In fact, it looked like she might pass out at any minute. Lena grabbed her under her arms to pull her up. Victory bore little of the weight herself, and helping her stand proved difficult. Still unsteady, Victory leaned into her, and Lena had to keep her arms around her so she wouldn't fall.

"Am I going to die?" Victory whispered. All of the strength had faded from her voice.

"No." Lena stroked her hair and squeezed her gently.

"I was going to be President," Victory said.

"You can still be President."

"You are beautiful."

Lena started to wonder if Victory's brain had gone funny. Before she came up with any sort of response, Victory kissed her. A tender kiss—the kind of kiss you shared with someone right after you shared *I love yous* for the first time or got engaged.

"Miss Lowell?" A security guard grabbed her arm. Lena felt more violated than afraid. They shouldn't see Victory so vulnerable. She hoped they wouldn't tell the Senator that his daughter had kissed a girl, as completely unimportant as that seemed right now.

The guard pulled Lena's arms behind her back and as he did so, Victory slumped back down onto the steps. "You are being taken into the custody of the state for questioning."

A gunshot rang out behind her. Lena winced automatically and waited for the bullet to hit her. It didn't. She looked up.

Jack stood in the lawn, holding a gun over his head like he had just shot a bullet into the air. Warren stood a few paces behind Jack, holding a gun well away from his body like a piece of smelly garbage. The guard took out his gun and pointed it at Jack. Lena saw the terror in the guard's eyes. He shook from his head to his toes.

"Put it down," Jack commanded.

The guard threw his gun into the grass, turned, and ran into the wooded area on the side of the house.

"Lena, let's go," Jack said.

Lena looked back at Victory. She could still hold herself in a sitting position, but barely, and did not seem to have the energy to show much emotion at the sight of a Wilde man shooting a gun on her front lawn.

"She knows something, but I don't know what yet," Lena said.

"No time," Jack said.

"I think she's dying," Lena said.

Jack looked at Victory and his face went gray. He ran toward her and kneeled in front of her, looking at her closely.

"Oh, God," he said. "I did this to her."

"What? How?" Lena asked.

"Help me," Jack said. He grabbed Victory by the arm, and then dropped it, as if her skin burned him.

Warren approached Victory and reached to help her up.

"No," Jack shouted at Warren. "Stay back. Lena, you help."

Warren looked baffled, but didn't protest.

"Warren, when we get to the car, you sit in front with me." Jack spoke through barely parted lips, looking like he tried not to inhale an odor. He had his face away from Victory as if she emitted an intense heat Lena couldn't feel.

CHAPTER THIRTY-THREE

Warren rolled down the windows. Something intensely evil choked the air. He didn't know if rolling down the windows would do any good, but he had to do something.

"What is wrong with that girl?" Warren asked. "I have never felt anyone with such disgusting energy, and I don't even think the amplifier is on."

"Don't worry about it," Jack said.

Warren glanced in the rearview mirror at Victory and Lena. He didn't even want to look directly at Victory. Victory leaned on the side of the door and looked passed out. Maybe she was the Devil. It seemed appropriate that the Devil would be a beautiful girl. He wanted to be as far away from her as possible. Somewhere in China, instead of in a tiny car sharing her air. Lena caught his eye in the rearview mirror. She must not feel the girl's energy. If she could, she wouldn't sit so close to her without so much as a wince.

"Why did we bring her again?" Warren asked.

"We need her to tell us where Will is. I know she knows," Lena said.

Warren used the control on the side panel to open the back windows, too, and the movement of the window roused Victory. She looked at Warren and squinted. He shut his eyes to stop her from catching his gaze. What did he think—that he would turn to stone if he looked at her? Well, better safe than sorry.

"It's okay. They're not going to hurt you" Lena said. Victory must have closed her eyes again because Lena said, "Wait, stay awake for a minute. Where is Will?"

"What?" Victory asked.

"Where is Will?"

"He is with my father."

"Where?" Lena demanded.

Warren hazarded a glance back at Victory. She put her head back against the glass and passed out again.

"Ugh," Lena said. "Where could he be?"

"I have a suggestion," Jack said quietly.

"Where?" Lena asked.

"Throughout the centuries, certain members of the government have conducted business requiring discretion," Jack said. "There are chambers under the Capitol, chambers to which only a few elite members of the most prominent political families have access."

"I know you'll just evade the question like always . . . but, how do you know?" Lena asked.

"It's where my lab is . . . was. I need to go there on any count, to treat the girl."

"Lab?" Lena asked.

"Access must not be as exclusive as you say, if they let you in," Warren said.

"There is one significant problem," Jack said. "There is no way we can get in. You need a key and a code, and I have neither."

"Where is the entrance?" Warren asked.

"There are several. The Capitol basement. The White House. The Pentagon." He sighed. "The only one I know of that's not heavily guarded might be in Capitol Hill. There is an entrance in the basement of the house that Lorelei shared with William Cole. The house has been in the Cole family for a hundred years, and they needed a secret underground passageway, apparently. It's the one I've used the most." Jack said. "Lorelei still owns the house and I think it's vacant."

"Let's go," Lena said.

The neighborhood the Coles used to live in featured elegant houses in tight rows. Ancient trees, cobblestone walkways, and oil lamps lined the narrow roads. Warren could easily picture horses clomping along drawing carriages.

Jack awkwardly parallel parked the car, bumping the two other cars on either side.

"There." He pointed to a three-story, white stone house with a cast-iron fence. The house didn't stand out from the others much, but had an aura of history about it. Warren thought he felt a different energy, like its significance had left a bruise on the universe. He shook away the odd thought.

Lena got out first and Warren and Jack followed her to the door. Boldly, she tried to just open the front door, but of course found it locked. Jack gave Lena one exasperated look before he picked up a rock from the garden and threw it into an ancient-looking, stained glass pane on the door.

"What is the matter with you?" Warren said to Jack.

"We just kidnapped a Senator's daughter at gunpoint and you're worried about a little breaking and entering?" Jack asked.

Jack reached his hand in and opened the door. He gestured for them to enter.

The house smelled like a museum, but with modern furniture, or at least nineteen-nineties modern. The living room looked like it came from a catalog. Normal people appeared to have lived here—not people who bomb a nation and kill millions of people. Although, Warren figured that even mass murderers needed things like couches and decorative rugs.

Lena went back to get Victory and by the time she had dragged her lifeless body over the threshold, she breathed heavily and looked livid.

"Why didn't you help me?" she asked. "We could have done it a lot faster. I think someone saw me with her. How do you think it looks to drag an unconscious woman into a house?"

"It looks better for you than it would for us," Jack said. "Maybe you're just helping a girlfriend who had too much to drink."

"I'm sorry," Warren said to Lena. "She makes me feel sick."

Warren helped Lena pull Victory onto the couch anyway. He grabbed a throw from the couch and wrapped his hands in it before touching her. It didn't seem like it helped at all. After he let go of her, his hands pulsed with pain.

"I know where she used to keep the key to the passageway," Jack said. "There are two doors. One uses a regular key. And you were clever enough to bring the key to the second door," Jack said to Lena.

"What?"

"Victory," Jack explained.

"She has a key?"

"She is the key. They added a lock that requires a DNA scan. It opens only for people from certain bloodlines." Jack pulled up Victory's eyelids to examine them. She didn't flinch. "Warren, could you come here, please?"

"Why?"

"Just come," Jack said wearily.

Warren kneeled down next to Victory. He thought he might throw up. He stared at a lamp to avoid looking at her.

"I know," Jack said. "I'm afraid this will be unpleasant, but I think we need to act now. Her pulse is weak. She might not make it to the lab. I need your help. I think it will take both of us."

Warren cocked one eyebrow suspiciously. "To do what?"

"I need you to lay your hands on her with me."

"You've got to be kidding," Warren said. "You don't actually think that will do anything."

"It will help to stimulate the energy inside her. It will help her heal. Just like the storm helped you."

Jack had already cupped her face in his hands and breathed heavily. Sweat beaded on his forehead.

All the instincts Warren had told him not to touch her. She was death. He held his hands out about a foot above her and hoped perhaps that would do the trick.

"Put your hands on her chest," Jack said.

"Uh . . . where?" His hands hovered over her breasts, although the thought of touching them was far from sexy.

"By her heart," Jack said impatiently. "I have my hands near her brain. Being close to the organs most necessary for life increases the effectiveness."

Warren put his hands up Victory's shirt and placed them right above her breasts. After only a few seconds, pain intensified in his fingers and crawled up his arms. He pulled his hands away.

"No," he said. "There is something wrong with her."

"What does it feel like?" Lena asked.

"When I touch her, I feel like I'm going to die. And I'm not being dramatic. I mean it literally."

Jack's hands trembled as he continued to keep them on Victory's face. "She has been given a virus that destroys Blue Energy. It's designed to kill Wildes."

"Then, why the hell are we touching her?" Warren shouted. "No wonder I feel like I'm going to die. I am."

"No. The virus won't transmit through skin to skin contact. You feel bad when you touch her because you feel what she feels. It's not really hurting you."

"No," Warren said.

"You won't get the virus," Jack said through gritted teeth.

"How can you be sure?

"Because I created it," Jack shouted.

Silence.

"Why?" Warren said.

"You know why. I hate the Wildes. But I regret creating the toxin and never used it. Many Wildes do deserve to die. But not you, and not Will, and not Victory. So put your hands on her."

"You son of a bitch," Warren said. "Traitor. As soon as I can manage it, I'm having you arrested again."

"Fine," Jack said.

"He's right," Lena said softly. "If you have the power to help, you should."

Warren took a deep breath and put his hands back on her chest. He closed his eyes and said, *I am not dying,* over and over in his head. The pain traveled from his hands and up his arms. When it got close to his heart, he thought for sure he would die, but he didn't, it just felt like a boulder sat on his chest. Why would he do this for a woman he didn't know? What if Jack had lied? He tried to push the thoughts out of his head. A life needed saving. That had to be enough. Even a stranger's life deserved a few minutes of pain. He focused on that to see if it would help. He thought *live, live, live,* and visualized blue light going from his hands into her heart. One way or another, she seemed to improve. Her veins began to look less pronounced and her skin returned to a more normal color.

After about a minute, Victory opened her eyes suddenly. She gasped and jerked away from Warren. To be fair, she had passed out and then woken up in a strange place with one Wilde man with his hands on her head and another with his hands up her shirt. Her resistance faded quickly, though. She sighed and closed her eyes. It did look like she felt some relief. A tear slid down the side of her face.

"Okay." Jack pulled his hands away, and Warren did the same.

Warren crouched onto the floor and curled up into a ball. His position probably didn't look very manly, but he didn't care.

"Are you okay?" Lena asked.

"I'm just going to lie here on the floor for a minute," he said.

"How do you feel?" Jack asked Victory.

She glowered at him and said nothing.

"Just rest here for a while. I'm going to help you," Jack said.

Warren's hands continued to shake when they walked down the stairs into the basement. Lena led Victory by her elbow and she didn't resist. Victory wandered along with them like a sleepwalker. The basement smelled like mold and dirt. Jack opened an air vent and felt around inside.

"Shit," he said. "The key isn't here anymore."

Jack examined a door that looked like it would have led to a water heater and tried to turn the knob. He then took a credit card from his wallet and slid it in the crack. After this didn't work, he kicked the door a few times.

Warren felt something cold against his arm. A key. Victory dangled the key from a chain and laid it on Warren's forearm. She didn't say anything, or even look at him.

"You have a key, too?" Warren said. "Does this open the door to the passage?"

She pursed her lips, like the stupidity of the question tasted bad.

"Thank you," Warren said, taking the key.

Jack looked at Victory for a moment before taking the key out of Warren's hand. He nodded to her and used the key to open the door.

They crowded inside a tiny chamber between two doors. The second door looked like it belonged on a space ship. Victory pressed her thumb onto a glass plate and the panel opened with a hiss.

Warren didn't consider himself to be claustrophobic, but he thought the narrow tunnel would test that theory.

Jack flipped a switch, and fluorescent lights hummed to life down the tunnel, and a vent above began to whir.

"The ventilation system will take a minute to really kick in," Jack said. "It's about a mile to the lab."

They followed Jack at a brisk walk. Anxious to get out of the enclosed space, Warren wanted to break into a run.

After what seemed like a very long time, Jack said, "We're under the Capitol now."

He pointed to the walls, now sparkling granite. The row of fluorescent lights ended, replaced by sconces. The doors now matched the rich mahogany doors to the offices in the Capitol above. No longer one long tunnel, the hallways turned off in different directions. To Warren, it seemed like a hopeless maze, but Jack walked with confidence like he walked through the rooms of his own home.

Jack slowed and kept his gun raised. Warren copied him with the gun Jack had given him. Lena walked so close to Warren, she kept stepping on his feet. Jack stopped in front of a metal door, unlike the others. He closed his eyes and looked deep in concentration. Warren first thought he listened for something, but then realized he *felt* for something. Warren concentrated on any energy coming from behind the door. It surprised him that he hadn't felt it sooner. The same dark energy that came from Victory seeped through the hinges of that door.

"He's here," Jack mouthed. "Stay."

Warren shook his head and tried to project, *No, I'm helping,* into Jack's mind although he seriously doubted he could project thoughts into people's minds.

Jack gave Warren and his gun a hard look, then nodded toward the door.

"Stay out of sight and watch my back," Jack whispered.

They entered a massive laboratory with all sorts of fancy-looking gadgets Warren couldn't name. Warren thought about how much Isaac would love this place, the lair of a brilliant madman. Warren had no opportunity to stay out of sight.

Brighton stood in the middle of the large, silver room, waiting for them to come in. He faced them with a cold smile.

"Well, well, well. Jack. I haven't seen you in ages." He nodded to Warren. "Mr. King, nice to see you again. Now, how may I help you, gentlemen?"

"He's still alive, isn't he?" Warren said. One corner of the room felt about as welcoming as the gates of Hell—that must be Will's dying energy. Warren couldn't look in that direction. His eyes simply wouldn't follow his brain's command.

"How much have you given him?" Jack asked.

"Hopefully enough to save his soul," Sam said.

"I can count on you, Sam," Jack said, "Rather work alone than give any common men access to your hidey-hole. What's to stop me from killing you right now?"

Sam seemed to pull a gun out of thin air. "You should have taken the shot when you had a chance. I'm a quick draw."

Warren tightened his grip around his gun. He felt protective of Jack, even though he considered Jack to be a villain. He wanted to shoot Sam, but he wanted to shoot the creature in the corner even more. He didn't trust his instincts. He knew some of them came from Blue Energy or his DNA, somewhere other than his own gut. *Only shoot if he tries to shoot you*, he said to himself, trying to fight back any other thoughts.

"You know, I'm glad you came, Jack," Sam said. "It really clears up a lot of things for me. Will really is your bastard son."

"Will is your best friend's son," Jack said. "Not mine. Kill Will and you don't hurt me at all."

"Not possible," he said. "He's full of the darkness that's in you."

"You're wrong." Jack's hands started to shake. "You and William screwed me over and thought I just ran into the bushes with my tail between my legs." He laughed humorlessly. "I got my revenge."

"Oh, did you, now?" Sam's eyebrows raised in mock interest.

"You should have left your baby-making to God," Jack said.

"What the hell are you talking about?" Sam asked.

"Preimplantation genetic diagnosis," Jack said. "Because of the genetic disease in their family, the Coles went to a fertility clinic. They had their embryos tested before implantation so they could select an embryo without the cystic fibrosis mutation. And guess which doctor examined the embryos? I decided to give William's first-born son the mutation that he hated so much. After years of working with the Wilde mutation to try and destroy it, I believe I know more about it than any man alive. I altered the embryo that became Will so that the only characteristic inherited would be the increased Energy. That way, Cole wouldn't see him for what he was, right away. I wanted him to raise him and love him. I wanted him to find out about it only after it would completely destroy him. Unfortunately, William didn't live to find out what I had done. But you . . . ." Jack laughed. "When I saw your file cross my desk, too . . . wow. That was just too good to be true. And then, when I heard what you named her . . . Victory. I loved it. You didn't realize that the victory was mine."

All the blood left Sam's face. Warren wondered if he'd had a stroke and died where he stood. But then, his face scrunched up like he might cry. The sadness only lasted about a second his before expression shifted to disgust.

"I knew something was wrong with her. She wasn't right. I never loved her like a father should. You robbed me of the daughter I should have had."

"Kill me if you want," Jack said. "But Will and Victory are innocent. You're just torturing them with the virus anyway. You know full well that it doesn't work."

"You know what . . . you're right," Sam said. "I don't have the patience for it."

Sam had looked so lost in his emotions that Warren could not anticipate what happened next. Before either Jack or Warren could respond, Sam took aim and shot into Will's corner.

Warren forced himself to look. His eyeballs burned in pain as he looked at Will strapped to a hospital bed. Blood blossomed onto his shirt from a gunshot wound to the heart. Before Warren could do anything to stop them, Lena and Victory ran into the room. Tears streaked Victory's face. Warren guessed she had just heard her father say he never loved her. Victory looked at Will, and then looked at her father. In what seemed like slow motion, she snatched the gun from Warren's hands and shot her father between the eyes.

White specks of light swam in Lena's vision. She would faint any second. She crouched down on the floor to keep from keeling over. Everyone in the room froze in a state of shock. Jack still pointed his gun at the empty space Sam had occupied moments before. Victory looked down at the gun like she didn't know how it got in her hand, and let it clatter to the floor.

Warren acted first. He rushed over to Will.

"Jack, help me!" Warren put his hands over the wound on Will's chest. "Jack!"

Lena gravitated toward Will's bed, still dazed.

Jack came to Will's bedside and put his hand on Will's neck to feel his pulse. The man on the bed didn't look much like the fresh-faced, charming politician she had known and cared for. Sweat soaked his hair and clothes, like he had suffered there for days. His pale skin had turned almost translucent. He looked like a ghoul, but Lena took his hand anyway.

"Help me," Warren said again. "We can put our hands on him."

Jack shook his head. "You can't bring someone back," he whispered.

"He's not dead. I can still feel him. We can keep his brain alive until paramedics get here."

"It's not enough."

Without a word, Victory stood beside Warren and put her hands on Will's chest, too. Jack shook his head again, but then darted off out of sight, like he'd thought of something. Without warning, Warren and Victory crumpled to the ground. A sudden, hot jolt of energy shot through Lena's body. She clung to Will's bed to keep from falling down.

The air around her felt thick, and she struggled to raise her head. Every nerve in her body fired at once and the energy pulsed through her heart with such force she feared she might go into cardiac arrest. She had the obscure and terrible feeling that her soul whipped around her body like a flag in a hurricane. She didn't care if Will lived or died, or even if she did. She just wanted it to stop.

Then, the feeling lessened considerably, but she still tingled over every inch of skin.

Jack pulled a large cylinder toward them and crashed into everything he passed. He veered from side to side like he walked the deck of a ship in a storm. As the machine got closer, Lena felt her nerves firing up again.

"I had to turn it down so I could make it back. I hope this will be enough." His voice shook.

"What is that?" Lena asked.

"Amplifier—as Warren calls it," Jack said. He started pulling wires out of a cabinet, dropping them several times. Lena helped him scoop them up. Jack looked like he had trouble staying on his feet.

"Thank you," he said. "Help me. Stick these all over his head." The wires had adhesive pads on the ends. After she did as he asked, she noticed that the wires connected to the cylinder.

"What are you going to do?" she asked.

"I used to test the virus on myself," Jack explained. "I used this machine to build my energy back up, so I could endure repeated tests. I'm going to turn it up all the way. You'll feel something, but the energy is routed through the wires now, so it won't be as bad."

Warren and Victory had surfaced, too, and eyed the machine fearfully. Warren started backing away from the machine and grabbed Victory's elbow to lead her away.

"That's a good idea," Jack said. He typed onto a keypad, and after a series of beeps, the terrible electric feeling surged through Lena again. She backed away from the machine, rolled into a ball on the floor and waited for the feeling to pass. If she felt this way, she couldn't imagine what it felt like for the others. After a time, the energy started to lift. She pulled herself up by grabbing the bed. The others still lay on the floor.

Will's eyes opened. Instead of feeling happy and relieved, she felt fear. Something had gone wrong. His eyes had become paler, almost white. His skin remained as pale as if he was a corpse, but seemed to faintly glow. He looked like Will's ghost.

Lena touched his leg. A prickle of energy met her fingers, but he felt solid.

Will watched her curiously but didn't speak.

"Will?" Lena asked. "Can you hear me?"

Will looked at Lena's hand on his leg and touched it gingerly like he'd never seen anything like it before.

"Yes," Will said.

"How do you feel?" Lena asked.

Jack pulled himself up shakily and stared at Will.

Will parted his lips to speak, but didn't.

Jack's put his stethoscope on an undamaged part of Will's chest. "He doesn't have a heartbeat," Jack said in a barely audible whisper. "I shouldn't have done this."

Dread crept down Lena's spine.

CHAPTER THIRTY-FOUR

Warren got up on his hands and knees. The massive flux of energy passed, but agitation still lingered in his body. The stiff muscles in his neck and chest made it hard to breathe. What the hell just happened?

Warren felt Lena's hand on his back, and then she grabbed his arm to help him up.

"You okay?" she asked.

"I think so," Warren said.

Jack and Victory had already recovered and huddled over Will's bed. The energy coming from Will had changed, still strong, but the darkness that came from the effect of the virus felt like a lingering odor; the source had gone.

With the amplifier buzzing right in the same room with him, the mess of emotions coming from the group of people around the bed formed a dark blob of agitation so intense and complex, he couldn't single out anything.

When Warren saw Will, he first thought, *zombie*. He had a bullet hole in his chest that didn't seem to bother him in the least. Warren knew that with Will strapped to the amplifier, he didn't feel the wound as much, just like Warren in the storm. But Will's wound made Warren's look like a paper cut.

Warren leaned toward Victory.

"I need to talk to you," he said.

She flinched away from him, like he had just stuck his tongue in her ear.

"You seem to hate Wildes a lot, considering you are one."

Victory didn't say anything. In fact, he hadn't heard her say one single thing since she killed her father. She didn't cry. If anything, she looked too dry. Like something sucked her life out.

"I'm sorry," he said, as kindly as he could. "I know you're upset. But I need your help. It's very important that I talk to the President. We need to tell her that Will is safe so that she calls back the troops. You must know of a way to contact her."

She pointed to her father's body.

"What?" Warren asked.

"Bring me his phone," she said.

Rummaging through the pockets of a dead Senator Brighton was surreal. He thought about what his past self would think if he had a glimpse of the future and saw only this moment. He found the man's phone and handed it to Victory. Victory dialed mutely, and then handed Warren a ringing phone.

"Sam, make this quick," said the President.

Warren felt like his throat might close up from nerves. She couldn't have given him a moment to prepare?

"Hey, how's it going?" Warren asked.

Silence.

"Who is this? How did you get this number?"

"I'm sorry. This is Warren King. I don't know if you remember, we talked that one time after I got arrested."

"For Christ's sake, I know who you are. Why do you have the Senator's phone?"

Warren didn't want to distract the President with minor details like, *the Senator's daughter shot him in the head and I robbed his corpse to get his phone.*

"I'm the King of the Texas Empire," Warren said. "Saul is just a decoy. He's a Beta. I'm the real King."

More silence.

"I know. Mr. Craven told me."

"Okay. Good. So, then you'll talk to me about a truce . . . or a treaty." Whatever word meant, *don't invade my country please.*

"You're hardly older than my son."

"You only have to be eighteen to be King of the Texas Empire," he said. "I'll get right to the point. I'm looking at your son right now. He's hurt, but he's alive. And if you're tracing this call, you'll know that I'm in Washington, D.C. Not far from you at all, in fact. The Texas Empire didn't kidnap your son. Jack, Lena, and I found him and saved his life. Now, do I have your word that you'll stop the invasion of the palace once you see that he's safe?"

"You'd better not be lying," she said.

Warren heard a hint of tears in her voice.

"I think you're a good President," Warren said. "And I don't think you want to finish the job your husband started. You're just doing this to save your son. So if he's okay, you'll pull out the troops?"

"Yes."

The President arrived alone. Warren wondered if she could even allow her security into the underground chamber. They had moved the Senator out of sight so they could try to explain before she saw the body. But she had eyes only for her son anyway. Warren guessed she would have stepped over the Senator's body without a word if they had left him there.

"Dear God," she said. She shot over to Will's side like they were magnetized, and kissed his palm.

Will considered his mother with a look of polite interest while she cried and examined his bloody chest.

Jack watched Will carefully.

"Will, who is the President of the United States?" Jack asked him.

Will paused for a moment, looking at his mother. "I don't know," he said.

The President gave Jack a panicked look. "What's wrong with him?"

"Memory loss can happen with trauma. Will, do you know any of the people here?" Jack asked.

Will studied everyone around the bed carefully. His pale, creepy eyes seemed to linger on Warren a little longer than the others. But he turned to Jack.

"You," he said. "You seem familiar to me."

"We've never met," Jack said.

Will looked troubled and pointed to Victory and Warren. "I know them, too. I'm sorry. I can't remember your names."

"Can you remember anything about them?" Jack asked.

Will considered them for a while. "Not really. We're close."

Warren thought Will had made some lame guesses, considering the fact he hadn't said anything about his mother, the woman whose tears ran down his arm. If Warren had to guess, he would have pegged her as someone he knew. Perhaps Victory, too, since she limply held his other hand, but Warren wouldn't have picked himself, the man standing farthest away from him, six feet back from the foot of his bed.

"And the woman sitting next to you on your bed?" Jack asked.

As Warren had thought, anyone in any state of being could tell by the fear and desperation in the President's eyes that the answer should be yes.

Will looked at her a long time before responding. "Yes, I know her," he said hesitantly.

"I'm a doctor," Jack said. "In order to help you, I need you to tell me the truth."

"I'm sorry," he said to his mother. "I don't remember you."

The President put her face in her hands.

"I'm so sorry," Will said again.

Jack put his hand on the President's shoulder and she shoved it away.

"He's stable. If we keep the amplifier on him, hopefully he'll be able to make it into surgery. How do you want to do this?" Jack asked the President.

She turned to Victory, Warren, and Lena. "You should go before the paramedics get here. You don't need to be involved."

She looked at Jack. "And you. I never want to see you or hear from you again."

"No. I'm going to stick around," Jack said.

"Excuse me?" she said.

"I'm going to stay to keep an eye on Will until he can get under another's doctor's care. Then, I'm going to turn myself in for killing the Senator."

"What did you just say?" the President asked.

"I'll explain," Jack said, but he looked at Victory instead of the President.

Victory stared back at him and didn't say anything.

"I owe you one, Victory," Jack said simply. "Consider this my apology for making you what you are."

CHAPTER THIRTY-FIVE

Warren had never visited any place as wonderful as The Holiday Inn and Suites in Richmond, Virginia. His bed had the same pretty girl in it every night, and he had hundreds of channels on the TV, Wi-Fi, free coffee and sesame bagels, and most importantly, he wasn't King of any of it. He was a regular guy staying in a regular room with his girlfriend. Of course, paradise didn't stretch very far. Even going into the hallway to get ice could get one of them recognized. At least they had an unexpected ally. He supposed it made sense to be nice to the people who had witnessed you killing your father.

Victory came to the door looking like an overdressed pizza delivery girl. She handed Warren the pizza box. He started eating a piece before either of them spoke.

"Here is the pizza you asked for," she said to Lena. Warren would call her tone robotic, but having met real robots, he knew that would just be an insult to them.

Victory wore a sleek navy pantsuit and had carefully applied makeup and done her hair. Her effort did not conceal the dull tone of her skin and reddened eyes. However, having just lost her father, people would not think twice about her distressed appearance.

"Come in," Lena said.

"He's awake and talking now. They say he's doing well," Victory said.

"Is his heart beating?" Lena asked.

Victory gave her a puzzled look. "Yes. That's what I mean when I say he's doing well."

"How long can we stay here?" Warren asked.

Victory shrugged. "I don't care."

"We can pay you back," Lena said.

"That's not necessary," Victory said with a slight smirk Warren interpreted to mean, *I am richer than God and your money is useless to me.*

"He ordered his hamburger with no pickles," Victory said to Lena.

Warren could never guess what Victory would say next. Who the hell knew what synapse told her to say that.

But Lena must have the same synapse, because she gasped. "No pickles!"

"Does that mean something?" Warren asked.

"Will does not like pickles," Victory said.

"He must be in there somewhere," Lena said. "Does he remember anything else yet?"

"I don't think so. He's trying, but I think he's just telling us what we want to hear," Victory said.

"How does he act?" Warren asked.

"What do you mean?" Victory asked.

"Is his personality the same?"

"I suppose so," Victory said. "He doesn't really say much. But he's polite. Friendly."

"Are *you* going to be okay?" Lena asked.

Victory frowned and turned grayer. "I don't want to talk about what happened. I'm going back to the hospital for a while, and then I'll pick up my mom at the airport. Then, there's the funeral."

"I've never seen your mom," Lena said.

"I haven't seen her in three years myself," Victory said. "She lives overseas. Probably coming back to hear the reading of the will."

Victory looked at Warren. "What are you going to do now?"

"I don't know, maybe watch a movie," Warren said. "Then, go down to the fitness room, see if I can work out for a while without being noticed."

"Don't be ridiculous," Victory said. "You know that's not what I'm asking."

"I don't know," Warren said. "Go home. Start my freshman year in the fall."

He lied to her, but he didn't trust this woman farther than he could fling her.

"When you're ready to check out, just call the front desk. I bribed the staff to keep quiet until you're ready to go back into the public eye. Hopefully, they will abide." Victory looked like she wanted to say something else, but after a pause, just said, "So, goodbye, then."

Victory turned and left abruptly.

"She creeps me out," Warren said. "And not just because she killed her father in cold blood."

"He shot Will," Lena said.

"I'm not saying the Senator didn't get what he deserved. But still . . . she shot to kill. You can tell she knows how to handle a weapon. Probably went to some fancy marksmanship camp for rich girls."

"You know you really can't just go home," Lena said. "You know who the other options are . . . no offense to Isaac. But whoever the King is, he'll surely be a tyrant. What kind of man just walks away and allows that to happen?"

Ouch.

"If you have all the answers . . . marry me. You can be queen, and I'll sit on my ass while *you* save the world."

"I'm not going to marry you just to be queen."

"Well, now you know how I feel. I offered you the world on a platter and you didn't want it."

"I do want it. But I'm not going to get it that way."

Warren raised his eyebrows.

"Well, I'm not going to walk away and do nothing," he said. "And I'm sorry that you think that's the kind of man I am. Maybe I was. But I don't have that choice anymore."

"I never really thought you would do nothing," Lena said. "It's not in your blood."

"Leave my blood out of it."

"What will you do, then?"

"I'm thinking maybe I'll be King long enough to make Texas a democratic nation. How . . . I have no idea."

Lena smiled.

"Obviously, I like that idea. But making Texas a democratic nation may not be as easy as you think," Lena said.

"When did you hear me say I thought it would be easy?"

"They're showing the story again," Lena said.

She un-muted the television. An aerial photo of the Palace at Waterloo displayed on the screen. Black gashes marred the partially constructed dome, and burned patches of grass covered the grounds.

Every time Warren saw it, he let out a sigh. "It's still standing."

"I'm sure he's fine. Don't worry." Lena rubbed his shoulders. "They were all safe belowground."

"Yeah, he's down there with crazy stabby David, the Caebellum girl, and I-think-I'm-a-real-boy Saul. Safe and sound."

"You need to call your mom," Lena said. "Let her know you're okay."

"I will. Soon. I just need to figure out what to say."

"How about, I'm alive and I still love you now that I know the truth about you."

"That sounds good. Write that down."

Lena rolled her eyes.

"A freak electrical storm turned a Presidential peacekeeping mission into a dangerous situation," began the female anchor.

"Do you think what they're saying is true?" Lena asked. "That no shots were fired, it was just planes crashing into the palace on accident?"

"I can see why people think it's a cover story, but you and I know that it could be true. I never saw the planes fire at the palace," Warren said.

"In a statement early this morning, the President assured the nation that the United States and the Texas Empire are still at peace and this was not an act of war from either side," the anchor continued. "She states that the United States will assist with the rebuilding of the palace."

"It sounds nice. I just hope both sides agree that we're not at war," Lena said.

"Me, too." Warren turned off the television and put his arm around Lena's shoulder. "I still owe you a proper date."

"You mean in public?"

"Let me guess. You're embarrassed to be seen with me because one of my earlobes is slightly smaller than the other. I'm a freak, I know."

Lena laughed. "I think I can get over the earlobe thing."

"I assume you know we'll wear disguises to the restaurant. I was thinking either a fake nose or a fat suit. You, of course, will be wearing a slutty nurse costume and a pink wig."

"Very inconspicuous."

Warren heard the distant rumble of thunder and opened the balcony door. An afternoon storm brewed on the horizon. The cool breeze smelled like rain.

Lena wrapped her arm across his back.

"It's just a thunderstorm," she said.

"I remember I once used to like them," Warren said.

He put his arm around her and pulled her close enough that he could smell her hair. They watched the blue streaks of faraway rain. Warren felt warmth spreading through his body that had nothing to do with Blue Energy. Just the God-given desire a guy had for a girl. He tried to focus on the moment. He wondered if he would have many more moments like this in his life. He used to think his life would be full of them. He would have gotten a good job, gotten married, had kids, coached Little League, and enjoyed a normal, happy life. His tombstone would have read, *Nice guy. Liked by all.*

He pushed the thought away. No use thinking about what would never happen.

ACKNOWLEDGEMENTS

I never would have achieved my publishing goals without the help and support of my family, friends, and colleagues. I am blessed with an amazing circle of supportive people, and I can't even begin to thank everyone who deserves to be thanked.

First and foremost, I want to thank my husband. He fully supported my goal to become an author, even when it wasn't easy—even when I stayed up until 4 a.m., neglected housework, and obsessed endlessly over query replies (or lack thereof). In fact, my entire family supported me completely, and never said that my goal of being an author was unrealistic or crazy . . . at least not to my face. I especially want to thank my mother and brother, who were the first to read *The Charge*, and have supported my writing goals ever since I handwrote my first novel in a spiral when I was fifteen.

I'm also grateful for the support of the online writing community at large. I'm not surprised that my family was behind me, but having virtual strangers from across the world step forward to help me, both amazes and humbles me. I want to thank the numerous critique partners and beta readers who helped me with *The Charge* and earlier projects, especially my most recent beta readers for *The Charge*, Alexandra Villasante and Natalia Jaster.

Of course, you wouldn't be reading this book right now if it weren't for the good people at Curiosity Quills Press. First, I want to thank one of the most hardworking people I know, Krystal Wade. She was the acquisitions editor that first read *The Charge* and gave me that long awaited "yes". And I want to thank Eugene Teplitsky and Alisa Gus for welcoming me to their crew of marauders. It has been a blessing to be a part of the Curiosity Quills family, an incredible group of supportive and talented authors. Thank you to all of my CQ brothers and sisters.

A big thanks to my cover artist Michelle Johnson and my editor Mary Harris who helped make *The Charge* the best it could be, and had to put up with me. I am also immensely grateful for the support of CQ staff members Jade Hart, Thea Gregory, and Courtney Worth Young – fantastic industry professionals, talented writers, trusted confidants, and all around awesome.

Last but certainly not least, I want to thank God for giving me the strength to never give up and for the wealth of blessings in my life that humble me every day.

THANK YOU FOR READING

Curiosity Quills Press
http://curiosityquills.com

Please visit http://curiosityquills.com/reader-survey/ to share your reading experience with the author of this book!

ABOUT THE AUTHOR

Sharon Bayliss is a native of Austin, Texas and works her day job in the field of social work.

When she's not writing, she enjoys living in her "happily-ever-after" with her husband and two young sons. She can be found eating Tex-Mex on patios, wearing flip-flops, and playing in the mud (which she calls gardening).

You can connect with Sharon at: www.facebook.com/authorsharonbayliss and www.sharonbayliss.com.

Theocracide, by James Wymore

In a time when Americans live isolated lives behind computer glasses that mask the harsh reality, Jason is forced to abandon this rose-colored fantasy as an unwilling part of his father's plan to assassinate the Undying Emperor. With aliens invading the world and his sister dying of an incurable flu they brought, he is pulled from his perfect life with an amazing new girlfriend and plunged into a dark game of intrigue and conspiracy against the most powerful people in the world. Is there any way to regain the respect of the girl he loves after committing Theocracide?

Nefertiti's Heart, by A.W. Exley

Cara Devon has always suffered curiosity and impetuousness, but tangling with a serial killer might cure that. Permanently.

London, 1861. Impoverished noble Cara has a simple mission after the strange death of her father—sell off his damned collection of priceless artifacts. Her plan goes awry when aristocratic beauties start dying of broken hearts, an eight inch long brass key hammered through their chests. A killer hunts amongst the nobility, searching for a regal beauty and an ancient Egyptian relic rumored to hold the key to immortality.

In a society where everyone wears a mask to hide their true intent, Cara must figure out who to trust, before she makes a fatal mistake.

Sweet Dreams are Made of Teeth, by Richard Roberts

Have you ever had the nightmare of being chased by a beast? Then you've met Fang. He'll be the first to admit that he's a very simple nightmare. All he knows is hunting your dreams and dragging them into the Dark.

He's not ready for his life to get complicated. He's not ready to be dragged into his best friend's schemes to make dreams so terrifying they break people. He's not ready to love, or to be loved, or to meet someone who makes him happy.

He's not ready to grow up. When he does, one thing will stay the same: he'll stay an artist, and he'll paint your dreams with fear until they're beautiful.

Wild Children, by Richard Roberts

Bad children are punished, turned into animals marked with their crimes.

Five children each tell a different story of what they became: One learns that wrong can be right, and her curse may be a blessing. Another is so Wild he must learn the simplest lesson, to love someone else. An eight year old girl must face fear and doubt as she dies of old age. Love and strangeness hit the lives of two brothers in the form of a beautiful flaming bird. Finally, the oldest child learns that what is right can be horribly wrong. Together they tell a sixth story, of a Wild Girl who doesn't seem Wild at all.

18 Things, by Jamie Ayres

A young girl struggles to live again after a lightning strike kills the best friend she was secretly in love with.

Her therapist suggests she write a life list of eighteen things to complete the year of her eighteenth birthday, sending her and her friends, including the new hottie in town, on an unexpected journey they'll never forget.

As she crosses each item off her list, she must risk her own heart, but if she fails, she risks losing herself and her true soul-mate forever

Once Upon A Changeling, by V.J. Chambers

Russ Knight found out his girlfriend was cheating on him when she gave birth at the junior prom and left the baby to die in a trashcan.

His girlfriend is trying to get the faeries to give her baby back. Russ doesn't buy it. But the baby starts swearing and begging to be taken back to Faerie. The kid he's raising is a faerie changeling.

To save an innocent life, Russ will face ancient faeries with razor-like teeth, wrestle snarling skeleton dogs, and, maybe worst of all, track down every guy his girlfriend was sleeping with last year in the hopes of finding the baby's real father.

Danger in Cat World, by Nina Post

On the verge of losing himself in his work, Shawn Danger, a homicide detective, investigates the murder of a reclusive heiress, but when he discovers a window to another universe and dozens of cats begin appearing out of thin air, he must embrace the unknown to solve the case.

Can Shawn embrace the unknown and find the answers he needs to solve the case, and can he act quickly enough to restore balance between the two worlds?

The Prince of Earth, by Mike Robinson

In 1988, young American traveler Quincy Redding is trekking across the misty terrain of the Scottish Highlands. She is destined for the infamous peak Ben MacDui, the summit of which soon finds her inexplicably debilitated and at the mercy of a malevolent entity.

The book spans twenty years, alternately following Quincy in her 1988 ordeal in Scotland as well as Quincy in 2008, when, as an adult, she begins experiencing abnormalities that threaten her family and her life—phenomena that may be related to what happened all those years ago.

CPSIA information can be obtained at www.ICGtesting.com
Printed in the USA
BVOW05s0515061115

426004BV00003BB/31/P

9 781620 072035